scarlett fever

ALSO BY MAUREEN JOHNSON

Suite Scarlett

Girl at Sea

Devilish

13 Little Blue Envelopes

The Bermudez Triangle

The Key to the Golden Firebird

MAUREEN JOHNSON

scarlett fever

Point

Library of Congress Cataloging-in-Publication Data

Johnson, Maureen, 1973–
    Scarlett fever / by Maureen Johnson. — 1st ed.
    p. cm.
    Summary: Fifteen-year-old Scarlett, who is beginning to get over her
break-up with Eric, stays busy as assistant to her theatrical-agent friend
who is not only promoting Scarlett's brother Spencer, but also a new
client whose bad-boy brother has transferred to Scarlett's school.
    ISBN-13: 978-0-439-89928-4 (alk. paper)
    ISBN-10: 0-439-89928-1 (alk. paper)
    [1. Family life — New York (State) — New York — Fiction. 2. High
schools — Fiction. 3. Schools — Fiction. 4. Actors — Fiction. 5. Dating
(Social customs) — Fiction. 6. Hotels — Fiction. 7. New York (N.Y.) —
Fiction.] I. Title.
    PZ7.J634145Sc 2010
    [Fic] — dc22

2009019322

12 11 10 9 8 7 6 5 4 3 2 1   10 11 12 13 14 15/0

Printed in the U.S.A. 23
First edition, February 2010

The display type was set in Helvetica medium.
The text type was set in Hoefler text.

Book design by Yaffa Jaskoll

For Agnetha Fältskog, Benny Andersson, Björn Ulvaeus, and Her Serene Highness Anni Frid, Princess Reuss von Plauen.

scarlett fever

ACT I

Gothammag.com
"Though this be madness, yet there is method in't": Hamlet *at the Hopewell Hotel*

So let's set the scene, shall we? Hamlet. *In a hotel. But not one of the grand palaces or tourist farms — a much rarer breed. A tiny, privately owned hotel. It would be fair, and possibly even generous, to call the place* distressed. *The floors squeak, a fine layer of dust covers everything, and most of the furniture in the lobby has an astonishing lean to it, so much so that I actually found myself cocking my head to the side at points.*

But what is equally obvious is the true style under the decay. It's there, like good bone structure. The place is an absolute Deco masterpiece: cherry wood, silver lightning-bolt motifs where you least expect them, poison-purple and tiger lily–orange tinted light from the colored lamps. You pass from the lobby into a modest dining room, now converted into a theater. Like everything else, the chandelier is lopsided, but deliberately so, pulled by a wire draped with silver gauze. The walls are bare but alive with the shadows of a hundred small, guttering candles. The room is in decadent disarray, as if a seedy royal wedding has taken place soon before.

Which, of course, it has. Welcome to the world of Hamlet.

Full disclosure: I wanted to dismiss this production as a gimmick, a cheap bag of tricks. Hamlet *in a hotel . . . and next,* Othello *in an office.* Macbeth *in a McDonald's. I've seen shows staged in every possible location, but the fact that this one seemed so tied to the establishment — with backstage access to guests — I assumed it was a new step downward in the ever-devolving state of the art.*

But this show works. I now think every *production of* Hamlet *should be staged in a broken-down hotel. This is the play where people constantly come and go — royals, courtiers, messengers, servants, students, performers — and events progress from bad to worse to terminal. All is uprooted in* Hamlet, *no one is sleeping in the right bed, and your stay may be much shorter than you expect. So a hotel . . . of course! Why not?*

This Hamlet *is also staged like a kind of carnival — a mad, strange circus. It's an uneven production, overacted at points (Stephanie Damler doesn't quite know where to pull back on Ophelia's insanity, and Jeffery Archson's portrayal of Horatio set my teeth on edge). But there are some true laugh-out-loud moments, mostly provided by the inspired clowning of Rosencrantz and Guildenstern, played by Eric Hall and Spencer Martin, respectively. In particular, when Martin careened through the crowd on his unicycle at the start of the show and had an encounter with a closed door — I actually spit-took my drink onto my companion's shoulder. And I'm not normally a spitter.*

Like all good things, it will come to an end, so get your tickets while you can. (SHOW CLOSES AUGUST 28, TICKETS AVAILABLE THROUGH TICKETPRO OR FREE TO HOTEL GUESTS.)

SAFETY FOR THE STUPID

It was four thirty in the morning, and Scarlett wanted answers.

Unfortunately, four-thirty-in-the-morning questions are often of a very different nature than, say, three-twenty-in-the-afternoon questions. At three twenty in the afternoon, the questions you might be asking yourself are, "What's for dinner?" or "I wonder if that button on my cell phone is stuck or completely broken and if I keep pressing it will I fix it or will it fall off?" You can wave those questions off with a quick swing of the hand. They scare easy.

The questions that creep around at four thirty in the morning are not the kind that can be easily dismissed. You can beat them with a shovel, and they'll just keep getting back up. "What are you going to do with your life?" they demand, pulling themselves from the ground with no visible damage. "Who are you, really?"

Hamlet was big on questions. "To be, or not to be," he asked peevishly, "that is the question. Whether 'tis nobler in the mind to suffer the slings and arrows of outrageous fortune, or to take arms against a sea of troubles, and by opposing end them."

In other words, why not just give up? What's the point? Life is rough — is it easier just not to bother? Lie here and do nothing?

Curl up and die? Scarlett Martin knew the whole whiny speech because she had seen the show every single day for the last four weeks, plus rehearsals. It's hard to miss a show when it's in your dining room.

The questions that Scarlett was asking herself at the moment weren't quite that dramatic. They weren't even that specific. What was going through her head was a querulous vibration with a questiony flavor . . . a general *"What the hell is going on?"*

She lay on the twelve-foot-wide main stage platform, her feet propped up on a unicycle ramp. A sheer purple curtain dangled just inches above her forehead. Higher up, silver banners and purple drapes hung from the set walls. Beyond that, tin lanterns were suspended from the ceiling. Around her, theatrical lights were attached to freestanding poles, and a hundred empty chairs pointed in her direction — an audience of no one.

This was the skeleton of the show, stripped bare of flesh and life. It had been closed for two days, and for those two nights, Scarlett hadn't really slept. She tossed in bed for a few hours, then took the steps down the four flights from her room (the elevator was much too loud to use in the middle of the night) and paced the set. She would not, would not, would not look at the pictures of Eric on her phone. Or the saved messages. She would do none of these things, because it was over.

Probably.

Most likely.

Which is why she would not look at . . .

Too late. The phone was in front of her face and she was clicking through the photos. She saw her finger doing it. It was like she wasn't even in control of her hand. It had gone rogue, disconnected itself from her brain. The hand wanted to see the photos. The hand *always* wanted to see the photos, clicking through them again and again, one hundred and fifty-four in all. Some were action shots from the show. Some were pictures she snapped in quiet when Eric wasn't looking. It was a minor point of pride for Scarlett that she had gotten very good at doing that. If you're going to be a stalker, she figured, you really should be *good* at it. The shame of failure was too great. Ideally, a good stalker could perhaps gain future employment as a spy. Fight crime. Go undercover. Save the world. Yes. That's what the world needed, someone good with a camera phone, someone prepared to spend five hours online looking at the same video clip, someone who really knew how to read into a status message. Surely, all very desirable skills should the perpetrators of terror ever really get into social networking.

The dining room doors opened and a tall figure appeared in the doorway, casting a long shadow as it came farther into the room. Scarlett sat up abruptly, startling the person and causing him to yelp and almost crash into a chair.

"Sorry," she said. "Didn't mean to startle you."

"God . . . what . . . Scarlett?"

Spencer was always the first awake at the hotel, fully dressed in his uniform: white dress shirt, black pants, and black tie. Unlike at the Hopewell, staff at the Waldorf-Astoria had to get dressed up for work. Also, the Waldorf-Astoria had staff — this was another major difference. Spencer worked the breakfast shift there and always woke at an unreasonable hour. He lived on almost no sleep.

"Why are you up?" he said, sitting on the edge of the platform.

"Just the heat," she said. "Our air conditioner broke again."

The part about the air conditioner in the Orchid Suite was true.

It used to freeze Scarlett and Lola with its powerful, energy-draining, light-dimming gusts, but it had recently given up on emitting anything aside from a painfully loud squeal. So they poached all night long in the hot, damp air. That had nothing to do with why she was awake tonight, though, and Spencer seemed to know that. He looked at the phone, still grasped in her hand.

"Expecting a call?" he asked, nodding at it.

The whole Eric situation had caused tension between Scarlett and Spencer for a little while over the summer, tension that had been resolved when Spencer punched Eric in the face during a fight practice, coincidentally just minutes after Eric sort-of dumped Scarlett and made her cry. The matter had been put down by all involved as an unfortunate accident. Spencer and Eric performed every night from that point on without a problem and everyone acted as if nothing had happened between Scarlett and Eric at all. It had all been swept away, just like the play. A moment of unreality, long past.

Spencer may have pretended all month long that all was well and maintained a never-wavering "I don't want to know" stance on the whole thing . . . but he had surely noticed Scarlett's nervous, careful behavior and inability to speak around Eric. Or Eric's excessively polite, excruciating efforts to make sure it was perfectly clear that nothing was happening. Scarlett had seen the other cast members jump in to fill the holes in the conversation when she and Eric were cornered together. The Eric situation was a lot of work for everyone. Never mentioned, but always there, always generating a crackle of unpredictable energy.

"It's nothing," she said.

"Yeah," he mumbled, rubbing his face tiredly. "I hope so. Come on. Since you're up, I need your help."

Just because she was awake at this hour didn't necessarily mean that Scarlett actually wanted to *do* anything, but she followed him along to the kitchen anyway. She sat on one of their large wooden prep tables while he set up the coffee station. That was his early morning task, and it only took a few minutes. He pulled a few script pages out of his back pocket and handed them to her.

"This," he said, "is killing me. The audition is at one. I have no idea what I'm doing. Help me think of something. Read the highlighted part."

"'Man holds two ends of seat belt in his hands,'" Scarlett read, as Spencer filled an industrial-size coffee urn with water. "'He is unable to figure out how they click together. He tries several times. He puts up his hand for help from the flight attendant.' Seems pretty easy."

"Seems easy. *Is* impossible."

He turned off the water and hauled the heavy urn up by its side handles, taking it out of the kitchen. He returned a moment later and sat on the counter. He unbuckled his belt, slipped it from around his waist, and held it up for examination.

"This is a seat belt," he said, "and I am the guy who can't figure this out. What is my problem? Look." He looped the belt around himself and jabbed the end at the buckle. "Seat belts are just insert and click. That's it. How do you play someone who can't figure that out? Why do they even do safety videos on planes?"

"If I flew," Scarlett said, "maybe I could tell you. What is this for, anyway? Air Stupid?"

"I know. This is my problem. I don't know how to play someone who doesn't know how to fasten a seat belt without acting like an idiot. But the airline won't want the person in the video to seem stupid, because I'm supposed to be playing their typical customer. So I have to *be* stupid without *looking* stupid. I can do looking stupid. Looking stupid is easy. But *this* is harder than Shakespeare. People get Oscars for playing the kind of guy who can't fasten the seat belt. It's a well-known fact."

"Do they give Oscars to people in airline safety videos?"

"They should," he said. "God. This is going to be another Day of the Sock."

It had been four weeks since the Day of the Sock, and yet there was no sign that Spencer was any closer to getting over it.

A casting director had come to see *Hamlet* on its first night. Spencer had impressed him with his skills — fighting, fake falling, backflipping, running into walls on a unicycle. The casting director brought him in to audition for a washing machine commercial, in which he was asked to play a sock stuck in an oversize fake dryer. Spencer spent a good eight hours in the fake dryer, getting callback after callback all day long, until it was down to just him and one other actor. Apparently, eight hours in a fake oversize dryer is not nearly as much fun as it sounds. Especially when the other guy gets the part, and all you get is a headache that lasts for a day and a half.

The Day of the Sock had come to symbolize a kind of curse Spencer thought had come over his career. It cast a pall over his ordinarily high spirits. Since that day, he had been going on auditions several times a week, but nothing was panning out. Casting directors liked him. They called him back again and again. But at the last second, someone else would get the part. Again and again and again. It was wearing him down.

"Maybe you've never been on a plane before?" Scarlett suggested, trying to sound positive.

8

"I've only flown twice, and even I could master the seat belt," he said. "Anyone can work a seat belt. A seat belt practically fastens itself."

He slumped down a bit, resting his elbows on his knees and running his hands through his dark hair. Scarlett stared at his black tie.

"The tie," she said suddenly. "What if you got it caught in the seat belt? You wouldn't be able to buckle it then."

This made Spencer sit up. He looked at his tie, then yanked on the knot to loosen it.

"Okay," he said, pulling the tie so that it hung low. "I just lean over a little when I'm trying to put on the seat belt, and . . ."

He made sure to dangle the tip of his tie into the imaginary clamp so that it couldn't catch.

". . . oh no! I can't figure out my seat belt!"

He increased his struggle, and began doing a very good simulation of choking himself with the belt-clamped tie. He somehow managed to make it look like it had tightened around his neck, and he gagged and choked and pulled himself all the way down to the floor.

"How's that?" he asked, opening his eyes in his death pose. "It's just a starting point. Obviously, I have to work that out a bit."

"I like it," Scarlett said approvingly.

Spencer got up and straightened out his shirt and tie. He opened the accordion guard on one of their large and dusty kitchen windows and surveyed the day. It was just before sunrise, the sky a heavy purple-gray, the air already thick and warm. A summer morning in the city, in the pocket of time when the heat was between merely uncomfortable and completely unbearable. Spencer just stared out at the small, paved area that separated their property from the apartment building behind them — just a little plot of concrete with a table and some chairs that no one ever used. He exhaled long and slow.

"What?" Scarlett asked.

Spencer just shook his head and snapped the guard back into position.

"Nothing," he said. "I should get going. Walk out with me?"

Outside, Spencer's bike was looking a little worse than usual. It had been the duct-tape special since he was in high school, but now one of the handlebars was bent up and forward, like the horn of a bull.

"What happened?" she asked.

"Oh yeah," he said, unlocking it. "A little present from yesterday. I went to pick up some new copies of my headshot, and when I came out, this is what it looked like. The whole frame is messed up. Someone must have nailed it with a car. I'm on a lucky streak these days."

He fastened the bike chain around his waist and squatted down, balancing the bike in his hands and examining the line of vision from seat level. The bike was clearly crooked. He rolled it along as they walked down the sidewalk, and it was obviously a struggle. It kept pulling in Scarlett's direction, sometimes nudging her, and he would drag it back.

"Can you really ride that?" she asked.

"I don't have much choice. It's mostly okay, except that it always wants to go left now, so I have to steer right to keep it straight."

"That's really bad in traffic. There's about a dozen ways to die on that thing."

Spencer stopped and looked at her like she was a genius.

"A dozen ways to die," he repeated. "That's it!"

"What?"

"I'm going to strangle this guy in a few different ways, besides the tie. I'll make everything dangerous. Like when the oxygen mask drops down, I'll strangle him on the cord. I can do the same thing with the inflatable life preserver. I'll make him the most inept passenger of all time. You always think of something!" He yelled some kind of farewell as he wobbled off into traffic at high speed.

It was just dawn now, a violent burst of sun breaking between the buildings on the east side. Scarlett pulled her phone from the pocket of her pajama shorts. The screen displayed the time, signal strength, battery life . . . but otherwise, its face was blank and stupid.

She sat on the front step of the hotel and watched Mrs. Foo, their dry-cleaner neighbor, open the gate in front of her shop. She waved to Scarlett. Scarlett lifted her arm to wave back. The arm felt tired. The first wave of weariness washed over her; still . . . there was something about this up-with-the-dawn thing. What if . . . she wondered . . . what if she made today the first day of a whole new era? She was literally up with the dawn. School started in less than a week. The show was over. In a few hours, she'd be seeing all of her friends together for the first time since the end of school.

This was the day to begin again, to put Eric behind her, to think about what came next. Something quivered in her, something made of enthusiasm or exhaustion, something that told her that this was the plan. This was the way.

She pulled out her phone again. This time, she gave her hand permission to pull up the pictures of Eric. There was an ERASE ALL button. All she had to do was hit it. That would be a good start.

Her finger hovered over the button for a moment, teasing it, just coming into enough contact. But she didn't press down.

No. Even better. She would go through the pictures one by one and erase them manually. That was more like a ritual, more cleansing. She would wipe out all one hundred and fifty-four of them right now, in her sleeping clothes, on her stoop, in the early morning sunshine in full view of Mrs. Foo and whoever walked by.

Picture one: a very early one of Eric, soon after they met. He was buying a sandwich and didn't even see her take the photo. Kind of historical. She would come back to that one.

Picture two: from an early rehearsal. Same thing. She would come back to these. Better to start in the middle. Back to the main menu. Scroll, scroll . . .

Picture thirty-nine: Eric in the theater. Very generic. A little blurry. Erasable. She took a deep breath, clenched her free hand into a fist, and hit the TRASH button. Picture gone.

Or was it? Did the phone save trashed pictures? She had no idea. She backed through the menus to check. No, it did not. The picture was gone. Only one hundred and fifty-three left to go.

Scarlett managed to prune twenty-three of the pictures before the second, heavier wave of exhaustion hit. She crept back up to her room, her feet heavy. Her sister Lola was already awake and in the shower. Scarlett dropped down on her bed and listened to the water run in the bathroom next door.

It was six thirty in the morning, and Scarlett felt herself falling under. But before she gave up and just let the sleep come, she said to herself, out loud, "I am making a new start."

RUE IS FOR REMEMBRANCE

After a few hours of fitful midmorning sleep, Scarlett made a second attack on the day and headed for the shower. It always took a moment for the Hopewell water pipes to figure out what temperature you wanted. The default setting was "death by ice or fire." Scarlett didn't care at the moment. She would take what came, and what came was cold. Bitter, impossible cold that almost felt good in the heat. She locked her teeth together and accepted it, letting it run down her back. As she reached for her shampoo, she got dangerously close to singing "I'm Gonna Wash That Man Right Outta My Hair," a song she learned when Spencer was doing *South Pacific* in high school. She stopped herself just as she opened her mouth. New start or not, there was a line to be drawn, and that line was singing musicals to yourself as serious psychological motivation.

Downstairs, the lobby was empty of people. There were a few guests still staying at the Hopewell, but the numbers were coming down dramatically now that the show was closed and the novelty of the theater-hotel was over. The dining room doors were open, and her father was up on a ladder on the stage platform, unhooking a wire and a silver banner from the tired chandelier.

"I'm going to meet Dakota," she called.

"Come here a sec."

Working on the set, her dad practically looked like a member of the theater company. He was in his mid-forties, but didn't look his age at all. He still had the floppy blond hair and trashy-hipster thrift store clothes of the art student he had once been. The older Spencer got, the more the two just looked like brothers, something that Scarlett found fascinating and strangely unnerving. Sometimes — okay, most of the time — her dad just didn't seem like someone who should be running a business. Nothing against her dad. Not everyone was born to run a hotel in New York. The job had been thrust on him. He'd fought it for a while when he was just out of college. But then he married his true love and had four kids, one of whom developed cancer. After that, like it or not, good at it or not . . . the hotel became his life's work.

"You know about the dinner plan for tonight?" he asked, releasing the last hold of the fabric and sending it drifting to the floor. "Dinner at Lupe's."

"Lupe's?" Scarlett said, pleased to hear the name of her favorite Mexican restaurant.

"Lola set it up. You four are going. Your mom and I are having a date night. It's sort of a back-to-school treat, and a welcome back for Marlene. So be back around five."

This last bit of information took some of the shine off of things. For ten wonderful days each summer, Marlene, the youngest Martin, went away. Her cancer survivor group had a camp in the Catskills where they threw one another into the lake and ate marshmallows, and peace would reign on the fifth floor of the

14

Hopewell. Scarlett loved her little sister, of course, but she was not prepared to lie and say she was fun to live with.

Her dad climbed down from the ladder and stared up at the chandelier, which was still crooked after being released from the wire that had been pulling it deliberately out of joint.

"Has it always been like that?" he asked.

"Kinda. It's a little worse now."

He *hmmm*ed, and the matter seemed to pass from his mind.

"Listen," he said, wiping dust from his hands onto his pants, "your mom and I were thinking . . . since Mrs. Amberson has moved out, and you have school starting . . . you have enough on your plate right now. We don't expect you to have to take care of the Empire Suite or any of the other rooms."

"I don't?"

"Well, Lola is around pretty much full-time this year, and Spencer's been doing a lot. And we won't have as many guests."

He tried to make that sound like it was a good thing that would just save them all a little time.

"And you have your job," he added. "How *has* your job been going?"

"It's fine," she said. "We've worked it out. It's just a few afternoons a week, a few hours here and there. It's not bad."

"Do you want to do it? I know it's college money, but that shouldn't be your big concern."

It was college money. It was a lot of college money. Somewhere out there, a bank account with her name on it was growing.

"All I'm saying is, you can quit. I want you to quit if it feels like too much. The show is done. You don't have to —"

"No," Scarlett said. "I want to do it. I . . . like it."

A piece of glass fell from the chandelier and landed on the silver fabric, like a dirty, loose tooth. It punctuated their conversation, bringing the matter to a close.

In Biology I, Scarlett had been taught that carbon was the building block of life. They forgot to mention the other element: Element M. Money. Money determined everything. You needed money for your health — they'd learned that lesson when Marlene's medical bills came in. (Though they were never supposed to talk about that. It was a Martin Family Rule.) You needed money for school. You needed money to get across the city, and to do things on weekends. You needed money to go away for the summer, like most of Scarlett's friends had. Summer in the city was hot and terrible, and outside of the city there were *opportunities*. If you had the money. Which most of Scarlett's friends did. Dakota, for example, had been in France at a language immersion program. She had arranged this little picnic in the park to celebrate the fact that they were all back and together. Only Scarlett had been here all along, because she was the most stone broke out of the group.

Scarlett knew better than to resent her friends for being more well off. But sometimes . . . sometimes it was just a *little* annoying that she had to lead a slightly different life from the rest of them. Her dad could pretend all he wanted, but it did make a difference that she had a job. And when the time came for her to go to college, if they could even afford it, every penny in that account would matter. Her friends had more choices about how to spend their time. They could "improve" themselves. She just had to take what she was dealt.

By the time she reached Central Park, Scarlett was feeling massively sorry for herself. She didn't exactly see herself as a character right out of Dickens — cleaning chimneys, eating soup made of fishheads and old shoelaces, getting sold to a local blacksmith for a few chickens and a dozen bars of soap — but it was still *pretty bad*. Add to that the fact that Eric was gone, and her tragedy was complete.

Her mood was in sharp contrast to the scene that had been prepared. She found her friends on a quilt of blankets and beach towels. Dakota had a real wicker picnic basket with white-and-green china plates and silverware strapped to the lid. There were cupcakes and tiny sandwiches — all, Scarlett was sure, made by Dakota herself. She had probably worked until four in the morning and then gotten here early to set up. Because that was the kind of person Dakota was. A true friend who spent her nights doing things for others, not wandering around sets looking at pictures and comparing herself to Hamlet. This was a smooth gear change from self-pity to guilt. Scarlett knew she should have gone to Dakota's the night before to help, but when you're obsessed, it takes up all your time.

Dakota had outfitted her tall, beanpoley frame in a little blue dress and pulled her dark hair up into two very strange little scrunches by her ears. She sometimes dressed a little bit like she was four years old, but she pulled it off about 80 percent of the time. Chloe and Josh were there as well. Chloe managed to be the kind of person you couldn't resent, even when she wore short short-shorts that showed off her tanned and toned tennis legs or flashed lasered teeth or wrinkled her nose job. At heart, she was a math genius and a closet nerd. And Josh, Scarlett's closest guy friend, was a goofy redheaded Brooklynite. His parents were both writers, and he was insanely well-read. He'd been in England all summer, supposedly studying literature. In reality, it sounded like he had been drinking beer and chasing every English girl who crossed his path. Josh was a little like that, but it was okay. The others would be coming soon — Mira, probably Hunter, maybe Tabitha. All of them happy, full of stories.

Yes, the summer was done, and everything was going back to normal. This was the part of normal that she was supposed to like, seeing all of her friends. But nothing felt right. She flopped down on one of the blankets and tried to make herself look carefree, but she landed on a stick and it dug into the meat of her thigh, causing her to start in pain. Slings and arrows. Always the slings and arrows.

"So," Dakota said quietly. "The show. Is gone. Today, right? Gone?"

Clearly, Dakota was going to waste no time in getting to the point. Scarlett shaded her eyes and nodded, still trying to look like she didn't have a care in the world, except for that leg wound.

"Good. So Eric's officially out of your house, and now we can get him out of your life and out of your head. Starting *right now*."

"I already started," Scarlett said. "I erased some pictures of him off my phone this morning. I'm making a new start."

"No," Dakota said. "Really."

"I'm serious," Scarlett said, taking a little offense at this. "I'm making a new start."

To be fair, Dakota had every right to doubt her. She had been a little *on message* the past few weeks. She had sent her friends accounts of every single exchange (or non-exchange, as the case may be) that she'd had with Eric. She'd made them examine photos and messages. She had asked for analyses of gestures they hadn't seen and looks she couldn't re-create. She had sent Eric's every move to the far corners of the Internet and the world. And she had made promises more than once that she was going to stop.

So that haunted, twitchy look in Dakota's eye came from bitter experience. But today was different.

"Today is different," she said.

"Look," Dakota said. "Think about it this way. You made out with Eric *twice*. You made out with Josh more than that."

At this, Josh looked over lazily, sensing his name was being invoked.

"What?" he asked.

"I was just saying that Scarlett made out with you more than she made out with this Eric clown," Dakota said.

"Oh yeah." Josh nodded and closed his eyes against the sun.

"It wasn't the same," Scarlett said. "Everyone makes out with Josh."

This was no insult to Josh, and no secret to anyone. Josh was a lovable idiot who was more than happy to let his female friends practice their making-out skills on him whenever they wanted.

"I haven't," Dakota said.

"Whenever you want," Josh said, rolling onto his back.

"I'm just trying to put it in some perspective," Dakota said, "because, you know, I hate Eric and I am trying to explain why he does not matter in a *new* way. For example, you spent more time making out with Josh than you did Eric."

"It's not the same thing," Scarlett said. "It's not just how much *time* you put into it."

"When did you guys make out again?" Chloe asked. "I forget."

"Last winter break," Scarlett said. "And it was different."

"It was three times or something," Josh said.

"Right," Dakota went on. "And notice how that didn't make you crazy? That is because Josh is a good guy, and Eric is a *cheat* and a *sneak*. He is a bad man. Everyone hates him. You have to *get in line* to hate Eric Hall."

"He's not a *cheat*," Scarlett said.

This conversation was a minefield, and with those words, she lifted her foot off a pressure device. Dakota was now set on tick-tick-boom.

"Let's break it down step-by-step," Dakota said. "Shall we? Eric made out with you while he had a girlfriend. A girlfriend of two years, down in . . . wherever it is he comes from. South Carolina or whatever . . ."

"North Carolina," Scarlett said, feeling the need for the facts to be accurate. "And I didn't know about her."

"No. Of *course* you didn't. He made sure you didn't. Because he was *cheating on her*. With you. And do not . . ." Dakota held up a finger on this. ". . . do not give me this stuff about how he really felt bad about it and how he was going to break up with her but he just wanted to wait until he got home. Do not."

"Yeah," Josh said, sounding very bored that this was happening again. "Don't."

"I'm not even thinking about him," Scarlett lied. "You don't have to . . ."

"Do you want to know how I *know* you're thinking about him?" Dakota cut in.

"Nope," Scarlett replied honestly.

"Because I checked that link to his commercial that you sent me. Remember how you said you were the only person who ever really watched it and how you were embarrassed because the view count was going up really fast? Well, it was at 356 two days ago, and now it's at 512."

Scarlett felt her stomach lurch. She had made one of the most basic of life errors, and she saw it immediately: Never give anyone evidence of your crazy.

"I watched it . . . a few times," Scarlett said, looking down. "You don't know it was me."

"It's a pizza commercial. You were the one who said you were afraid he'd notice because you were the only person in the world who would watch it besides him."

"Some people *really like pizza*," Scarlett countered. "And I'm wrong a lot. Can we be done now? There's a bee on your drink."

"Can I make a suggestion?" Chloe was chiming in. Scarlett loved Chloe dearly, but she was a notoriously flirty and flaky dater. She had gone through a total of four "relationships" over the summer. As far as she was concerned, the average life cycle of a couple was a week. If they were *very* serious. Taking relationship advice from her was like taking flying lessons from a kamikaze pilot — someone who thought the only way to land was nose-first into the ground.

"Why don't you call him?" she asked. "Why don't you go and see him? Sometimes you just need to make out one last time to get it out of your system. I've done that."

"Do. Not. Do. That."

That was Dakota, of course.

"I'm always here," Josh added.

Scarlett's problem — the ruling issue of her life right now, her secret inner turmoil — had become a conversational Frisbee. Something to toss around on a bright summer's day when there was nothing better going on.

"I'm making a new start," Scarlett said again.

And then, of course, the phone began to ring. She had set it on the blanket beside her. Dakota got to it first and snatched it away.

"Who is it?" Scarlett said anxiously, her voice betraying her.

"It says 'AAA,'" Dakota replied. "AAA? American Automobile Association?"

Sadly, many people made this mistake. They had been getting a lot of calls from stranded drivers recently.

"Give it," Scarlett said, holding her hand out.

The phone rang again.

"Who is AAA?" Dakota asked, holding the phone back a bit.

"Just give it to me for a second. . . ."

The phone rang again.

"That is not an answer."

"It's my boss," Scarlett said with a sigh.

"Oh no. No, no, no." Dakota stuck the phone under her leg. "Not her, either."

"You don't understand," Scarlett said. "You don't know what she's like. Just let me call her and she'll calm down. It's only been three days since she moved out of the hotel. She has separation anxiety."

"That doesn't mean she can call you every ten minutes to do something stupid while she's out getting her butt waxed."

"Thanks for that mental image," Scarlett said. "That's something she might do, if her butt was hairy. Which it probably isn't . . . Great. Now I'm imagining it. Remind me to repay you."

"*De rien.* God, go away for one summer and I'm replaced with an entire cast of freaks. I am never leaving again."

The phone started ringing again. Each ring pierced Scarlett. Mrs. Amberson didn't have a special ringtone, but Scarlett could just tell when she was calling. The calls had a keening, urgent quality.

"Please," Scarlett said. "She won't stop until I talk to her."

Ring.

"You can have your phone back if you tell her that you are staying here today with us. And we will all take turns patting your head and helping you heal your broken heart. That is what is going to happen."

Ring.

"Fine!" Scarlett said, her anxiety peaking.

The phone stopped ringing as soon as it was back in Scarlett's hand. She stared at it for a moment, wondering if she could just let it go, ignore the call.

"Don't," Dakota said. "Don't call her back."

"You don't understand," Scarlett said again. "She won't stop."

The phone started ringing again, proving her point. Scarlett answered it instantly, preparing herself to tell her boss that she was not available, but she had no chance.

"Where are you?" Mrs. Amberson snapped. "I am getting in a cab right now and coming to get you."

"What?"

"I'm aware that it's your day off, but it's an emergency. *Address,* O'Hara!"

"I'm in the park," Scarlett said, moving away and lowering her voice. Dakota was squinting suspiciously.

"What's the closest street?"

"I don't know," Scarlett said. "Sixty-seventh or something? On the west side?"

"I will be there in five minutes."

Scarlett snapped the phone closed and faced her friends. Dakota was staring intently and seemed to have taken a very dim view of the situation.

"She didn't really give me a choice," Scarlett explained, getting up. "She's on her way."

"I didn't really hear you fighting her off," Dakota said.

"It's her boss," Josh said. "You can't fight off your boss."

"Her boss isn't normal!" Dakota shot back. "People are allowed to have days off. School starts in two days. This is all the time we get!"

It was useless for Scarlett to try to explain that this was her fate. Outrageous fortune. Hamlet had made some good points after all.

LUNCH IS FOR SUCKERS

It had only been a few weeks, but Scarlett couldn't remember a time when she didn't know Mrs. Amy Amberson — the longest-staying Hopewell guest of recent record, with her tall, yoga-taut former-dancer body, her stories of the disco and punk scenes in New York, and her endless tea drinking. Once you entered her world, you forgot where you came from. You forgot there was any world of which she was not a part. She made sure of it.

Mrs. Amberson had lived in the Empire Suite for ten weeks over the summer, and had immediately enslaved Scarlett on arrival. (Well, not enslaved. She paid well. But it still felt like enslavement.) Scarlett had come to accept that Mrs. Amberson was going to live with them forever, when, just a week before, she announced that she had accumulated too much stuff to be confined to the Empire Suite any longer. It was time to set down more permanent roots. A friend was leaving the city, and she was going to take over her apartment. She'd been moving for three days now. Though out of the building, Mrs. Amberson was hardly out of Scarlett's life. She was a bit like malaria in this respect — once you had her, you never really got rid of her.

Which is why Scarlett was standing on the corner of Sixty-seventh and Central Park West when her cab pulled up. And when Mrs. Amberson threw her long body across the backseat and yelled, "Get in!" . . . Scarlett got in.

Mrs. Amberson was dressed in a sleek black day dress, one that showed off every inch of her toned frame and smoothly muscled arms. Her exact age was unknown. She had to be older than fifty, that much Scarlett knew. But she seemed to defy time by eating a lot of seaweed and brown rice and working out two hours a day, keeping her dancer's physique in perfect working order. Her short hair — shiny, light colored brown with a stripe of chestnut cut through the center — was perfectly spiked. She was dressed for some kind of business.

The cab shot off with such force that Scarlett's head snapped back against the seat. They headed south along Central Park. Mrs. Amberson had gotten much more fidgety now that she had stopped smoking, and she repeatedly flicked the window switch. Each flick sent a burst of hot air into the backseat.

"Where are we going?" Scarlett asked, wincing as her curls were blown in her eyes.

"To Perestroika. A fabulous new Russian place. Very Soviet chic with a devilish czarist twist."

"Why?"

"A client, O'Hara. A new one."

"*Two* clients?" Scarlett said. "How will we cope?"

The Amy Amberson Agency (four weeks old) had just one client, and that client was Spencer. It was the AAA that had sent him on the Day of the Sock and all over to the doomed auditions he'd been on in the last month.

"Chelsea Biggs," Mrs. Amberson said, ignoring the remark. "Ingénue of that new musical, *The Flower Girl*."

"I've seen the commercial," Scarlett said. "Does she sing that song 'Pick Me'?"

"That's the one. This is Chelsea."

She reached into her bag and produced an eight-by-ten photo with a résumé printed on the back. Scarlett had to clutch it with both hands to keep it from flapping in the gust of air that came out of the suddenly opened window. The picture was of a girl, very pretty, but very generic-looking, as if she had flattened her every feature with some kind of computer program that makes you into the average ideal: straight hair, big teeth, dimples, big brown eyes. A boring kind of pretty, Scarlett decided. That's what it was.

Scarlett flipped the picture over and tried to read the small print of Chelsea's perfectly prepared résumé. Chelsea had a massive list of leading roles in musicals at regional theaters, at least a dozen television commercials, and ten major print ad campaigns. Her training section was terrifying — eleven years of training in five styles of dance, ten years of singing training, eight years of acting training. Just looking at this piece of paper made Scarlett's ego curl into a tiny ball for protection.

"I'm sure you've heard about *The Flower Girl*," Mrs. Amberson said. "They're calling it the worst musical in twenty years. No one thought it would make it out of previews. But it stumbled along — sometimes, things do. The worst ideas sometimes manage to find traction. I honestly believe the only thing that works in the entire show is Chelsea. This girl holds that train wreck together."

She tapped the photo for emphasis.

"The problems are too serious for her to hold it together for long. But she has star quality. A little birdie named Billy told me that she landed the part without representation — quite a feat — and now she is looking for an agent."

That would be Billy Whitehouse, an old friend of Mrs. Amberson's who had gone on to become one of the most famous acting coaches in New York. Billy had literally written the book on voice work and was highly respected all around Broadway. It was probably Mrs. Amberson's connection with Billy that made so many people want to sign with her.

"That show may last two more weeks, maybe three, and then the jaws of hell will open and drag it back into its depths. Then she will need work. Which means she will need an agent. And Billy has waxed rhapsodic about the Amy Amberson Agency to her. We have a real shot."

"Why did you need me for this?" Scarlett asked.

"Because Chelsea is fifteen. You are fifteen! You can relate."

"She's also on Broadway. I can't relate to that."

"Of course you can, O'Hara. Ah . . . here we are. And there they are."

They were on Fifty-third Street. Mrs. Amberson pointed at two sunglassed females on the sidewalk. She tapped on the driver's window.

"Go around the block, please."

He shrugged and continued right past the restaurant.

"What are we doing?" Scarlett asked.

"Do you want them to think that this is the only thing we had scheduled all day? Have you learned nothing in your time with me?

We can't have it seem that we had nothing better to do than to come here. We must always seem like we have come from a busy morning, full of appointments, even if we have not. Once more around the block will have us getting there just two to three minutes after them. That is enough to make us look busy, without making them wait too long."

Mrs. Amberson managed to make herself sound winded when they got out of the cab.

"Chelsea! Miranda! It's been an absolute *madhouse* today, but we're here now. This is Scarlett, my right hand. . . ."

Chelsea Biggs wore no makeup. Her skin was pale, but had a soft glow, speaking of lots of exercise and facials. She wore a red sundress with an aggressive pattern of interlocking circles. Her mother wore a nearly identical dress, but in a plain red.

"I thought Russian for lunch," Mrs. Amberson said, leading them inside. "The Russians are the true masters of theater, after all. It seemed appropriate. By the way, I *love* the dress, Chelsea, I appreciate a bold pattern. Come now, in we go. . . ."

The restaurant was like a cement bunker with exposed steel beams, covered in bright Futurist art — big red paintings of raised fists and tractors and sewing machines. But the seats were oversize and plush. They were seated at a large table near the window, Mrs. Amberson and Scarlett on one side, Chelsea and her mom on the other. The menus were stiff, heavy pieces of cardboard with single sheets of paper tabbed to them. Mrs. Biggs stared at hers with kind of distasteful curiosity, like she'd been handed a crime scene photo.

"Russian?" she said. "We don't eat Russian."

"Well," Mrs. Amberson said, "first time for everything. So many things in life we just don't think to do. It's always been my personal goal not to miss *anything.*"

Chelsea sat high and straight in her seat, smiling even as she read the contents of her menu. Scarlett got the feeling that Chelsea was programmed to smile at all times, in all situations, even at nothing, in the dark, with no one around. Mrs. Biggs scowled at the menu for a moment.

"I guess you could have the smoked salmon with no goat cheese," she finally said to Chelsea. "Would they make that omelet with whites only? I don't know what most of these things are. . . . Maybe you could have the veal appetizer. Do you think that's small?"

This question was to Mrs. Amberson, who was watching this with a fixed smile, as if this was the most delightful exchange she'd ever heard.

"I am sure it is reasonably sized," she said.

"Reasonably? Is it under 500 calories? Aren't they supposed to put the calories on the menu?"

"In chain restaurants," Mrs. Amberson said. "Not in an establishment like this."

This was not good enough for Mrs. Biggs. She shook her head.

"Chelsea's on a strict fifteen hundred a day limit and she's already had . . . what have you had?"

"Four seventy-five," Chelsea replied automatically.

"Four seventy-five? What did you eat this morning?"

"I had to have a protein smoothie before school. I was dying after the gym."

"Why didn't you just have a protein bar?" Mrs. Biggs asked. "Those are only two hundred."

"I was *really* hungry. We did an extra twenty minutes of weights. I made up for it, I promise."

"Promises won't help you if you put on twenty pounds."

This entire exchange flew past like a horrible and wholly unexpected burst of gunfire. There was no anger in it. It was so repulsive that Scarlett had to look down at her menu, where her eyes landed on a description of some blintzes with sour cream. Oh, she was so having that . . . both because she wanted it, and just to make Mrs. Biggs stare. They were enemies now.

A man came over with a basket of beautiful breads. Scarlett was starving and leaned over to see which one she wanted, but Miranda Biggs was already shaking her head.

"No," she said. "No bread here."

"I haven't had bread in a year and a half," Chelsea said, as if this was understood everywhere to be a kind of accomplishment.

It took another ten minutes of examining and discussing the menu before anything else could happen. Scarlett's stomach was grumbling. Having seen the basket, the bread was all she could think about. She wanted one of those dark slices of black bread. It would be amazing with some nice, salty butter. She wanted that so much. If Scarlett was going to keep her mind off Eric, she was going to need some food to do it.

"If you'll allow me," Mrs. Amberson said. "I am highly sensitive to dietary constraints. I'll order you some pickled fishes and lean proteins, with very limited dairy and carbohydrates. Now, Chelsea, how do you feel about caviar?"

"That's fish eggs," Mrs. Biggs said with a shiver. "And pickled fish? Still, at least it's not cooked. No oil."

The bread guy passed just close enough for Scarlett to reach over and extract a slice of black bread. This encouraged him, and he plunked down a large bowl of butter pats, all molded with the embossed shape of the hammer and sickle. Chelsea stared at the butter, possibly because of the design, or possibly because she hadn't seen butter in a while. There was longing in her eye. She kept looking at it all through the agonies of ordering, and then she snapped right back into her straight-backed perky setting.

"We're talking to several agents," Mrs. Biggs said. "We have meetings set up with most of the big agencies. But Billy Whitehouse said we should meet with you."

"I've read all his books," Chelsea cut in. "He's amazing."

"Isn't he?" Mrs. Amberson said with a smile. "Billy's an *old* friend. We go *way* back. We were contemporaries. I was a performer then, and he was just developing his system. I like to think I played my role in that."

To Scarlett's knowledge, Mrs. Amberson's role in helping Billy develop his famous voice system was letting him sleep on her couch for a few weeks about twenty-five years before. For this accommodation, he had paid dearly. Mrs. Amberson dropped his name in every possible circumstance, and it carried a lot of weight.

"Billy saw Chelsea perform and came backstage to speak to her," Mrs. Biggs said. "He called her an exceptional vocal talent. Which she is."

"My strong point is my voice," Chelsea said. "We're trying to bring my dance up to the same level."

"Mostly contemporary," Mrs. Biggs added, "but she also does ballet once a week, just to keep in condition. Plus she has a personal trainer once a week to work on strength training."

"Very impressive," Mrs. Amberson said, but her voice sounded a bit dry. She took a sip of water and watched Mrs. Biggs from over the top of the glass. "Tell me, how do you manage it?"

"Chelsea goes to the Professional Children's School," Mrs. Biggs replied. "Or she will when she starts next week. They have a flexible schedule for, well, professionals."

"My schedule will be pretty regular," Chelsea replied. "I go to the gym at six in the morning, three days a week. Then I'll go to school from eight thirty to two, Monday through Friday. Except on Wednesday I'll leave at noon because I have to do a matinee at two that day."

"Flexible schedule," Mrs. Biggs said again. "It really is an amazing school. I was looking at the contact list for her class, and you should see some of the names on there. We sat there picking them off from television shows, theater, movies. It's so exciting now that Chelsea can be with people who are . . . like her. Chelsea's always been very motivated. All of this is her idea. She always wanted to be an actress. It's all her idea. If she wanted to quit tomorrow, well, I'd have a heart attack, but . . ."

Chelsea gave a little laugh on that.

". . . but if Chelsea didn't want to do this anymore . . . then, you know, we'd talk about it, and if she really didn't want to do it . . . but that would never happen."

"Right," Chelsea said plainly. "This is my life."

"It really is," Mrs. Biggs said. "It's her whole life. And obviously, we've invested a lot into her success."

"That," Mrs. Amberson said, "I believe."

There was a pause as the food arrived. Chelsea examined her fish to make sure no one had hidden cheese or candy bars or lumps of solid fat under the slender, pink strips.

"Of course, I understand the appeal of the big agency," Mrs. Amberson said. "You absolutely must meet with some. Absolutely."

Mrs. Biggs helped Chelsea with her fish exploration, lifting up a corner with her knife. She grimaced and made a "eat that if you want" face. She hadn't ordered anything for herself except a cup of coffee.

"The problem, of course," Mrs. Amberson continued, "is that they have many, many clients, and if you're not one of their biggest, they tend to forget that you are alive. You hear such *horror* stories. A boutique agency like mine is much more concerned with nurturing clients and building careers. I work with people like Billy to guide performers in the *right* direction. . . ."

Scarlett drifted a bit as she ate her cheese-and-sour-cream blintzes. Her brain traveled to an imaginary class at NYU, where Eric stood in front of a room of fellow performers, smiling, introducing himself as they worked around the room. His class was probably at least half made up of girls. Probably very pretty ones. Maybe ones like Chelsea who never ate bread. Hungry, crazy, ridiculously attractive girls who could act, who would take one look at that country boy with his honest face and natural skill . . . They would size him up and mark him for their own. They would fight for him. Every day, another one would throw herself in his path, taking advantage of his Southern manners, suggesting extended kissing scenes in plays where they weren't even required. And with every passing day, Scarlett would be more and more forgotten, until she was Scarlett Who? That girl from the hotel? The one who was fifteen, not an actress, the one who ate bread almost every day?

"Of course," Mrs. Amberson was saying, "Scarlett here is my secret weapon. . . ."

Scarlett blinked. The whole mental episode evaporated.

". . . and she goes to that wonderful school on the Upper West Side . . . what's it called?"

"Frances Perkins," Scarlett answered, still reeling a bit from what she had just imagined.

This caused Mrs. Biggs to sit up a little straighter.

"Isn't that funny!" she said. "That's where Max is going!"

"My brother," Chelsea explained. "We're all moving from Binghamton, so he's transferring."

"It's a good school, isn't it?" Mrs. Biggs asked. "We looked at the private schools, but Frances Perkins was even more highly recommended than most of them. And, obviously, the private schools are all expensive."

Mrs. Amberson leaned over to refill Chelsea's glass with sparkling water.

"What a remarkable coincidence!" she said. "It's always good to have someone on the inside to show you the ropes."

"He's pretty good at figuring out ropes," Chelsea said. "He can be . . ."

"He's very bright," Mrs. Biggs cut in. "But he won't know anyone there, and he can be very . . ."

"Spirited?" Mrs. Amberson offered, when both the Biggses ran out of words. "Like so many young men of talent and intelligence? I understand completely." Her voice had dropped that one half-tone that took it from smoothly polite to conspiratorial. That tone reverberated up Scarlett's spine, signaling danger. "I have a little idea, just a little one, purely outside of our discussion here. I've seen your wonderful show, but Scarlett hasn't. Maybe she and Max could go together. It would be good for him to have a familiar face on his first day. Scarlett could tell him about his new school, give him a little advice."

Scarlett was a bit surprised to hear herself being farmed out this way — but it was Chelsea who seemed the most outraged by this idea. She tried to control herself, but Scarlett caught the look of utter disgust she flashed across the table. As if the mere idea of Scarlett going to *her show* with *her brother* was just taking this whole thing a bit too far. The expression faded within seconds, as she regained control of her facial muscles. But Scarlett had seen it.

Mrs. Biggs, however, latched on to this idea with all enthusiasm.

"I'm sure we could arrange some tickets to *The Flower Girl*, couldn't we, Chelsea? You have loads of unused comps!"

"Sure," Chelsea said, her voice sounding a little hollow. "Whenever you want. I have some for tomorrow's matinee if you want."

"Wonderful," Mrs. Amberson said. "That's settled then! At the very least, that's a connection we can set up, no matter what happens professionally."

Scarlett was about to thank her for letting them all have a say in the matter, but restrained herself.

"Now," Mrs. Amberson said, "shall we be daring and order a crème brûlée and four spoons? We don't have to finish it, of course, though they are quite small and think of the protein . . . but let's make a decadent gesture. I *insist*!"

A PLAGUE
OF ACTORS

"Isn't she a gem?" Mrs. Amberson asked on the cab ride back.

"Yeah," Scarlett said under her breath. "She's the Hope Diamond. Isn't that the one that kills you?"

"I heard that, O'Hara. It was quite funny, actually."

"Did you see that look she gave me?" Scarlett asked. "When you said that thing about me going to the show with her brother?"

"No, I must have missed that," Mrs. Amberson replied. She was futzing around in her massive purse for the tea tree oil sticks she had to chew after eating in place of her cigarette. "It's not Chelsea that concerns me. It's her mother. What a piece of work that woman is. She's exactly the kind of stage parent I can't stand. I think it's hilarious how the most deluded ones always say, 'Oh, we'd leave this all behind tomorrow if little Chelsea here didn't want to dance! She loves to wake up at the crack of dawn and work all day long until she drops! It's all her idea, I just ride along with it!' Of course it is. The constant, hammering pressure has nothing to do with it. If Chelsea tried to walk away from her show, there'd be bloodshed and psychological warfare in that house, mark my words."

"So why do you want her?" Scarlett asked.

"Because . . ." Mrs. Amberson dug harder for the sticks as her need increased. "There's a lot of very good buzz about Chelsea, and I have no doubt that she could end up being quite a big deal if she's managed correctly. Think about that, Scarlett. Her success is your success. And a good agent could be a useful buffer between her and mommy dearest. I'd love a chance to give that bloodsucking harpy Miranda a run for her money. I'll eat her for breakfast."

The tea tree oil sticks were recovered, and Mrs. Amberson hastily opened the box and shoved one in her mouth.

"Oral fixations are so cumbersome," she said, easing back into the seat and chewing contentedly.

"*If* she signs with us," Scarlett said. "Her mom didn't seem that into the idea until you said . . ."

And then, Scarlett realized that something had just happened. That she had been moved like a pawn in a chess game. She didn't know the overall strategy or what her fate was to be — but she felt it as clearly as if an enormous pair of fingers had picked her up by the head and moved her a square or two.

"Why am I going to this show?" she asked.

"It's a free ticket!"

"You said it's horrible."

"Yes, but it's barely two hours."

"Why?" Scarlett asked again.

"What's the first rule of this agency?" Mrs. Amberson asked. "Our first rule is . . . and make a note of this, O'Hara . . . you must *always do a little spying*."

"It is?"

"Yes. And that's exactly what I did. Before we met Chelsea, I took one of the dancers from *The Flower Girl* out for cocktails on the roof of the Met and got the whole story on the family. The wild card here is Max Biggs. Max is sixteen and generally considered to be the family liability. Quite bright by all accounts — he did get into your school, after all. But there have been issues along the way. He is less motivated than his sister, but his mother is convinced he's a latent genius."

"So you want me to go to a bad show with him," Scarlett said. "For what? How does that help?"

"I want you to get a good look at him. You'll be going to school with him, after all. Just go to the show. Talk to him a little. We need to seem to be everywhere — you at the school, the show. Signing with us will just feel inevitable after a while. It's just a show, O'Hara. You see shows all the time. Is that asking so much?"

It was, but Scarlett shook her head no. She was trained to obey. It was sad.

The cab approached Mrs. Amberson's new apartment, which was on Fifth Avenue, on the east side of Central Park. It wasn't too far from the Hopewell, actually, a five- or ten-minute walk at most. But those few blocks seemed to span several worlds. This was a lush neighborhood of embassies and museums. The park was the front lawn, fifty city blocks of emerald green grass, ponds, and paths. Even by the standards of the neighborhood, this was a nice building, twenty chalk-white stories of parkside elegance, with a long green awning that extended almost to the curb to protect its residents from rain and snow and sun.

"Do me a favor, O'Hara," Mrs. Amberson said, shaking the nearly empty box of tea tree sticks. "Run down to the health food store and get me more of these? Also, some more umeboshi plums. I'm out."

Clearly, Scarlett was not released for the day. Not yet. Her boss went through umeboshi plums — small, gray, salty things that came in a tiny plastic container — at an astonishing rate. This was a common and easy enough errand, though. She was there and back in a few minutes.

The lobby of Mrs. Amberson's new building was cold and beautiful, from the marbled walls and floor to the gleam of the brass mailboxes to the buttery leather sofas off to the side. The man on duty was new to Scarlett. He was shaped roughly like a postbox, but moved with slightly less grace than a postbox might if it freed itself from its moorings and went for a stroll down the street. He was spraying the delicate orchid on the coffee table with water, pumping the bottle hard, as if the orchid had said something offensive about his mom. The orchid shook under the onslaught. He took his time setting down the bottle and coming over to the desk. Things really went wrong when she told him that she was going to 19D. He seemed to take it as a personal affront.

"The freight elevator *closes* at *six*," he said, pulling on his name tag for emphasis. His name was Murray.

"Okay?" Scarlett said.

"At six," he said again. "When you gonna be done? I got to keep the lobby clear. When you gonna be done?"

Scarlett looked around at the lobby, which was empty.

"I can't have you moving boxes through here all day. And sofas. And chairs. I gotta keep the lobby clear."

"It is clear," she said.

"*You* have to get *your stuff* up there by six," he said. "The freight elevator closes at six. I lock it then."

"It's not my stuff," Scarlett said.

"What? I gotta lock it at six."

"Yes, but . . ."

"Hey! I gotta keep it clear!"

"Six," Scarlett replied. "Got it. Six."

He picked up his phone. Scarlett could just hear Mrs. Amberson's voice on the other end, and she didn't sound happy.

"You can go," he said, disappearing behind his *New York Post*, still making noises of general disapproval. "Six o'clock. Remember."

Scarlett turned the corner, around the bank of gleaming brass mailboxes with the marble shelf, to the elevators. She stabbed the button several times in her annoyance.

"What time was that?" she said, in a low, mocking voice. "Six? Was it six? Did you say six? Oh wait . . . six?"

"Hey!" Murray called loudly. Scarlett blanched, wondering if he'd heard her. She poked her head back around the corner to see him holding up a bundle of large envelopes bound together with rubber bands. Scarlett walked back to collect it.

"Gets a lot of mail," the guy muttered. "Always going to get this much mail?"

Murray didn't seem to like anything that involved doing his job, like greeting people or letting people move in or getting packages. As someone who lived in a hotel, Scarlett recognized his resentment of visitors, and while she sympathized, she didn't approve of it.

"Probably," she said, taking the three dozen or so large envelopes he pushed in her direction. Mrs. Amberson had posted an ad in *Back Stage*, advertising her services. The headshots and résumés had been coming steadily since, dozens every day. Scarlett had always known there were lots of actors in New York — but she didn't know there were *this* many who apparently thought that working with Mrs. Amberson sounded like a good idea. Yes, there was always going to be this much mail.

"Six o'clock," he said again. "You tell your boss."

Scarlett rode the elevator up to the nineteenth floor. It was a fancy elevator, quiet and efficient, unlike the one at home. She was deposited in a dark hall with lush blue carpeting. Scarlett walked to the end and let herself into 19D.

There was no denying that Mrs. Amberson's new home was a step up from the Hopewell. It was a massive, airy space, with a long string of windows facing the park. There were white sofas that hadn't been there the day before, a plush white rug on the hardwood floor. The built-in bookcases were still empty, but there were unopened boxes everywhere. Only one area of the apartment was completely set up. That was the large desk, bulletin board, and file cabinet unit that served as "the office." These pieces of furniture formed the physical structure of Mrs. Amberson's new business.

"I'm here!" Scarlett called.

No reply.

Scarlett wandered deeper into the apartment, over to the board of photos featuring their one and only client. Mrs. Amberson had paid for an expensive photo shoot and had Spencer photographed in a dozen different ways. There was Spencer in a T-shirt, looking young and tech-savvy, ready to do a computer commercial. There was Spencer in a suit, looking like a hard-boiled young attorney. Over on the left, there was Spencer in a sleek dress shirt with an unbuttoned collar, doing his best sexy face. On the right, there was comic Spencer, doing a handstand. There were a few other photos on the board — photos of the production of *Hamlet* at the hotel, carefully posed stills of various scenes. There was Spencer in his loose-fitting suit, balancing perfectly on his unicycle next to . . .

Eric.

Even in the comic outfit, with his expression set in mock alarm, it was such a good picture of him. He was supporting Spencer as he tilted backward, and you could see just how strong and graceful he was.

Okay. So she had looked at that one. She would be fine as long as she didn't look at the next one, the close-up of him as he stood alone onstage. She would not look at that. No. She would not. Except . . . she was already doing it. There he was, his shirt hanging open to the third button. That wide mouth that was always on the verge of a slow smile . . .

"You know what would be great," Scarlett mumbled to herself, "is if I could get some *more* reminders . . ."

"O'Hara!" a voice yelled. "In here!"

The voice seemed to be coming from the kitchen, but the kitchen was fully visible from the living room — just a sleek pathway of granite and stainless steel, divided off by a bar where you could sit and eat. Scarlett walked around and found Mrs. Amberson sitting on the sparkling floor, wrestling the Styrofoam insert out of a box. She had changed into her normal clothes — stretchy yoga stuff. She had a pair of scissors in her mouth. Her lips were holding the tip, in a dangerous and unbalanced way. She took them out to speak again.

"Did that *maniac* talk to you?" she asked. "Every time I even *cross* the lobby that deranged hobbit comes after me, screaming about boxes. I have read the building rules. Repeatedly. I can move in from nine in the morning until six in the afternoon. That is my right."

She passed the scissors to Scarlett a little too roughly, almost stabbing her in the palm.

"What does he expect?" she went on, gripping the box with her knees and yanking away. "That no one should ever be allowed to move in or out?"

The contents of the box yielded to Mrs. Amberson's efforts, and she produced a sarcophagus of foam, which she managed to crack through to reveal a stainless steel electric kettle.

"All this packaging," she mumbled, rubbing the little foam niblets from the kettle's surface. "That's an ice shelf crumbling right there."

She pulled herself off the floor and placed the kettle on the granite counter, then opened a cabinet to reveal three packed shelves full of boxes of organic herbal teas. She plugged in the kettle and filled it from a bottle of spring water. It set to work with a polite hiss.

"New headshots," Scarlett said, holding up the bundle of envelopes. Mrs. Amberson reached for them and started ripping them open, tossing the envelopes to the floor and extracting the glossy headshot photos and résumés. Once you'd seen a dozen headshots, you felt like there was too much sameness in the world. Pretty people smiling big smiles, sometimes leaning forward casually, sometimes leaning against something. Or you'd just get a big close-up of their beautiful eyes and perfect skin and teeth. Actors. So many actors.

"Tea?" Mrs. Amberson asked, not looking up from the parade of faces.

"Is there coffee?"

"O'Hara, you know that caffeine is the great dehydrator. It's like a vampire. Invite it into your body and it sucks all the moisture right out. That's the real fanged bandit. It will drain you dry and . . ."

The rest of the remark was lost under the keening cry of the kettle, which apparently couldn't take the vampire comparisons anymore. Mrs. Amberson switched it off, then fiddled around in her herbal tea emporium for a moment, putting a spoonful of this dried-up thing and that dried-up thing into a tea ball, finally dropping the whole mess into a cup and covering it with hot water.

"We'll let this steep for a moment, O'Hara. That is a very potent brew. Some very special teas and ingredients in there, from a very special shop in Chinatown . . . some of them not entirely legal in the United States. This stuff is better than any medication on the market, and certainly a lot faster and better for you. I feel that the word 'detoxify' is overused, but that is exactly what this does. Now, these new headshots . . ."

She flipped through them all again for a few seconds each. The few that she thought were worth a second look she set on the side of the counter. The majority of them she dropped in one big sloppy pile. Scarlett picked up her tea and sniffed it carefully. It smelled like cooked pencil shavings and just a tiny, tiny bit like burning plastic. She set it back down again.

"God," Mrs. Amberson said in disgust, "I'm just not getting the quality that I'm looking for. I've set my bar, and it's high."

She pushed the photos to the floor in dismissal.

"What's wrong with those?" Scarlett asked, looking at the faces of actors around her feet. They looked sad and desperate now, smiling all around her shoes, asking to be picked up. They had done nothing wrong. They just wanted a chance.

"No spark," Mrs. Amberson said. "You can see it at once. You know when you see it."

"How can you see a spark in pictures? They all look the same."

"Exactly." Mrs. Amberson gulped down some tea, even though vast clouds of steam were still coming off of it. "They all look the same. We need Chelsea. She's the key. She's our next step."

Scarlett picked the pictures up from the floor and piled them on one of the bar stools. She had to do that much for them.

"That's all for today," Mrs. Amberson said. "Oh, but you have to deliver something very important. Do you see that large envelope over there on the bookcase? Take that with you. Your brother has an audition tomorrow for *Crime and Punishment*! He's reading for the part of a young pervert! He'll enjoy that!"

"*Crime and Punishment*? You mean, like, to be on the show with Sonny Lavinski? The *Crime and Punishment*?"

Scarlett liked *Crime and Punishment*. Everyone liked *Crime and Punishment*. *Crime and Punishment* had been on TV as long as she'd been alive. It had four spin-off shows and was on in reruns pretty much all the time on one network or another. And wisecracking lead detective, Sonny Lavinski, was pretty much her favorite character on any show. Everyone loved Sonny Lavinski.

"I've been talking to the producers for a while," Mrs. Amberson said, "since one of the directors came to see *Hamlet*. They have real interest in him. I've been working on this for *weeks*, but I didn't want to say anything until it came through. Make sure he looks at the pages *tonight*. The audition tomorrow is at four. I have a very good feeling about this one."

BAD OMENS

The moving van had come while Scarlett was out and the stage platform and lights were gone. Only the chairs remained, scattered around in a confused fashion. *Hamlet* was truly over, and the room was once again an underused, dingy dining area. Scarlett took a moment to stand alone in the empty room, listening to the echo of traffic outside, the creak of the floor. The feeling of loss was so profound that for a moment, she couldn't breathe. Something wonderful had happened here — something confusing, but wonderful — and now it was gone, and it would never come back. The show was permanently over.

She probably would have started crying, but she was startled by a noise behind her. Quick little steps in the lobby.

"There you are," Lola called. "I was worried you'd be late for dinner."

Lola had been cleaning. Unlike most people, Lola cleaned while wearing neat and formfitting black pants and shirt, with a little white pocket apron tied around her waist. She carried a little caddy of furniture spray and cloths. Her hair was pulled back in a loose, flattering knot.

Lola was the second-oldest Martin, just three months out of high school. She had taken a "year off" to work at home at the hotel, instead of going to college like all of her friends. Of course, there was no money for college, but that was never mentioned. Lola always acted like her service was completely voluntary. She was unfailingly, sometimes infuriatingly gracious. She was also a strange throwback to some other generation of Martins — white-pale with a fragile build. If she had been a character in an old romance story, she would have been the lovely maiden at court, the one with the terrible wasting disease who had to be married off before she dropped elegantly dead.

"I've been thinking a lot about these chairs today," Lola said, pushing one of the many scattered dining room chairs into a patch of sunlight. There were many styles of chair in the room, but the one Lola had was one of the old ones, part of the fancy original set from when the dining room was decorated in 1929 and all the furniture matched. They were made of deep cherry wood, with backs carved into stylized flowers. Some of them still had the threadbare original cushioned seats, covered in yellow silk with a pattern of silvery birds.

"I've been trying to think of a way to get these chairs refinished and reupholstered," she said, testing one of the legs. "It would probably only cost a few hundred dollars."

"A few hundred dollars?" Scarlett said, settling herself in one. They creaked, too.

"Maybe a thousand. Or two. But I think it's important. They're really good chairs, and I feel like we need to make a good impression right here, on the doorstep. If people come in and see frayed fabric . . . well, people notice."

"We could put them in the basement if they look bad," Scarlett said.

"The solution for everything isn't 'put it in the basement,'" Lola said.

This had been the solution for as long as Scarlett could remember, but she didn't care enough to argue the point.

"That's true," Scarlett said, picking at the threads. "It never works in horror movies. The thing always escapes and eats you. Or someone finds it and then you have to kill them. And then you have two secrets in the basement. Basements are bad."

"I've researched this," Lola said. "After Mrs. Amberson told us about the man who designed this place, J. Allen Raumenberg. We could be sitting on a fortune, literally. He was a really famous designer. The pieces are just in such bad condition. If we could get them fixed . . ."

"You're probably right." Scarlett held up her hands in surrender. "But we can't afford to."

Lola sank down in the chair opposite Scarlett.

"I know," she said. "I just can't help thinking about it. This place could be a showpiece. A good cleaning, a little fixing . . . it's not even that much money in the grand scheme of things."

"Every amount of money is a lot of money when you have no money."

"It would be an investment, though." Lola stared into a thready patch of fabric for a moment and worked her finger into the seat stuffing. "Did I mention I had an interview at Bubble Spa the other day? It went really well. Even though I was fired from Henri Bendel, my old manager still loves me, so I got a really good recommendation. I think I've got that one in the bag. I'm hoping they'll give me twenty hours a week. I could make a ton on commission there. That stuff is easy to sell. Makeup, skin care . . . I can sell that stuff in my sleep."

This was true. When it came to selling beauty products, Lola had Jedi powers. She'd only been fired because she took off too many days to go places with her ex-boyfriend, Chip, who didn't understand that when you had a job, you were supposed to go all of the days you were scheduled to work. But it wasn't his fault. Lola had done the skipping.

"That's great," Scarlett said.

"It's something. I mean, I like sales. Oh, and you heard we're going to Lupe's, right?"

"Yeah," Scarlett said. "With Marlene. Let the happy fun times begin."

"Scarlett . . ." Lola admonished.

The Martins were, on the whole, a fairly open family, but Marlene was one subject no one was allowed to touch. She was the elephant in the room. They all knew that it was Marlene's medical bills that had caused so many of their problems. Talking about this, ever, in any context, was not allowed. Scarlett even wondered if they were allowed to *think* about it. The other thing that you really weren't supposed to mention was Marlene's personality, which was not entirely composed of sunshine and rainbows. She responded a little differently to each member of her family, with Lola at the top of the pack and Scarlett at the far, far bottom. Marlene's normal greeting for Scarlett was a contemptuous glance, and (if she was very lucky) a little side-brush out of the way.

"I'm going to go upstairs," Scarlett said, getting up. "To put on my biggest smile! How's this one?"

She gave Lola a wide, alarming grin. Lola just shook her head and picked up her cleaning caddy.

Scarlett had nothing to do upstairs. She sat on her bed in the Orchid Suite and watched dust motes float in the sun for a few minutes. She examined the crack in her windowpane that prevented it from being opened more than halfway. She watched her neighbor on her roof deck. The neighbor, who was about seventy, was often proudly naked, especially in the morning. Today she was setting some kind of art project, a big collage, out on a table and spraying it with some kind of substance in an aerosol can.

Her sheets needed washing. She hadn't stripped them and taken them downstairs in more than two weeks. Bad hotel daughter. That would be a good thing to do. Or any of her laundry, really.

Or she could watch that commercial. Her laptop was right under her bed. One little view . . . Dakota would never know.

She hit PLAY.

The commercial was for a pizza chain, and Eric was playing a guy who accidentally set himself on fire while cooking dinner (which is why he had to order the pizza). Scarlett had seen the commercial many, many times before she met Eric. It was kind of funny, but it didn't make much of an impression. Once she knew Eric, though, the commercial was her obsession. She knew every expression in every frame.

The flames, Eric told her, were part real and part CGI. When the fire just started at the stove, that was real. His shirt had been treated with some chemical, and he wore protection underneath. They put him out after just a few seconds. When he fell to the floor and started rolling around, and when he tumbled through the window, those were all fake. At the end, he was seen bobbing up in his neighbor's swimming pool, fully dressed, soaking wet, shirt clinging to his body. (Though he looked much smaller on television than he did in life, which was the opposite of what Scarlett had heard about what the camera did to you. The real-life muscles were well-developed, but you couldn't see them on TV. Which was fine by Scarlett. This was a secret the world did not need to know.)

The commercial took two days to shoot, and Eric earned enough from it to pay for four years of college in his home state, or one year of the extremely pricey NYU acting school. He auditioned. He got in. He opted to blow it all on NYU and take his chances. He'd moved to the city for the summer and scored a part in *Hamlet* as Spencer's partner, and that was that. That was where their lives connected. A pizza commercial.

Scarlett was about to add a few more forbidden viewings to the counter, when there was a knock at the door. She slammed the computer shut and shoved it off her lap.

"It's open," she called.

A very tan and freckly Marlene stood in the doorway with a duffel bag. To Scarlett's amazement, Marlene came over and gave her a tight, businesslike hug. Then she sat on the edge of Scarlett's bed. There was something about her expression that chilled Scarlett. It was a kind of peacefulness. An even-temperedness. No scowl or evil look or shifting eyes. She just sat there, all prim and vaguely saintlike.

"I'm home," she said.

"I see that," Scarlett replied.

"I missed you."

Scarlett coughed in shock.

"Camp was good," Marlene went on. "I won the award for canoe-ing. Want to see?"

She opened up her bag, shuffled around through the dirty shorts and shirts and still-damp bathing suits and produced a small plastic trophy with a picture of a canoe on it. Marlene had never bothered to share something like this with Scarlett before. Scarlett had learned from television that the appropriate big sister reaction to this sort of thing was praise, but it seemed like too big a leap. Maybe she should start out slower, by fact-finding.

"How did you get this?" Scarlett asked. "What's it for?"

"*Canoeing.*"

"Right, but, was it a race, or . . ."

Marlene squinted a bit, probably sensing Scarlett's weakness and confusion, but she kept playing the politeness game. There was maybe a little tension in the jaw area, though. A sign of strain.

"It was just for *canoeing*," she said.

"It's great," Scarlett said, turning it over once in her hands and passing it back quickly.

The trophy was stuffed back into the bag. Marlene idly twirled a lock of hair around her finger and looked around the Orchid Suite.

"When did your hair turn curly?" she asked.

"It . . . was always this way."

"Even when you were a baby?"

"As long as I've had hair, it's been like this."

Unlike Scarlett and Lola, who were pure, total blonde, Marlene's hair was slowly going a burnished red-blonde. It was long now, too, not quite curly and not quite straight. For a long time, it had been so fried by the cancer treatments that it was patchy and thin and fell out in big clumps, clogging the bathroom drains. Now that she had some hair, Marlene played with it constantly, obviously proud of it.

"I thought mine might grow in curly," she said. "I like your hair. I wish mine was like it."

You can't complain about how big and unruly your hair gets to someone who's happy to have hair at all. Scarlett guessed that Marlene knew this and had cornered her, conversationally. This was a politeness death match, and Marlene was winning.

"Have to go unpack," she said, with an unnerving smile.

When Marlene got to the door, she turned and gave Scarlett a knowing look — the kind of look one spy might give another spy when she realizes that they are both spies and no one else is aware of the fact.

"Your outfit is pretty," she said, and shut the door. "And it's time to go. Lola's waiting for us."

Scarlett sat there in shock for a moment, stirring only when she heard her phone buzz. There was a text message from Dakota that read simply: *I saw you do that. Don't do it again. I AM WATCHING!*

Lupe's wasn't far from the Hopewell, just a few blocks uptown, in the hustle of the Upper East Side. For the whole walk, Marlene swung her arms playfully like a little girl and chatted to Lola about camp. She even turned a few times to try to include Scarlett in the conversation. But Scarlett could now see something cold and steady in her eye. Some terrible plot was afoot. Everyone conspired against her. Her friends. Her boss. Her eleven-year-old sister. It sounded paranoid, but it was true. *Hamlet* was gone and Eric was gone and she was doomed.

Spencer called and met them halfway, skidding up on his unsteady bicycle. He pulled it up on the sidewalk and rolled it along.

"Audition go well?" Scarlett asked. She tried to make her voice sound normal and pleasant, but it cracked a bit. Luckily, someone hit a car horn and this was lost.

"It was good," he said, taking a deep breath after his ride and wiping some sweat from his hands onto his pants. "They kept me for a few hours. They laughed at the tie thing. They laughed even more at the oxygen mask thing. They had me read eight times. I'll find out tonight whether or not I got it."

The bike snaked and banged into his side, and he had to keep lifting the front wheel to make it go straight again.

"That doesn't look good," Lola said, noticing the bike. "I'm glad you always wear your helmet."

Marlene rushed ahead of them, which was a common behavior. But this time, she did it to get the door of the restaurant and hold it open for them. Spencer stayed behind a moment to lock his bike. Lola went through, and Scarlett fully expected Marlene to move aside and let the door shut in her face, but she stood there, waiting for both her and Spencer. No one else in the world could hold a door open with the bitter determination of Marlene.

Once she had herded her three older siblings inside, she stepped in front of them and backed them into a very loud corner of the festive, red-tiled lobby filled with piñatas and a decorative old-timey red gas pump.

"Stay here," she said to the three of them. "I want to show you guys something."

"Did you see that?" Scarlett whispered to Spencer. "She *held* the *door*. And when she got home? She *hugged* me. She showed me her canoeing trophy. She said I looked pretty. She said she *missed* me."

"That's a little disturbing," he admitted. "Maybe she just *really* liked camp?"

"Camp does not do that," Scarlett said. "Unless she went to camp at Lake Prozac."

"She could be on new pills."

"There's nothing wrong with her," Lola said, obviously having overheard. "She's so proud of that canoeing trophy. . . ."

"You're not listening," Scarlett said. "The only time Marlene feels bad about missing me is when she's thrown something at me."

Lola laughed one of her oh-Scarlett-what-a-wit-you-are-but-I-have-no-idea-what-you-are-talking-about laughs.

Spencer was looking intently over both of his sisters, into the depths of the restaurant.

"Lola . . ." he said.

"You just need to give Marlene a chance," Lola was rambling on.

"Lola . . ." Spencer repeated, and this time, his voice was a warning.

Scarlett immediately saw the cause of his concern. Someone was coming toward them. They had been led into a trap.

DINNER IS ALSO FOR SUCKERS

Coming at them through the melee of waiters and bright yellow chairs and blue tables and guacamole carts was Chip Sutcliffe, Lola's ex-boyfriend.

"I didn't do this," Lola said quickly. "I swear."

Scarlett believed her. Lola's constant, unfailing composure completely fell away for a moment, and she backed up gracelessly into a dark corner by the host stand, bumping her head into a low-hanging piñata of a yellow cab.

"So this is a coincidence?" Spencer asked. "We just stumbled on Chip while he was on a mad, lonely hunt for tacos?"

Lola shook her head in confusion.

Chip paused in his progress and stood by a large cactus, prodding it gently with one outstretched finger. Marlene had his other hand and was tugging him along, trying to force him onward.

"I told you," Scarlett said, pointing. "I *told* you." She was glad to have her worst suspicions vindicated — Marlene *had* been up to something. There was nothing quite like the sweet, sweet nectar of being right.

"You have to be kidding me," Spencer said. "You told me *you* were taking us out."

"I was covering for Marlene," Lola said, flustered. "She wanted it to be a surprise."

"How the hell would Marlene be able to afford this?"

"You know how she gets stuff through Powerkids. I figured she had a gift certificate or something and was sharing it. She gets all kinds of things. I didn't know!"

"So what do we do now?" Scarlett asked. "Want to have family dinner night with your ex?"

"Well, we can't leave," Lola said.

"Why?" Spencer asked.

"We're here for *Marlene*," Lola said.

"If Marlene wants to have dinner with Chip, let her have dinner with Chip."

Something very strange had come over Scarlett's older sister. There was a totally foreign blush to her paper-white cheeks, and she was rocking a bit on her low heels.

"Don't leave me," she said, clutching them both by an arm. "Please. Don't leave me. Tomorrow, he's gone. He goes to Boston for school. You won't have to deal with him anymore."

"I thought the day you broke up with him was the day I didn't have to deal with him anymore," Spencer said, looking at the tiny, pale hand that gripped his wrist.

"You weren't that picky on the day he saved your show. You owe him."

This, sadly, was true. Chip had played a large part in making *Hamlet* happen by distracting their parents on a day-long cruise on the Sutcliffe family boat, giving Spencer and Scarlett enough time to load in an entire cast and stage a show. He did this after Lola had broken up with him, no less.

"Look," Lola said, when neither Spencer nor Scarlett responded to that statement. "Maybe . . . I don't know. I want to stay. But I can't stay here alone. And Marlene must have gone to a lot of effort, so, let's just stay, okay? It's a free dinner at our favorite restaurant. It could be worse. I'm just going to go to the ladies' room, and then we'll stay, okay? Okay?"

She accepted their stunned silence as a yes, nodded tersely, and tiptoed off to the ladies' room behind her.

"This is so bad," Spencer said, leaning up against the decorative old-fashioned gas pump behind him. "This is so, so bad. . . ."

He trailed off, and his face stiffened into a neutral mask as Marlene dislodged Chip from the cactus and brought him over.

"Stay here," she commanded them all. "I'll get us a table."

Chip had really outdone himself tonight, outfitwise. The pants were stripy, the shirt was a different color and seemed deliberately too small, the tie a different stripy still. Ridiculous as it was, there was no doubt in Scarlett's mind that what Chip was wearing cost a fortune — that perhaps, if you touched him, an alarm would go off somewhere. Not that Scarlett had any plans on touching him.

He took a careful step in Spencer's direction and extended a hand of greeting.

"What's up?" he asked.

Chip seemed understandably nervous to be facing the Martins once again, because even he knew that Scarlett and Spencer weren't his biggest fans. Scarlett's dislike was fairly tepid, but Spencer genuinely couldn't stand him and had never hidden that fact. Chip had no real personality; at least, Scarlett had never seen it. It may have been one of those things that stayed hidden most of the time, like a groundhog.

But that wasn't the problem. Chip's crime was something he couldn't really help. He was rich. Seriously rich. Bona fide, century-old, New York society, private school rich. To be fair to him, Chip never bragged about his wealth, nor did he appear to care that Lola and her family came from a totally different financial league. He was not snobbish. If anything, he acted like he'd recently landed on the planet and was charmed and fascinated by the things he found there. The magical underground "subway" train that transported people all over the city. Credit card limits. Doing your own laundry. Having a job. Chip gazed in wonderment at it all.

This trait, however innocent, had never been very endearing to Spencer or Scarlett. Scarlett thought Chip was dull and a little dim. Spencer exhibited something that ranged from profound irritation to seething hatred. Scarlett always assumed that this had something to do with seeing a guy a year younger than himself, who had an endless spending limit, no known vocation, and no pressure to accomplish anything right away. Chip would get four years of college to continue his lacrosse-playing and shirt-buying, and maybe a year or two after that, before anyone asked him what he planned on doing with the rest of his life.

He loved Lola. Of that, no one had any doubt. He loved Lola with a kind of palpable, squeamish love. His eyes followed her when they were in a room together, and when she left, his brain seemed to go into a sleep mode, waiting for her reappearance. He cared enough about Lola to extend his hand to Lola's tall, unpredictable older brother who had fixed him with a gaze of stone. Scarlett had no idea what Spencer was going to do with the extended hand — so many things were possible in his world — but he merely shook it. Even Chip seemed surprised by this.

"I like your tie," Spencer said.

Chip grabbed the tie reflexively with his free hand.

"Oh . . . thanks. I just got it. I've been looking for one in this color for a while. They don't make this shade that often, so . . . anyway, I found it at Hugo Boss and . . ."

Spencer's face had frozen in a tableau of slightly exaggerated interest, inviting Chip to keep digging his hole, keep talking about his tie until the universe finally went *poof*, rolled itself back into a ball, and took itself home.

Lola quietly emerged from the restroom. Chip opened his mouth to say some kind of greeting, but failed. Lola smiled shyly and put her head down.

"Chip got a new tie," Spencer said. "I did something with a tie this morning, Chip. Want to see?"

Before Spencer could demonstrate his strangulation method, Marlene reappeared.

"Table's ready!" she said.

"Guess we should sit," Lola said, knocking Spencer gently out of the way as he reached for Chip's tie. "Lead the way, Marlene."

As she walked off, Lola mouthed the words "stop it" over her shoulder, and Spencer pointed to his heart, as if he had no idea what she could possibly mean.

"Remind me to kill Marlene later," he said quietly to Scarlett. "Just in case I forget. Let's eat and get this over with. And eat a lot. Order *everything*."

At the table, Lola and Marlene were positioning themselves on a bench seat against the wall. Chip was milling around, trying to do the mental math about where he should sit. He backed up on Scarlett and Spencer's approach, letting them take whatever seats they wanted. Spencer delayed sitting down, hesitating between two chairs for over a minute. Chip eventually got so nervous from this that he excused himself.

"Sit!" Lola exclaimed when Chip was out of earshot.

Spencer gleefully took a seat next to Scarlett. A trayful of organic guava smoothies arrived, unbidden. These were the best drinks in the place, but were also shockingly expensive.

"Chip is trying to win us over with fancy fruit drinks, huh?" Spencer asked, accepting one.

"I ordered them," Marlene said. "I also got guacamole."

"Spencer," Lola said, "be nice!"

"I was," he said, straightening the napkin on his lap. "I was being very nice. I was asking him about his nice tie."

"I know what you were doing."

"Yes, but could you prove it in court?"

"Spencer, please . . ."

"What? I'm telling you, *nice* is my middle name. Right, Scarlett?"

"Your middle name is Reynolds," Scarlett said, sipping from her smoothie.

"Just one night," Lola said. "Please, Spence. Don't bait him. He's trying to be friends."

"Kind of a pointless activity, don't you think? Considering that he's your ex, and he's leaving the city tomorrow?"

"Stop it, Spencer!" Marlene said, a note of absolute authority in her voice. "Don't ruin everything!"

Spencer shrugged and sat back, folding his arms over his chest in temporary surrender.

Chip returned just as the guacamole cart came rattling up to the table. They all watched a man with an alarmingly wide smile whack avocados in half and smash them to bits in a huge stone mortar. It looked like a carefree job, one that helped you get out all your aggressions and frustrations. Scarlett watched him enviously as he smacked down the pestle, grinding in the garlic and onions and cilantro. He would never need therapy. Anytime he had a problem, an avocado would meet a terrible death.

"Obviously, um, tonight's on me," Chip said as the waiter approached. "I just thought, you know, dinner . . ."

"Thank you," Lola said politely. She was doing some kind of napkin origami in her lap.

Once they had ordered half the menu (Spencer wasn't kidding), a fog of silence fell on the table. Lola and Chip kept slipping looks at each other, being tediously, horribly coy. Unlike the silences between Scarlett and Eric, these were full of meaning and potential, and Scarlett wanted no part of them.

"What are you majoring in?" she asked, breaking the silence. She didn't care, it was just the only question that sprang to mind.

"Oh . . . yeah." Chip shuffled his utensils. "We, um, we don't have to pick our majors for a year or two. So I'm just taking a bunch of classes. And probably row. I guess. They row a lot. In Boston. They have a . . . big river. I forget what it's called."

"The Charles," Marlene said. "I looked up your school online, and some stuff about Boston."

Sometimes, Marlene could be really creepy. She could get away with it while she was eleven, but it was going to be a problem really soon.

"Oh right," Chip said, smiling. "Yeah, I knew it was a name."

"You knew the name was a name?" Spencer asked politely.

Scarlett thought she felt a kick brush by under the table.

"I won the canoeing trophy," Marlene said. And this time, she provided an explanation. An extremely long one. The trophy had apparently been the result of some all-day adventure course where Marlene had to navigate around the lake. They were treated to descriptions of every single girl in Marlene's bunk (she didn't like them, except for one named Zoe, who sounded like she was now Marlene's little lieutenant). Chip listened intently. A conversation about eleven-year-olds rowing around a lake was one he could keep up with. And he was a rower. Paddling techniques were exchanged. This had a softening effect on Lola, who liked it when anyone paid attention to Marlene.

After a while, Chip must have felt like he had to share his attentions with another Martin, and so he finally turned to Scarlett.

"Hey, Scarlett," he said. "Good summer?"

"I . . . guess?"

"Are you still seeing that guy?" he asked. "Ed . . . no . . ."

"Eric," Scarlett corrected him, far too hastily.

"Right," Chip said. "Eric. Nice guy. From the show, right?"

"Right . . ."

Spencer fell back in his chair and looked up at the red-tiled ceiling, probably wishing that it would choose this moment to collapse.

"That guy was an idiot," Marlene continued. "He was just messing with Scarlett. And he was really —"

"Marlene!" Lola said brightly. "Tell Chip about the Powerkid of the Year competition. Marlene is being considered for . . ."

The interruption only confirmed Marlene's suspicion that she was onto something worth talking about.

"Eric was gross," Marlene went on, leaning toward Chip. "I hated him, and . . ."

"Hey, is this one spicy?" Spencer said, making a wide reach across the table for the Scotch bonnet salsa, the one that glowed an alarming yellowish-green. Before anyone could answer, he filled a chip with a massive scoop and ate it.

The reaction that followed, while certainly exaggerated, was not entirely fake. The gasping and grabbing all the glasses of water — the banging on the table that drew the attention of all the nearby diners and the waiter — all of it was designed to kill this avenue of conversation. Marlene took the hint this time.

Dinner passed by slowly. Now that he had convened the Martins, Chip had nothing to say to them. It was a puzzling exercise of silences punctuated by the sizzle of fajitas and the endless consumption of pricey smoothies. Marlene tried to keep filling the air, but after a while no one was even pretending to listen to the canoe stories.

Just as they finished up, Spencer's phone rang.

"I have to take this," he said, springing out of his chair. He returned a minute later. Scarlett could tell from the tightness of his jaw and the way he fixed his eyes on the table and didn't play around anymore — the call had been about the audition, and the news had not been good.

"Anyone want dessert?" Chip asked cheerfully.

THE PRICE OF FAILURE

Out on the sidewalk, the group waited uneasily in the humidity and the falling dark as Chip called for his car to come around. Now that she was fully stuffed, the lingering scent of hot, frying tortilla chips made Scarlett feel ill and heavy.

"Since we're here," Chip said with forced casualness, "the boat's just sitting up at the basin. We could go for a ride. Last one of the summer."

Oh, so *that's* what tonight was all about. The boat. A trip under the stars, looking at the gleaming lights of Manhattan. The dinner at Lupe's was the goodwill gesture, the setup. Aside from the fact that Lola kind of hated boats because they made her puke, it was a great plan, well hatched.

For a second, Scarlett hated Lola, hated that people went to efforts like this to get her back. They ate dinner with their enemies to be near her and went after her in watercraft. She looked to Spencer for support — for him to make a joke or exchange a look with her — but he was staring off down the street and didn't even seem to notice.

"Yes," Marlene said definitively. "We have to."

Lola shifted a bit on her heels and swung her purse in a ticktock motion by her knees.

"I guess since Marlene wants to go, I can go."

Chip looked like he might cry. His eyes took on that congested tone of emotion.

"I think I'll just go home," Spencer said.

"Me too," Scarlett quickly seconded. "Busy day tomorrow."

There was no doubt in Scarlett's mind that their responses had been predicted. Even Chip could correctly guess that Spencer and Scarlett would not come along. The car pulled up that moment, allowing Chip the opportunity to quickly recompose himself back into his usual, ever-cool prepster self.

"We can drop you off at the hotel," he said. "Or . . ."

"We'll walk," Scarlett said. "But thanks."

Marlene was already climbing into the air-conditioned, leathery depths of the car, not even bothering to wait for the driver to come around and open the door for her. Chip didn't tempt fate by trying to shake Spencer's hand again, so he simply gave a guy-nod in his direction. But in his flush of emotion, he decided to give Scarlett a hug. This had never happened before and caught Scarlett entirely by surprise. She stiffened in nervousness.

"Good luck in school," he said.

"Oh . . . thanks." She felt the need to do something in return, so she gave him a quick squeeze in the rib region just as he was letting go. He renewed the hug. Then neither of them seemed to know what to do for a moment. Chip broke contact suddenly and ducked into the car.

"Emo Chip hugs," Scarlett said. "Who knew?"

Spencer *mmmm*ed and walked on, digging his hands deep in his pockets.

"Was that call about the commercial?" Scarlett asked.

Another *mmmmmm*.

"Sorry," she said. "They're idiots."

"Guess it was overkill, huh?" He raised his eyebrows a little, wryly noting his own joke. "At least they called. They usually don't bother."

It was just light enough that they could cut through Central Park to get home. They descended the steps of one of the south gates. It was quiet. Most people had filtered out for the evening. The last of the dog walkers and joggers hurried past. The ducks slept on the lake. Scarlett heard rustlings in the undergrowth, probably rats and mice who were getting ready to take over for the night. The park lights blinked on all at once, flickering a bit as they were stirred into action.

"It was another Day of the Sock," Spencer finally said. "I should have known. They laugh. They *always* laugh. They make you do it over and over again, and then they give it to someone else. Why do I even bother?"

"Because you're really good?" Scarlett said.

"It doesn't matter what I am. It doesn't matter how I do. Like with the sock thing. I did so much better than the guy they cast. They just thought it was funnier because he was *short*. For my height, I did *way* more tumbles. Didn't matter. Too tall. That job would have solved my problems for a year. It's all luck. And I'm not lucky."

"Come on," Scarlett said. "It was just an airline safety video. You don't want that."

68

"It was *work*," he said pointedly. "I can't keep this up forever. At some point, something has to give. *Hamlet* was a fluke. Mom and Dad *clearly* know that things aren't going well. I'm not acting. I'm not in college."

"You never wanted to go to college," Scarlett said. "Everyone knows that."

"Sure . . ." he said distractedly. "That's not the point. The point is . . . I'm feeling poor, Scarlett. Well, I always feel poor. I feel poorer than normal."

"Is this because we just saw Chip? You can't compare. Chip's never *made* any money. He has no skills. He gets his money from his family."

"Does it matter where it comes from?" he asked.

"You know it does."

"I'm not so sure anymore. If I was a Sutcliffe, I'd be able to audition forever. But I'm not. We just don't have money. We have to make things work."

"Wait!" Scarlett said, remembering her good news. Spencer stopped and waited as she retrieved the script from her bag. "You have another audition. A good one! For *Crime and Punishment*! My favorite show! Everyone's favorite show! More important than a safety video! You have to learn these pages tonight."

She held out the envelope. Spencer looked at it with the same enthusiasm he might have mustered upon being offered a half-used jar of outdated mayonnaise from a complete stranger.

"It's a waste of time," he said.

"It's *Crime and Punishment*!" Scarlett repeated.

"Everyone auditions for *Crime and Punishment*. I'm not going. I can't deal with another useless open call."

"It's not an open call," she said. "Mrs. Amberson said they asked for you specifically. They saw you in *Hamlet*. They're really interested in you."

"No offense to your boss, but she always says that."

"Audition!" Scarlett said.

"Even if I get the job, it's what, one day's work?"

"So?"

Spencer stopped and sat down on one of the benches along the winding path.

"How do I put this?" he said, sinking low and looking down over his chin. "I'm the oldest. And I'm the guy, which means that I can't be a huge failure."

"Like I can?" she asked.

"I mean I don't want to be your loser older brother who never went to school and doesn't have a real job."

"Lola's not in school," Scarlett said. "She doesn't have a *real job*. She's taking time, just like you did."

"Lola's different," he replied. "And you know what? She's *not* fine with it. Seeing her friends go off to school or off to something new and interesting and cool? And you're still at home? It sucks. I know. I went through it. I guess Lola's the smart one, anyway. Date rich. You saw them in there. He's back, for sure. I give it a week. One week and it'll be back on. Mark my words. I'll be unemployed, Chip will be around every day . . . it'll be just like old times."

"Listen . . . to . . . me," Scarlett said, punctuating the words by slapping the envelope on his arm with each one. "The character they want you to play is a twenty-year-old millionaire. An evil twenty-year-old millionaire who kills people. And Mrs. Amberson said he's a perv and that you would like it, so would you at least *stop whining and read it?*"

He sighed and accepted it, removing the small sampling of pages inside. He slid over on the bench to be directly under the pathway light. She watched his eyes flick back and forth across the page.

"Do it for me?" she asked. "I am not going to forgive you if you could have worked with Sonny Lavinski and never even tried."

Spencer looked slightly helpless in the face of such a basic request.

"Fine," he said. "For you. And for the irony."

Back at home, Scarlett found herself staring at the closed computer on her lap. She had a little time before Lola came home. On every other night that she had some time like this, she had used it to watch Eric's commercial a few times. (Or, if Dakota was right, about a hundred and fifty times.) This had to be the day that she broke the cycle.

"I am making a new start," she said to the computer. "If I try to look at the video, I need you to explode."

The computer made no promises.

Scarlett opened it gently and turned it on. It was a hand-me-down from Chloe and always slow to start. She didn't mind. It was her computer, and it worked well otherwise. Though her fingers almost twitched from wanting to open the page with the video, she forced them to instead open a story she had been trying to write. This was the only benefit of the last few weeks — she had been fueled by a desperate desire to say things. And sure, the story was about a girl who broke up with a guy, but at least she had done some research.

Lola glided into the Orchid Suite around nine thirty, carrying a bottle of ginger ale. She was a little ashen around the eyes and under the cheekbones.

"You okay?" Scarlett asked.

Lola nodded and took a long sip of the soda.

"I was a little queasy at first, but then I was fine. We went really slow and it was smooth. The ginger ale helps, though. I'm sure you and Spencer had fun picking the whole night apart."

"He's learning some lines," Scarlett said. "I've just been here."

Lola considered this as she let down her hair.

"So?" Scarlett said.

"It was . . . fine."

But to Scarlett's eyes, it looked like it was more than fine. Lola brushed her hair over and over in a calm, meditative way. That was a content Lola. Spencer was probably right. It was only going to be a matter of time before Chip was back in the picture. Some people did get back together with their exes. Just not Scarlett.

"You look like you have something on your mind," Lola said. "Is everything okay?"

"I'm trying not to think about it," Scarlett said.

Like everyone else, Lola knew exactly what that remark meant.

"I know it's hard," she said sympathetically, "but that's the best way to handle a breakup."

"Who ever broke up with you?"

Scarlett knew the answer to this. It was: no one. No one had ever broken up with Lola. Lola had had three boyfriends, and she had broken up with all three. She was loyal, long-term, and everyone wanted to keep her.

"I don't know what I'd do if someone I really liked broke up with me and I had to see him every day in my house," Lola said. "But you did, for a whole month. I saw how hard you had to try every day. We all saw."

This was the first time all day anyone had given her any points for effort. Scarlett felt her eyes well up a little, and she looked away. Lola understood her. Lola cared.

"So what do I do?" Scarlett asked.

"I . . . um. I think you keep doing what you're doing, you know? You seem to have it under control."

"Right," Scarlett said. "My plan is working so well so far."

"That's the spirit! Have to go wash my face."

Lola may have cared, but she was also out to lunch, drifting away on her boat of love with the Chipster. She had no ideas, because she had no experience. She floated off to scrub herself with whatever elderflower-ginger-vitamin C concoction she had leftover from her days at the beauty counter, and Scarlett swallowed the fact that she had set herself on a course of action . . . and, while she was sure everyone wanted her to succeed, she was on her own.

ACT II

A SPIES OF NEW YORK EXCLUSIVE!

WHAT IS THIS WE ARE HEARING . . . from the set of Crime and Punishment, *the police procedural/courtroom drama that has been an integral part of our lives since we were just tiny spies? Is there trouble in our favorite fictional police precinct?*

RUMOR IS . . . Donald Purchase, who plays our beloved Detective Sonny Lavinski, is unhappy with the current story line and is restless for a change. A well-placed source tells us that Donald wants out.

"Donald is a great actor," our source told us in confidence. "But he's been playing Sonny Lavinski for fifteen seasons now. He's had offers from Hollywood for years. This time, he's ready to take them."

The idea of Sonny Lavinski leaving Crime and Punishment *is enough to make us drop our morning brandy. We have grown up with his dry witticisms and his sense of justice. His gravelly voice has nursed us through many a hangover. We have seen him fight terrorists, save children (and a seal) from an explosion at the Bronx Zoo, and single-handedly prevent the poisoning of the Central Park reservoir. We were there when his wife died, and when he found new love in the form of Denise "Wow, she's way too young and way too hot for him but* because he's Sonny Lavinski we will accept it" Shapiro. And though we have never seen his daughter, Daisy, born in the first episode, her mysterious school projects and much-discussed talents have never failed to amuse us.

Is Sonny really leaving us? Because we will have to book extra sessions with our therapists now.

"Completely untrue," Donald's rep told us. "I don't know where you're getting this information, but Donald isn't going anywhere. He just signed on for three more seasons. Donald loves New York, and he loves Crime and Punishment."

We are reassured, somewhat. But we will never truly be content until we are sure Sonny is staying. We suggest locking him in a cage located on some prominent city landmark where we can go and visit him every day.

Sonny, you belong to New York. Our love is strong. And more than a little obsessive.

THE FLOWER BOY

In the late summer, waking up on the fifth floor of the Hopewell Hotel was like waking up in a greenhouse. The heat rose to this floor, making the air in the Martin quarters swampy and thick. It puckered the fine, eighty-year-old silk-spun wallpaper, bowed the wood in the door frames, and popped the occasional tile in the bathroom as the floor underneath buckled. Scarlett fully expected to open her eyes one morning to a fully developed jungle — vines covering her furniture and maybe a monkey sitting on the head of her bed, picking through her ever-expanding blonde curls as if they were a bush that might contain delicious fruit.

Scarlett had almost gotten a full night's sleep to make up for the past two nights, but the scream of a fire truck pierced her consciousness somewhere around five in the morning. Lola gave up and just got out of bed. Scarlett stayed where she was until ten, dozing on and off. In her dreams, the show continued, but things changed whenever her sleep was broken. Sometimes she was in the play. Sometimes it was a musical. Sometimes the performance crept into the upstairs rooms. But always, Eric was there, and Scarlett tried to hold on to that as long as she could, grasping the tail end of the dream, trying to keep herself asleep. Finally, a knock on the door ended it for good.

"What?" she yelled, pulling the sheet over her head.

She heard the door open. If it was her parents, they would have just said what they wanted and shut the door. Spencer usually came in loudly, often bouncing off the end of the bed or singing. The person at the door was silent, which meant that it was Marlene. Scarlett removed the sheet from her face to confirm this.

"What?" she asked again.

Marlene glided into the room, coming right up to the side of the bed. She was close enough that Scarlett could actually feel the residual coolness on her little pink summer pajamas. Marlene's air conditioner *always* worked.

"You can go first," she said.

Marlene said this as if she was proclaiming a beneficent royal decree, one that would cause much barefooted dancing amongst the peasantry.

"First for what?"

"You," Marlene said again, a slight touch of annoyance in her voice, "can go first. Into the bathroom."

This was weird on many levels. The first, of course, was that Scarlett hadn't even made a move for the bathroom yet. The second, more comprehensive reason was that Marlene didn't let Scarlett go first for anything. In fact, Marlene usually lingered at the end of the hall, waiting for Scarlett to try to get into the bathroom, just so she could run for it and slam the door in her face.

"Oh," Scarlett said. "Okay."

Marlene continued to loom at Scarlett's bedside for a moment.

"You're welcome," she finally said, ominously, before backing out of the room.

Scarlett immediately pulled the sheet back up to make a protective cocoon of purple cotton. Why was the day starting off like this? Sirens, fine. But Marlene coming into her room for the sole purpose of freaking her out? And now what? Now she had to go to this horrible show to see Chelsea the Wonderful.

No point in asking why this was all happening. Best just to get up and get it over with.

Broadway is in the beating heart of Manhattan, at that flashing, wonderful series of intersections known as Times Square — where billboards are stacked on top of one another, where the massive hotels and flagship stores live, where thousands upon thousands of tourists crowd the sidewalks and spill into the street. Scarlett wormed her way through until she could see the massive glossy posters of Chelsea and her fellow cast members that were plastered to the front of the theater.

Scarlett looked around for anyone who might be Max, as she had been told he'd be there with the tickets. But the doors had opened, and it was hard to keep track of anything in the great press of people forcing their way through.

At exactly three o'clock, Scarlett felt someone come up behind her and turned. A guy was standing there, roughly her same age, just a few inches taller. He was obviously related to Chelsea — same squarish jaw and strong cheekbones, same long, narrow eyes and dark eyebrows. But where Chelsea looked like she was permanently wearing a bright, happy mask, this guy looked like he was built for battle, as if nature had endowed him with natural protection against the countless punches to the face that his life would surely deliver. His button-down shirt and jeans were recognizably of the right style, probably from some reasonably good store, but they had been ridden hard and put away wet. And he had curly hair — loose, floppy, overgrown curls. Waves, really. (Scarlett was judgmental on this subject.) And he smelled powerfully of detergent or some kind of strong, artificial scent.

So this was Max — the Other Biggs. He stared at Scarlett openly, working from the crown of her wild, blonde head right down to her feet.

"You're Scarlett," he said. "You work for Chelsea, right?"

"I work *with* Chelsea," she corrected him. "*For* an agent. And she hasn't signed yet."

"Right," he said, thrusting a ticket at her. "Whatever. Here. This is yours."

"So," Scarlett asked, "you're seeing this with me?"

"Looks that way."

"Have you seen it before?"

Max sighed in annoyance and looked over her head and around at the crowd, his eyes glazed over in boredom. He said nothing else. Scarlett took her place at the end of the line, behind the other latecomers. Though Max was silent, she could feel him behind her. He was only two or three inches taller than she was, but he had a *presence*, like his shadow was made out of heavy particles and essence of thundercloud.

Every time Scarlett went to a show on Broadway — which, admittedly, wasn't often — she was always struck by how the theaters felt smaller than she expected them to be, even though they clearly held hundreds of people. And the strange, muffled quality of the seating area — the plush red seats and thick carpets, everything to drown out the noise of the audience, all while providing luxury.

Turns out, though, that nothing drowns out the noise of two teenagers attempting to get to the two middle seats of the second row when the rest of the second row is occupied by senior citizens in matching tour group T-shirts. They all had to stand, some with great effort, to let Scarlett and Max squeeze along. The lights dimmed as they made their way and the orchestra started to rumble in preparation to play. Max was behind Scarlett and kept stepping on the backs of her shoes as they worked their way along. Scarlett struggled to find her seat as the last bit of light died out. There were five seconds of silence between the last test-squawk of the violin and the start of the overture. Max filled these by saying, "Did I mention that this show is a soul-sucking piece of crap?"

A hiss in the dark from someone close by — and then it began.

Max may have been a jackass, but he wasn't wrong. The show *was* a soul-sucking piece of crap. It was set in the 1940s, at a wedding in which absolutely everything was going wrong. Everyone was in love with someone they weren't supposed to be, including the bride. Everybody told their secrets to the flower girl, played by Chelsea. Each song bled indistinguishably into the next, grinding away at the nerves. The jokes were predictable, yet the audience laughed. The songs were generic, yet they clapped.

And yet . . . Chelsea had genuine talent. Her voice was rich and low. Chelsea was fifteen, but she was playing a younger character, and she wasn't being annoying about it. She didn't make faces or make her voice higher — she just *acted* younger. Genuinely younger. Scarlett found herself wishing that she wasn't as good as she was, or that she would be a bad singer. But no. Chelsea carried it all the way through to the end of the act one showstopper, "Pick Me," her signature song. The audience erupted in praise that continued until the lights came up.

Scarlett felt hollow inside, like she'd just discovered something terrible about humanity that would never really leave her.

"I told you," Max said conversationally. "It sucks. But people are dumb. Look at these people. They seem to like it. People like bad things."

These people were a little hard of hearing, but not that hard of hearing. One of the ladies of the group, a fierce-looking woman with bright, dyed red hair, wheeled around on him and gave him a look.

"Why did you come if you hate it so much?" Scarlett asked.

"Because it pisses Chelsea off," he replied. "Why are *you* here? Are you a wannabe actress or something? Is this your pre-famous job?"

"No. It's *just* my job."

Max leaned back and put his feet on the back of the still-occupied seat in front of him. He poked a finger into a hole that was developing at the big toe of his sneakers. "You go to my school, huh?"

It seemed to Scarlett that since she was there first, *he* was going to *her* school, but this was not a point she was going to debate.

"Guess so," she said flatly.

"You live in a hotel, too, right?"

"Yep," she said.

If he started in on the "you live in a hotel, you must be really rich" thing, she would be compelled to punch him in the ear. But that is not what happened.

"I looked it up," he said. "It has really bad online reviews. My favorite one called it the Hope Not! Hotel. The Internet is funny."

"You must have a lot of friends," she said.

Max finally smiled, accepting the engagement. It was a hard, unpracticed smile with clenched lips, like he didn't quite know how it was supposed to be done.

"Nope," he said. "Are you really popular? Introduce me to everyone. It would be awesome to be popular. That's what agents do, right? Make people *popular*."

"I open mail," Scarlett said.

"Okay, but . . ." The topic of agents was clearly one that interested him. He shifted in his seat to face her. "How did you end up doing this if you're not an actress? Did you try and were just really bad at it?"

"I'm *not* an *actress*," Scarlett said again.

"So you like hanging around actors? I need to understand this."

"Can we not talk?" Scarlett suggested.

"Whatever you want."

Max reached into his breast pocket, drew out his earbuds, and plugged them into his ears. He kept them in even when the show started up again, the low drone of his music buzzing out. The second half was a little preferable to the first, if only because it was only twenty-five minutes long. Chelsea sang a long, long note that caused the audience to burst out into applause. Scarlett saw Chelsea's gaze come down and land right on the two of them. Scarlett found herself clapping harder, but not really knowing why.

As the lights came up, a woman with a headset hurried over and signaled to Scarlett.

"Chelsea wants to know if you'll come backstage," she said.

Max appeared to be asleep, so she left him there and followed the woman up one of the small sets of steps off to the side of the stage.

They went behind the curtain, into a dark world of the plain pine-board backs of sets, cables, computers, and ropes. And tape. There was so much *tape* in theaters. Tape all over the floor. Tape on the walls. Thick industrial stuff in silver and some that glowed in the dark, marking weird little hieroglyphs in the shadowy places. The woman hustled her through a crew that was dragging the last set off to the side, through a heavy door that led to a cinder block hallway full of doors and clothes racks. A few people she had just seen onstage stood around, talking to one another or on their phones. Wigs had been pulled off and shirts were unbuttoned. Up close, Scarlett could see the thick makeup on all their faces — orangey pancake and fake facial hair stuck on with glue on the men, and alarmingly thick blue eye shadow and many layers of red lipstick on the women.

"Here," her guide said. "Go down there. She's the third door on the left."

Rough signs had been put up on all the doors, computer printouts with just their names. Scarlett knocked, and a cheery voice called for her to open the door. Chelsea sat at a small table in front of an illuminated mirror, plucking off fake eyelashes.

"Scarlett! I saw you out there! I'm so glad you came! So? Was it okay?"

"Great!" Scarlett lied.

"Really?"

"Really," Scarlett confirmed, again, in a lying way.

"Because today was really kind of an off day. It just felt like we were low energy, but I guess it was okay, right?"

"It was really good," Scarlett said, but the enthusiasm that had colored her voice had faded. Chelsea noticed the downgrade.

"God, it's such a bad feeling when you feel like not everyone is really there, you know? You can really feel it when some people just aren't present."

Scarlett decided that from now on she was just nodding, because apparently, if she answered, the conversation would go on forever. This didn't help, either. Chelsea went on for the next five minutes about some "energy problem" that may have been real or totally imaginary. She pulled off her costume and stockings, stripped all the way down to her underwear without a second thought, took off her bra, put on a different one, pulled on yoga pants and a T-shirt . . . talking all the while.

"Sorry you had to come with Max," she said. "He hates this show. Where is he?"

"He's . . . um . . . I think he's still out there?"

"Huh," Chelsea said. "I didn't even think he'd stay for the second act. I'm really sorry you had to come with him. I don't even know why he showed up. I know he hates the show."

So that was what Chelsea's sour face had been about the day before. It wasn't about Scarlett going to the show. It was about Max. That made Scarlett feel a bit more charitable toward Chelsea.

Chelsea's phone started to ring, and she answered it and spoke with it balanced on her shoulder as she tugged on her shoes. It was her mom, Scarlett quickly figured out. Chelsea began to give her a blow-by-blow rundown of the show. Scarlett saw an opportunity. If she left now, she could escape the rest of this conversation, or any potential "let's go and do somethings!" that might be coming. Because she was getting that feeling from Chelsea. Scarlett pointed at her watchless wrist and smiled and shrugged and waved and did everything but hold up cards that said she was going. Chelsea made a sad "oh no!" face and a confused gesture that Scarlett knew meant "wait!" But she chose not to understand, and backed her way out the door. She got a little lost backstage trying to find the street exit, and wandered into a closet full of costumes and some kind of informal tech meeting. Finally, the glowing EXIT sign beaconed her to safety.

Except that Max was waiting for her outside, leaning against a NO HONKING signpost.

"So what do you do now?" he asked, earbuds still plugged into his ears. "Run back and tell your owner what you saw?"

"How did you know?" Scarlett asked. "Can you read my mind? Are we . . . the same person?"

Scarlett started for the Forty-ninth Street subway station. Max pulled himself off the sign and followed — not directly, but a few steps behind. In any other neighborhood, Scarlett could have outdistanced him quickly, but the crowds in Times Square are slow and ponderous and thick. It can be difficult to break through a large group, or dodge all the people who stop abruptly in the middle of the sidewalk to take pictures of one another. When they finally reached an intersection he didn't plan on crossing, he got close enough to make himself heard.

"See you in school," he said.

THE SECRET WEAPON

Actually, Scarlett did need to check in with her owner and tell her what she had seen.

When Scarlett arrived at Mrs. Amberson's apartment, some cabaret songs were blasting. Mrs. Amberson's bedroom door was ajar.

"I'll be right out!" she shouted.

Scarlett sat down at her desk, under the big screen of photos, willing herself not to look up, and failing. It was time to take these pictures from *Hamlet* down and start filling that space with something new. Scarlett looked around for the most recent pile of headshots. She could put up a few of those, give those people a chance, change the scenery a little. She was shuffling around on the desk, trying to find them under the piles of magazines and paperwork that had accumulated in the last twenty-four hours, when she felt something pass over her foot. Something alive. Something that had some weight. Something with short fur. Something warm. Her New York–raised brain told her that the thing was too big for a mouse, and something too big for a mouse usually meant rat, because bunnies didn't usually make it into multistory apartment buildings and set up house in the walls.

She remained perfectly still for a moment, not wanting to scare the thing, because scared things bite. The thing got off her foot and appeared, slipping guiltily out from under the desk. It was potato-colored, with the torso of a squirrel and eyes like two massive black olives on opposite sides of its head.

This is when Scarlett decided it was time to scream like a tiny, tiny girl.

The bedroom door flew open, and Mrs. Amberson emerged in a flowing black day dress. She had a remote control in her hand, and her arm was already extended, zapping her stereo and turning down the sounds of 1930s Berlin that were bouncing off the walls.

"What's wrong?" she asked.

"There's a thing," Scarlett said, backing up and pointing. "Animal. Thing . . . thing . . ."

In a moment, her brain processed the fact that this was not an oversize rat. It was a dog. A very small, very unattractive one — one that seemed painfully aware of its low status on the food chain.

"Oh yes," Mrs. Amberson said. "That's Murray. Isn't he lovely?"

Murray was many things, but lovely was not one of them. It was hard to tell if he was covered in light fur or if that substance that held him together was just baggy flesh. He had tiny feet the size of quarters that made low, almost tap-dance-like noises as he shifted on the floor.

"He belongs to my friend Moo. She's gone to South America for a yoga retreat, so I'm watching him for a little while. She dropped him off this morning. The dog's actual name is Mr. Peabody, but to us he will be Murray, after our friend downstairs. Big Murray met Little Murray when we went out for wee-wees earlier. It was a wonderful moment."

Mr. Murray Peabody lurked by the kitchen and quaked so hard Scarlett thought one of his eyes might fall out.

"He seems nervous," she said.

"Oh yes," Mrs. Amberson said contently. "Life, to Murray, is just one long seismic disturbance. And he has quite an eclectic list of fears. Bags. Baby strollers. Canes. Hot-dog carts. Trash bags. Hats. Sneakers. And he absolutely hates the plants in the lobby! They give Murray the tinkles! Don't they, my hairless little anxiety attack?"

In reply, Murray accidentally shook his own legs out from underneath of himself and had to sit down.

"Murray the doorman *hates* Murray the tinkler," Mrs. Amberson said smugly. "He's also vegetarian. Isn't that wonderful? Moo leads a very ethical life and has raised him entirely on grain and vegetable-based dog food. A Xanax or two mixed in there probably wouldn't have hurt, but I feel that would take away so much of his *charm*. . . ."

"How long do you have him?"

"Until Moo works out some chakra issues. It's no problem. Large dogs require resources. Our friend Murray is a green alternative to a normal pet. Now, tell me all about Max."

Mrs. Amberson used to sit on the tiny window ledge of her room at the Hopewell and smoke nonstop. She still tended to sit near windows out of habit, twitching slightly from the lack of nicotine. She propped herself up on a low table and leaned against the window glass, all of the city and sky sprawled out behind her. She tapped her index and middle fingers together, squeezing an imaginary cigarette between them.

"He's an antisocial freak," Scarlett said.

"Elaborate."

"He trashed the show while we were in the theater and everyone could hear. He seems to hate people. He made everyone around us hate him, and me."

"I see," Mrs. Amberson said. "A *layered* personality."

"Layers of what?"

Mrs. Amberson waved her hand thoughtfully and brushed the question away. Murray attempted to climb into a small decorative pot near Scarlett's feet. She reached down and moved it before he knocked it over and broke it. He watched, awed, as she lifted the massive object into the air with one hand, then he stuck his head under the sofa flap.

"He likes you," Mrs. Amberson said.

"That's like?"

"You should see what he does when he *doesn't* like someone. You're very likable, O'Hara. That's why you're my secret weapon!"

"What does that mean?" Scarlett asked.

"It means that while you were out with Max, I put in a call to Miranda Biggs. You see, Miranda is very worried about Max. I don't know if you noticed this, but Miranda Biggs is a bit consumed by her children's careers and talents. She has Chelsea under control. Max is a different story. Miranda feels a certain lack of control when it comes to Max, and control means a lot to her."

"And?"

"And we spoke about how *reassuring* it might be to have a pair of eyes on him at school."

"Oh no," Scarlett said. "No . . ."

"Put on your business hat, O'Hara," she said. "We are a small, unknown agency. Soon we will be famed and feared and described as elite, but now we're just a few boxes on the floor of an apartment. We were never going to get in just by going for Chelsea. She could have signed with any big agency. We needed an edge. You are that edge. And that is why she just agreed to my offer of representation. Congratulations to us! We have a second client!"

Scarlett knew that she was supposed to express some excitement here, but she wasn't giving in.

"I am *not* spying on Max," she said.

"Oh, you misunderstand me," Mrs. Amberson said. "Just the fact that you will be in the same school, just the *suggestion* of a spy, that was enough. It's not spying . . . it's just a kind of insurance policy."

"I don't have to actually *do* anything, right? I don't have to call in a daily report of what Max is doing?"

"Of course not! All you have to do is go to school like you normally do. It sounds to me like Max was not happy about moving to New York City. I can't say I blame him. Miranda dragged him along when Chelsea got her part on Broadway. He has no reason to be in the city. Mr. Biggs remained behind. He runs a golf course. I don't think their home situation is very warm and fuzzy. The point is, they have no connections here. No friends. No network. Miranda finds you to be a very reassuring presence. She was thrilled that you went to Chelsea's show with Max."

"I'm not going anywhere *else* with him."

"Of course not. I promise you, this will not affect your life. It will simply be harder for Max to skip school and lie about it knowing that someone may be watching."

"But I'm *not* watching," Scarlett said. "Just so we're clear. Because I plan to stay as far away from him as possible."

"Avoid him as much as you like. We have achieved our goal. We have signed Chelsea. Once Miranda sees the wonders I'm going to do for her daughter's career, she'll forget all about you. In fact, this will really affect you in no way. I will deal with Chelsea entirely. And like I said, there is nothing special you must do about Max. It's all so wonderfully *simple*. Now, how is my *favorite* client doing?" she asked.

"He's depressed."

"Depressed? Spencer? Those words don't seem to go together."

"He feels like a failure," Scarlett said. "I think he wants to give up acting. He's feeling broke, like he's not getting anywhere. I had to talk him into going to that *Crime and Punishment* audition."

"Oh," Mrs. Amberson said, waving a hand in dismissal. "All actors go through moments of doubt. We just haven't found him the right part yet. I have some potential auditions lined up for next week. Here's one . . ."

She picked up some script pages that sat on the table, next to her.

"'Actor needed to play overactive bladder,'" she read. "'Five foot eleven or taller.' Audition's tomorrow."

Scarlett took the pages without comment.

"And you never know about *Crime and Punishment*. I'm telling you, they were very interested in him. Have to rush out now. I need you to take Murray for his walk. The leash is on the doorknob, along with some plastic bags for you-know-what."

When Scarlett got home, she headed to the kitchen to get a drink. She found Lola there. It was strange to find *any* Martin in the kitchen. They had three refrigerators and two underemployed stoves, all ready and waiting to produce food for dozens of people who never came to eat. And none of the Martins were very gifted in the preparation department. As proof of this point, Lola stood at the large wooden worktable, picking bits of eggshell out of a bowl.

"How do people do this?" she said. "I can never break an egg right."

"What are you doing?" Scarlett asked.

"Learning how to make muffins. They're really cheap to make — cheaper than buying them from the bakery. We just filled up four rooms, more spillover people from a tour. Mom and Dad are up there getting them ready and Spencer is helping move the air conditioners."

There were only a few really usable air conditioners and televisions at the Hopewell. These were shuffled around quickly whenever new arrivals came. If there weren't many people around, you could have both cool air and entertainment. But four rooms meant that decisions had to be made. Scarlett's mom was very good at reading people and figuring out their priorities — what comforts they just liked, and which ones they could not live without.

"So I was making these for the morning," Lola went on, continuing her dismal fishing expedition. The egg didn't just look broken — it looked like it had exploded. The slivered remains of shell were piled on a small dish.

"Maybe you should start again," Scarlett said.

"I have half a dozen eggs in here," Lola said. "I feel bad wasting them. It's not that bad . . . Look! I don't see any more!"

She held out the bowl proudly. Scarlett saw a few little flecks that were probably shell, but they didn't seem worth mentioning, because she noticed something far more interesting, and it was on Lola's wrist. She was wearing the Cartier watch that Chip had given her after their breakup. Lola followed the trail of Scarlett's gaze and clutched the watch self-consciously.

"Oh," she said. "Yeah . . ."

"What does that mean?" Scarlett asked.

"We're not anything yet," Lola said. "But, you know . . . he was never the problem. Not really. It's his friends that are the problem. And in Boston, he'll have new friends. It'll be different. He asked me to a start-of-the-year dance at his school, and I said yes."

"You're going to a *dance*?" Scarlett said. "You didn't mention that last night."

Lola's inability to dance was the stuff of Martin family legend. In a straight line, there was no one more graceful. Lola could ebb and flow from room to room or down the hall in any heels you threw her way. But throw in a quick step and a turn, and she was on the floor in a heap. Her condition had long been labeled "dancelexia."

"Who's going to a dance? What?"

Spencer appeared at the kitchen door. He jumped up to swing himself from the door frame, something he always felt compelled to do as he came into the kitchen.

"I am," Lola said, turning to face him.

Spencer let go and dropped to the ground.

"Seriously?" he asked. "And . . . where? Who with?"

When she played with the watch, Spencer understood at once.

"I knew it," he mumbled in Scarlett's direction. "I told you."

"Can we just skip the part where you complain about Chip?" Lola cut in quickly. "Just this one time? Because I need to ask you a favor. I was thinking, since you know how to dance . . . I mean you took dance every day in school, right? I've seen you dance in loads of things. I was thinking . . . maybe you could . . . teach me, a little? Just enough to get by?"

It took a massive effort for Scarlett not to laugh.

"I'm not really a dance teacher," Spencer said.

"I know that!" Lola said, her voice getting bubbly. "Just show me a few steps? Come on. You know how. I just don't want to fall or embarrass myself. I thought, if you could just teach me a little this week, I might not break my leg, and if my leg isn't broken, I can pick up some of your chores. Like, I could do the recycling and the trash until the end of the month. . . ."

Spencer folded his arms over his chest.

"Fine," he said unenthusiastically.

"He took that better than I thought," Lola said when he had gone. "Is he feeling okay?"

Scarlett decided to trail along after him and find this out for herself.

"Hey," she said, catching him at the elevator. "You gave in on that kind of fast."

"Why fight it?" he replied as he punched the UP button.

"Did you go on that *Crime and Punishment* audition like you said you were going to?"

"I did it this afternoon. I guess they were in a big rush."

"And . . . ?" Scarlett asked, unable to contain her excitement.

"It was an audition," he said with a shrug.

"Was Sonny Lavinski there?"

"No. And can we not talk about it anymore? I'm just . . . I did it. Like I promised. Okay?"

The elevator finally appeared, and he pulled the gate back. Spencer slumped against the sunburst. He noticed the script pages in her hand and pointed to them. "What are those?" he asked.

"These are . . . nothing."

"That bad, huh?" He held out his hand. "I think I have to see them now."

Scarlett reluctantly passed over the overactive bladder pages. Spencer read through them, expressionless, and passed them back once they reached the fifth floor.

"I should probably go to this," he said, turning toward his room. "It'll probably make the Day of the Sock a happy memory."

LIES EVERYONE KNOWS

Frances Perkins High School inhabited a remarkable building high up on Central Park West. It was red and gold brick, and grand, with two large, round towers on the ends, high gothic arches for windows, and a long porch with porticoes like some kind of Italian villa. The plaque on the front of the building said it was the site of "one of the city's oldest hospitals," but it was common knowledge that it was an old mental asylum. It was given up as a lost cause sometime in the 1970s, when many of the patients were released and the neighborhood got too rough, possibly because it was full of former mental patients. They hid up on the large wall of rock that jutted out of the park at 104th Street and jumped down on people from above and presumably ate their brains. Everyone knew this.

Everyone was wrong. The Frances Perkins building had never been a hospital for the insane. It was built as a sanatorium for people with tuberculosis. That's why the walls were rounded. The rich family that sponsored its construction erroneously believed that tuberculosis germs could not thrive in rooms without corners. So the building had been misunderstood since its construction.

Whatever its original intention, Frances Perkins now housed some of New York's brightest. Getting in was a tough process. Applicants needed excellent grades and high test scores to win a place in its hallowed, curvy walls. It attracted the nerds and readers and general academic types, and students didn't have to be rich to go, because it was a public school.

Due to some technical glitch, the schedules had only been e-mailed out the night before, and then frantically sent around to everyone for comparison. Scarlett had slightly lost the lottery on this one: French, International Politics, third-period lunch (a useless, quiet quasi-breakfast that everyone used to finish homework or sleep), Trig (for that post-lunch crash), Art History, English, American Government, and Biology II.

"Your schedule sucks," Josh said matter-of-factly, as they met up on the sidewalk before going in. "Wanna make out?"

"You just asked me that yesterday," Scarlett said, studying her classroom map to see how long it was going to take her to get between classes. "You usually only ask every month or so."

"I've been away for a few weeks," he said, heading off to his locker. "Just making myself available."

"Got it," Scarlett said. "Thanks."

The first day was just an exercise to take attendance, assign seats, pass out some paperwork, and give the teachers a few minutes to explain what nature of misery they had cooked up over the summer. Lots of work had been done. There were shiny new linoleum floors, fresh coats of paint covered up the scratches on the lockers, new plastic signs were screwed to the classroom doors. Someone had clearly been splashing some money around to bring some fancier items, like the sleek monitors mounted on the hallway walls that ran a constant, hypnotic listing of welcome back messages and classroom locations.

The most money of all had gone into the cafeteria, with its shiny new salad bar, a large vat of free fruit, the cereal station, and a coffee cart. There were new silver tables with sleek orange chairs and outlets on the floor for laptops. Also, there was a sign on the counter tacked to a piñata that read WE ARE BRINGING BACK TACO FRIDAYS!

Scarlett basically registered the following: French would be exactly the same as the year before; International Politics would be an overwhelming wash of bad news and maps; Trigonometry would just have to be dealt with with clenched teeth; Art History would be over at the end of the quarter but would probably be interesting; English would have been better with another teacher; American Government brought out the closet activists; Bio II was the saving grace. It was with Ms. Fitzweld, who was young and smart and covered with all kinds of old-school tattoos of broken hearts and hula girls that she attempted to cover up with long sleeves and arm warmers. She had been Scarlett's Bio I teacher, so Scarlett knew all about her. Dakota's mom was her doctoral advisor at Columbia. So they were set in two ways: Dakota was massively good at this stuff, and Ms. Fitzweld was inclined to like them.

As soon as she got into the lab, Scarlett grabbed one of the last remaining workstations. They each sat two — one seat for her, one for Dakota. She started to unpack quickly to claim the space. A minute later, she heard a bag land in the seat next to her. She turned to see Max sitting down on the stool.

"That seat's taken," Scarlett said.

"I don't see anyone."

"It is."

"But don't you think we should get to know each other? I do. I think I'll sit here."

He hopped up on the lab stool. Scarlett quickly scanned the room. The terrible game of musical chairs had begun. People were jostling for spots before the bell rang and everything was set for the year. That was how Ms. Fitzweld did things. So this was the *most critical three minutes ever.*

And Dakota was out there somewhere. She would be expecting Scarlett to protect her seat.

"Seriously," she said more urgently. "That seat is for someone. She's just being slow."

"Survival of the fittest," he said. "That's biology."

Dakota finally arrived. She had taken her time, thinking that Scarlett would be all over the saving-the-seat thing (they had worked this out in advance). So she was startled to see Max in her place. At that moment, the last completely empty station was taken over. Now they each had at least one person in them.

"That's my seat," Dakota said, hurrying over.

"I didn't see your name on it," Max replied.

"What, are you six? And who are you?"

"A good, good friend of Scarlett's," he said. "We went out yesterday."

Dakota turned to Scarlett in confusion.

"This is Max," she said unenthusiastically. "He's Chelsea's brother."

"Who's Chelsea?" Dakota asked.

"An actress. From that show *The Flower Girl*."

"This has to do with your job," Dakota said, her eyes narrowing. "All bad things come from your job. I hate your job."

"I don't have a job," Max said. "I'm really lazy. And I cheat. You should know that, since you'll be sitting next to me all year. I cheat like you wouldn't believe."

Dakota turned away from him and focused on Scarlett.

"He needs to move," she said. "You need to move him, now."

"What am I supposed to do?" Scarlett asked. "Pick him up?"

Max opened his arms wide, offering Scarlett a chance to have a go at that. Ms. Fitzweld noticed that Dakota was still floating free with no seat.

"McMann," she said, "over there. There's a spot in the front."

She pointed to a spot in the front row across the room.

"But . . ." Dakota began.

"No buts. Over there."

It was settled in an instant. Dakota crossed the room and sat down with Doug Taylor. In a moment, an entire year of pain was established. Scarlett saw it roll out in front of her, like a great scroll full of spidery writing, listing the many unfortunate moments that would come her way for the next nine months.

Scarlett was filled with the overwhelming urge to shove him off the stool, send him toppling to the linoleum floor. Of course, that would result in immediate suspension, or maybe even expulsion. The school had a very, very strict policy about violence. Not that she would ever have done it anyway. But it made for a beautiful moment of fantasy. Max brought out something violent in her, some evolutionary hangover from chimp days when it was okay just to knock another chimp out of the tree when he got on your nerves.

Must have been good to be a chimp.

He leaned close again, as he pretended to reach down for something. Again, Scarlett got a strong whiff of something floral and artificial coming from what seemed to be his hair.

Scarlett tried to rivet her attention to the whiteboard as Ms. Fitzweld started grinding through her overview for the year — a tedious and yet anxiety-causing recital of expectations. As much as she tried to engage, tried to stimulate that part of her brain and personality that paid attention and cared deeply about her academic future . . . all she was really aware of was Max's looming presence, nine inches to her right. He was drumming his long fingers on their lab station, and beating his foot in *an entirely different rhythm* against the cabinet below. It could not be ignored, this double-stranded beat. It wove itself around her mind. It demanded all of her attention.

Meanwhile, everything important she needed to know for the year drifted by. Five-hundred-pound textbooks were distributed from a cabinet, along with goggles, gloves, and plastic aprons. Syllabi were handed out, along with the exam schedule.

"You and me," Max said, when the bell rang. "All year. You and me."

Scarlett was not in the best of moods when she stopped by Mrs. Amberson's apartment on the way home to walk Murray. Murray's leash was ridiculous. It looked like a studded red bracelet on a string. Scarlett yanked it from its hanging spot and walked toward Murray. Murray took one look at the leash and started backing up, his black eyes widening.

"It's okay," Scarlett said in the calmest voice she could muster.

Murray trembled violently as the leash was attached, and refused to move, so Scarlett picked him up. After a furious shake, he hung limp in defeat. She angrily grabbed a plastic bag as she carried Murray out the door and down the hall to the elevator. She set him down when they reached the lobby.

Murray the doorman narrowed his eyes when Murray the dog came skittering along next to Scarlett.

"That dog," he said, coming from behind his desk. "You gotta do something about that dog."

Dog Murray quaked at the sight of Doorman Murray and hid behind Scarlett's ankles.

"It's not my dog," she said. "He belongs to Moo."

"To who?"

"To Moo."

"To me?"

"Not to you. To Moo."

"What does that mean? You gotta do something about that dog. That dog keeps making a mess on my floor. Three times today!"

"I think his nerves are bad," Scarlett said.

"I don't care 'bout nerves! I can't have this dog doing that in my lobby! I can't have that! You gotta do something about that dog! You tell your boss she's gotta do something about that dog!"

Something was going on down near Scarlett's right foot. She was dismayed to find a slowly spreading puddle forming around it, and quickly withdrew her shoe and hurried Murray to the door before this was noticed.

Once outside, Dog Murray came forward and surveyed the landscape. Finding it preferable to the horrors of the lobby, he shot straight out, straining the leash and catching Scarlett unawares. She was in no danger of being dragged along — Murray weighed no more than a grapefruit — but she hated to see him straining his neck against the leash, so she quickened her pace to relieve the tension.

She picked him up to cross the street to the park side, where the tree canopy sheltered the sidewalk from the late afternoon sun. The summer had gone so fast. It would hold on for a while, but soon there would be coats and hats and gloves. Scarlett hated her coat. She had gotten it because it was on sale. It was black and kind of shapeless and always made her miserable when she put it on. Plus, it wasn't warm. The thought of the coat depressed her a bit, and fall and the coat suddenly became one in her mind. The entire season would be tainted by it. Winter, too. The coat blanketed the calendar. She knew it was stupid to let the thought of a coat bother her, but there it remained in her thoughts, blanking everything out, covering up the shiny and the happy.

The first day of school *could* have been good. Unlike a lot of people, Scarlett kind of liked school. Not the work. Not the getting up in the morning. Not sitting through class. Okay, not 90 percent of all things that school entailed. But she liked Frances Perkins. There were so many ways school could end up in New York, mostly bad — super snotty, run-down, cutthroat. Frances Perkins had the best mix of people. A lot of people came from arty or academic families. There were rich people, but they had opted to go to a public school, which meant that they were usually down-to-earth.

Other bonuses: no serious sports or extracurriculars. The school seemed to figure that if you were smart enough to get in, you would be smart enough to figure out something to do with yourself in the middle of New York City. There were opportunities to volunteer or intern in situations far better than the school could come up with. If you wanted to play a sport, play music, be in a show, write for a magazine or website . . . it was all right on the doorstep, if you had the ambition. If students wanted to organize something on their own, like a show or a yoga class, they were pretty good about giving you some space and a few bucks. So there was no pressure to become the officer of this or the captain of that, and the school's favorite, if unofficial, team was their dodgeball team called "We Are Nerds." They wore their numbers on pocket protectors and battled weekly with Bronx Science and Stuyvesant in a field in Central Park. It was the only game worth going to.

In short, it was a good place.

And then, Max. He had invaded, like the snakefish, which creeps over to the local pond on its amphibious belly in the middle of the night and destroys the happy ecosystem. All the hard work she was doing to restart her life and be happy was going to be undone by some insane guy with a mysterious agenda. He had blocked Dakota from sitting next to her, and she had no doubt he was going to make his presence known every single day for the rest of the year. She would have to look at that smug face all day at school, and then deal with his sister's waxy mask of professional perfection all the rest of her time. Team Biggs was going to break her.

"Come on, Murray," she said, giving the leash a tug.

But Murray was transfixed, having made tentative contact with a dog that somehow managed to be smaller than he was, yet still visible to the naked eye. Scarlett picked him up and tucked him under her arm. She felt him stiffen with fear as they crossed the street and approached the apartment building.

"He's cute," a voice said.

"He's not mine," Scarlett replied, almost as an apology for Murray.

Then her brain registered the owner of the voice.

THE FEVER

Eric Hall was a nice Southern boy, from Winston-Salem, North Carolina — once the strapping, blond star of his high school theater department. He seemed to drag along puffy white clouds and blue skies from some other corner of the earth. He was the kind of guy who smiled easily, who you imagined smelled of fresh-cut grass and his grandma's peach cobbler, who tanned on the first day of summer, who was liked by all who met him. You could easily picture him on a horse, something Scarlett did a little too frequently, and not always appropriately dressed in equestrian gear.

He'd gotten a haircut in the last few days. She liked it a little longer, but this was good. Cleaner. Crisper. With the sunned-out blondish end bits clipped off. Being a blonde herself, Scarlett was kind of bored of the color. The darkness was nice, and unfamiliar. She heard herself speaking, but there was a mumbled roar covering up the words in her mind. It must have been something about coming inside.

"She sent around business cards to the cast," he said. "I thought I'd stop by. Just finished class. And when I saw you walking down the street with . . ."

"Murray," Scarlett said, the name strangled in her throat.

"What?"

That was from Murray the doorman, who was watching them with ill-concealed disgust.

"Not, no . . ."

Scarlett was stuttering a little. She took a second to control her voice.

"Not you. The dog. The dog is Murray."

"That dog's name is *Murray*?" Murray asked.

Eric picked up on Scarlett's signal that they should move quickly, quickly to the elevator. She tucked Murray the dog under her arm like a football. The elevator doors closed silently as velvet curtains, not like the great, end-of-the-world squawk that the gates of the Hopewell elevator made.

"He didn't like that answer," Eric said.

"He's not a Murray fan," Scarlett explained. "Also, his name is Murray."

"Is that a coincidence?"

"No," Scarlett said. "It's just my boss making a statement."

"Amy's a piece of work."

On that note of truth, the doors opened again, and the nineteenth floor hallway awaited them. Mrs. Amberson probably wasn't even here. Scarlett knew she should mention this. Except that she had now lost the ability to speak, and all she could do was embark on the death march down the thick blue carpet to 19D, Eric sauntering just behind her, Murray stepping on her feet in his haste to get to shelter. She opened the door with her key, which Eric noted with a little tuck-up of the chin.

"Own key, huh? She couldn't do anything without you."

Scarlett scooped Murray from the ground, where he had been scratching an ineffective paw at the door. As gestures went, this was like throwing a rock at the moon in an attempt to knock it out of orbit. It was nice to have Murray in that respect — only he had less control over his situation than she did over hers.

Scarlett called out for Mrs. Amberson, just in case she was ensconced in her bedroom and maybe about to emerge half-undressed. There was total silence.

"I think she's out," Scarlett said, gripping Murray tight. She mustered the courage to look at Eric now. Maybe he would just leave. That would make sense, since the apartment's occupant wasn't there. But he didn't. He walked right inside, making appreciative noises as he took in the airy living room with its white furniture, and straight to the windows that looked out over the park.

"Don't these kinds of apartments cost, like, millions?" he said.

There was something in his manner that made Scarlett feel like it was somehow her fault that Mrs. Amberson lived in a very nice apartment, and that she had to make excuses for it.

"It's actually her friend's," Scarlett said. "She's subletting it for cheap."

"When you say cheap, you probably don't mean the kind of cheap I go for. Because I go for *cheap*. Where I come from, a car on the lawn is considered landscaping."

He wandered past the desk, pausing to look at the photo array, which now included five pictures of Chelsea. He lingered on the photograph he was in for just a moment, then sat on one of the silver bar stools and swiveled. He slipped into one of those slow smiles of his — the ones that said, "I'm so irresistible and harmless."

Scarlett sat down on the sofa, holding a quivering Murray firmly on her lap. She told herself that if she could just calm Murray, she would be calm. But Murray would never be calm. He was an exposed, throbbing nerve, set loose into the world in the form of a dog.

"Things getting back to normal at home?" Eric asked.

"We don't really know what that means," she replied.

This resulted in an even slower, more dangerously charming smile. Murray vibrated like a cell phone in a box, impossible to ignore.

"Spencer still complaining about that day with the sock?" he asked.

"Yeah," she said, unable to keep herself from smiling — a queasy, wracked smile that hurt her face from the inside. "He's mentioned it once or twice. A day."

"God, I've never seen him so mad. Well, actually, I have, but . . ."

He laughed a quick, terse laugh and looked down. *Of course* he had seen Spencer angrier. Like right before Spencer's fist "accidentally" hit his face. Because of Scarlett.

Tension took over her body. Murray could feel what she suppressed. In protest, he broke free from her grip in terror, rocketing across the sofa. Unfortunately, a nervous Murray was a tinkling Murray, and he dribbled an erratic, golden trail across the white fabric before making a heroic leap from the armrest and splatting on the ground. Scarlett didn't want to bring attention to the fact that there was dog pee next to her, because that is considered unsexy in most cultures, but it was impossible to hide against the snowy whiteness of the sofa. It didn't help that Murray was making rapid, insane circuits of the room, his little nails acting like ice skates against the polished floor, sending him speeding and sliding and skidding into every single piece of furniture. Every blow just propelled him faster, bouncing him from kitchen bar to end table to desk to chair to potted plant, around and around.

Eric watched this with a detached, clinical interest.

"When did Amy get a dog?" he asked.

"He's borrowed," Scarlett said. "And he has issues. He has *every* issue."

"Yeah, I can see that. We should get that out before it sets in."

He was pointing at the yellow pee road next to Scarlett. He got off the bar stool and went into Mrs. Amberson's tiny kitchen. Scarlett could hear him rummaging around, and a moment later he returned with a bottle of sparkling mineral water and a roll of unbleached paper towels. He calmly started drizzling the water on the spots and blotting them up with a paper towel.

"I should be doing that," Scarlett said.

"I have four dogs back home," he said. "I'm used to this. You city people, living in your fancy hotels, you don't have to deal with animals like we country folks do."

"You should see some of the things we *do* have to deal with," Scarlett said. "Hotel guests make dogs seem really clean."

He laughed a little.

Scarlett grabbed some towels and started on the opposite end of the sofa. She tried to work long and hard on her spot, holding her ground, but Eric was clipping along. Soon, he was next to her. His arm rubbed against hers. He didn't seem to notice this, but it went on for almost a minute, this gentle brushing.

When she was trying to forget about Eric, she had to make an extra effort to erase the mental image of his arms. They were extraordinary arms — not gross, steroid big, but full and solid, just large enough to slightly strain the fabric of his shirt. They were even developed on the lower half, from the elbow to the hand, so that he had to have a really big watchband to make it all the way around his sturdy wrist. One day in a hot, empty theater, those arms had lifted her up like she was nothing at all.

Scarlett had to steady herself, even though she was kneeling. Eric stopped moving, but his arm was still touching hers. Just barely, but it was, maybe just a millimeter of contact she could feel through her whole body. He turned, his face just inches from hers, looking her right in the eye. They were alone in an empty apartment (except for Murray, who had calmed down and was meditatively chewing on the inside of his own thigh).

"Come here often?" he said, slipping into a leer.

Scarlett tried not to smile. A smile would be giving in — to what, she didn't know. But he kept the face up until she cracked. The wall was down completely.

"Gotcha," Eric said, clearly very satisfied with himself. He stood, taking the wad of used paper towels into the kitchen to dispose of them. Scarlett grabbed the water and the roll. They shuffled for position at the sink, sharing the soap and the flow of water, washing their hands. But the current passing between them was impossible to ignore. He moved back to make room for her but didn't leave the small room. He just leaned against the refrigerator until she was done.

"So," he asked, "you're good?"

"Yeah," Scarlett said, picking up an empty ice cube tray and twisting it. "I'm . . . good."

"And school?"

"Same crap, new year. But, good. I guess."

"NYU is scary," he said. "I guess I knew when I moved to New York that I wouldn't be the big kid on the block anymore, the guy who got all the leads in the school show . . . but I didn't know *how* much better everyone would be."

He pushed his hands into the pockets of his shorts and let out a long sigh — the song of insecurity.

"You're good," Scarlett said before she could help herself.

The speed of the compliment seemed to ruin whatever feeling was in the room.

"I guess I should get back," he said. "I have a rehearsal in an hour. But I just wanted to drop by. Say hi to your boss for me?"

"Sure," Scarlett said. She tried to sound casual, but her voice had gone all croaky. He looked at the granite floor for a moment, black and twinkling with golden flecks of mica.

"Okay," he said, "so . . ."

Some decision was being made. Something was being considered. They were so close. Scarlett had the mad urge to step forward and grab him around the waist, hug him close. He would be, at the very least, too polite to push her away. He would hug her back, and he would look down into her face, and then they would . . .

No. You can't go flinging yourself at people. Especially people *you are trying not to think about* even if they are standing in a tiny kitchen with you and even if you have just cleaned up dog pee with them.

Eric didn't know what words should come next, either, so he held up a hand of good-bye and retreat, backing up out of the kitchen, the apartment, and Scarlett's life in general.

It took her almost forty-five minutes to calm back down, most of which was spent on the phone to Dakota.

"Let's have him killed!" Dakota suggested cheerfully.

"I'm serious," Scarlett said. "Help me. I'm under a table."

"Is that a Shakespeare expression? Like, 'Gadzooks! I am under a table, milord! Prithee, handeth me the pointy stick for to stab the cad!' Is that what you mean?"

"I mean I'm under a table."

This was true. Scarlett was crouching on the fluffy white rug under the unused dining table on the side of the living room. She had no idea why she was doing this, except that it seemed kind of safe there.

"He came to see me," Scarlett said, getting back to the matter at hand. "Why did he come to see me?"

There was a long pause on Dakota's end of the line.

"He didn't actually come to see you," she finally said. "Think about it. Where do you work now?"

"For Mrs. Amberson."

"Who is an . . ."

"Agent," Scarlett said. How had she been so stupid? Eric wasn't standing around in front of Mrs. Amberson's apartment building hoping to see Scarlett — he wanted to see her boss. He wanted to see *an agent*. The fact that he had run into Scarlett was purely accidental. Her brain was so hopped-up on hormones and adrenaline that she couldn't see what was going on.

"You okay?" Dakota asked after a long pause.

"Fine," Scarlett replied. "I'd better go."

"Call me if you need me, okay?"

"Thanks."

She hung up and dropped her phone into the thickly piled rug and willed herself to think. So he had come here. So they had spoken. So he really just wanted to talk to her boss. Big deal. So what if she had to wrap her arms around herself to make the quivering feeling stop, or that she wanted to run out and find him, follow him, see where he went and who he talked to and if the girls in his class were as pretty as they were in Scarlett's nightmares. She had seen him, and she had lived. That made her strong, right? You didn't win the war until you faced your foe, and she had just done some full-on foe-facing, which was both brave and alliterative.

The intercom buzzed, startling Scarlett so much that she popped up her head and whacked it on the underside of the table. Downstairs, Murray had to be holding his finger down on the buzzer on purpose, because it was a solid, unbroken sound, one that could rip any thought in two. No wonder Dog Murray looked the way he did.

Scarlett crawled out of her hiding space rubbing her head and answered.

"Messenger," Murray growled. "You gotta come sign. I'm not sendin' him up. He's got a motorbike runnin' outside. Can't have that bike outside."

When she got to the lobby, she found a motorcycle courier in a white helmet waiting for her with a clipboard. He tipped up the visor on her approach.

"AAA?"

"Yeah," Scarlett said, taking the clipboard and signing. She was passed a thick envelope.

"Can't idle that bike outside my door . . ." Murray was saying, as Scarlett crept off to take the package upstairs. She carelessly ripped it open in the elevator, remembering her last ride upstairs one hour before, when Eric had been by her side. So this was how her brain was going to be — constant replay.

She yanked out some papers as she reached the nineteenth floor and looked at them ruefully. Some other dumb script to file some-where on Mrs. Amberson's desk.

And then she noticed the front page: CRIME AND PUNISHMENT, EPISODE 391, "CROSSFIRE." SHOOTING COPY, DO NOT DUPLICATE. There was another paper attached, a list of times and locations, and a name at the top: SPENCER MARTIN.

SUCCESS COMES CALLING

For the first time since Scarlett had declared her new start, things actually felt like a new start. The news about the show was so tremendous and startling that it actually blew away the clouds that Eric had dragged into her field of vision. This morning, it was blue skies.

"Know what I've decided?" Spencer asked.

He was sitting on the front desk (which you were never supposed to do, but no one was around but Scarlett), making a paper hat out of a spare *New York Times*. He jumped down at the sound of the elevator cable grinding its way down. "I've decided to get rid of my bike and buy a new one. I'll make enough this week to do that. I unlocked it, and I'm leaving it for anyone to take. My gift to the world."

"The world will thank you," Scarlett said. "Nothing the world needs more than a bent death machine covered in duct tape!"

"I know!"

The elevator opened to reveal Marlene, dressed carefully for her first day of school. She'd been playing with the curling iron again, her hair half-curled, half-bent into those strange triangular forms that appear when the barrel isn't twisted correctly.

"Morning," she said politely. "I'm going to make toast. Do you guys want toast?"

"I always want toast," Spencer said.

She turned her stare to Scarlett.

"No . . . I'm — I'm good."

Marlene nodded and dutifully set off through the dining room to the kitchen.

"She wants something," Scarlett said, watching her go. "I have no idea what, but she wants something."

"If she wants to make me toast, I'm okay with that," Spencer replied. "Why can't you develop more interests like that?"

"I have to work for your agent, who gets you on television shows."

"That's fine. As long as I'm being served in some way. That reminds me, I need to start making some contractual demands. You can't look me in the eye when you talk to me, I want someone to take all the bubbles out of my Coke, and I want a professional beekeeper on call at all times. Walk me through it one more time? You have a second, right?"

They'd gone through the script four times last night, but Spencer was all nerves. Scarlett was the known expert on the show, and Spencer wanted to make sure he understood what was going on.

"Okay," Scarlett said. "It starts off when the police find a body in a Dumpster. Sonny Lavinski and his partner, Rick Benzo, catch the case. That's the term. 'Catch' the case."

"And Benzo is always wrong?" he asked.

"Always," Scarlett said. "No one likes Benzo. See, Sonny used to have this really good partner named Mike Mulligan who knew that Sonny is always right, but Mike got killed by a subway train three years ago when he was trying to save a baby. See, this woman had stolen a baby . . ."

"Too much history," Spencer said, shaking his head. "So Benzo is always wrong and Sonny is always right. . . ."

". . . and it looks like a robbery, but Sonny Lavinski knows it's not. Sonny has a kind of sixth sense for these things. The trick in every episode is that Sonny is always right, but he usually doesn't find the evidence that he's right until *way late in the story*. So it's always a race for time for Sonny to find some kind of physical thing that proves his theory. In this case, there's no purse, no ID, but blah, blah, blah . . . lab stuff, lab stuff. The lab guy is pretty funny. His name is Pez. Pez ties the body back to *you*, David Frieze."

"Dropped out of Harvard to start an online porn empire," Spencer added. "Millionaire at twenty. Fancy penthouse. Smug and disgusting. Very smart, so *not* like Chip."

"But you have an alibi, so they can't arrest you, even though Sonny knows you did it."

"Which I did," Spencer said.

"You almost admit it, that's how sure you are you won't get caught. Benzo totally misses this hint and keeps saying it's a robbery, but Sonny keeps investigating you. Sonny follows you and annoys you in public at a club, so you have a little snark-off with him, which he wins, because Sonny is awesome. Then all of this illegal porn stuff turns up on Sonny's computer the next day. You obviously hacked it and put it on there. You do not mess with Sonny Lavinski. He is so going to take you down now."

"And he does?" Spencer asked.

"He *so* does. He stays at the station all night until he figures out how you did it, then he goes to your apartment at about two in the morning and drags you out. You have a big face-off. Then you call a fancy lawyer, it looks like you're going to get off, but then Sonny nails you in court, and you're found guilty. And you get really mad and start screaming and they have to drag you out."

Spencer nodded, then closed his eyes and started silently mouthing his lines to himself.

"What I don't get," Scarlett said, looking at the script again, "is that this sounds like the first episode of the season, the one that's supposed to be on next week. I read the summary online. Don't they shoot these things weeks or months in advance?"

"They do," Spencer said. "They were kind of weird when I talked to them on the phone this morning. They were kind of hinting that something was going wrong and they were really, really behind. That's why this schedule is so crazy. The days are, like, eighteen and twenty hours long. But I don't care as long as I have a job."

Marlene came out of the kitchen with a stack of toast on a tiny green plate. There were about eight pieces.

"I buttered it," she said, setting it down. "Want jam?"

"You need to ask?" he replied.

Marlene returned to the kitchen. Scarlett stared at the tower of toast, trying to make sense of it.

"Why?" she asked. "Just . . . why?"

"Because things have changed," he said, grabbing the top piece and taking a huge bite. "The curse of the sock is over."

Day two of school, and it was already tiring. Scarlett was jealous of Spencer and Lola. They didn't have to go through this anymore.

Spencer would spend his entire day on the set of her favorite show, with her favorite actor. He would meet Sonny Lavinski. The great, the beloved Sonny Lavinski. Lola had a less enviable day, but at least she didn't have to leave the hotel if she didn't feel like it.

And she? Would cycle through overly bright, curvy hallways, trying to jump-start her brain in academic mode after months of inactivity. This was the first full-length day, when she had to come with all of her obscenely heavy new books.

Eric leaked back into her mind as the day progressed. He was there in French (French was supposed to be romantic, though she never really knew why). He was there when they talked about the free university systems of Europe in International Politics (Eric went to a university). He was there in English (a love sonnet of Shakespeare's). He was there in Trig (no reason, just showed up). He was there in Art History (a painting of some naked dude in the overhead slides). He put in an appearance in American Government (a map of the country, he was from the South). He only moved aside when replaced by Max's smirking face in Biology.

Max had gone to some trouble today. He wore a wrinkled dress shirt and an even more wrinkled tie and jeans with huge bend-splits at the knees that revealed patches of hairy-guy legs. And his only goal during Biology was to make Scarlett lose her mind.

He used a variety of methods. Sometimes it was sitting too close to Scarlett and watching over her shoulder, looking at everything she wrote. He drummed his fingers constantly. He tried to stand pipettes on end. He switched their Bunsen burner on and off every time Ms. Fitzweld turned her back. Sometimes he was content with just the flame, but if she was really not paying attention, he would hold his hand low over the flame, or tempt it with bits of paper. More nerve-wracking were the times when he did nothing but perch at the edge of his stool, smiling brightly, as if *about* to do something at any moment. When she scrawled unfriendly comments to ward him off, he wrote little notes of thanks back.

"What if I told you I really needed to pass this class?" Scarlett asked at the end of the period. "Not just pass, but do really well."

"I would say . . . suck it?"

"What is your problem?" Scarlett demanded. "You don't even know me."

"I'll tell you," Max said, leaning over and speaking way too close and low into Scarlett's ear. She could feel his breath, warm against her neck and earlobe. She shivered involuntarily. "I heard that you're going to be watching me all year," he said. "Like my own Secret Service."

"I am not spying on you," she said.

"Sure you aren't," he said almost under his breath, getting up.

There was another heavy load of manila envelopes waiting in the lobby when Scarlett got to Mrs. Amberson's building, enough that they had to go into a box.

"I had to *find* this box," Murray the doorman said, and he meant it to sting. "For your mail."

"It's a great box," Scarlett said soberly.

"Are you bein' funny?"

Scarlett scurried to the elevator without answering.

Up in the apartment, Mrs. Amberson was sprawled out on her back on a white rug, eyes closed.

"Ignore me, O'Hara," she said. "I'm in Savasana."

Scarlett stepped over her to set the box on the desk. She opened the envelopes, headshot after headshot. The next job was to sift through the equally massive pile of postcards that were advertising shows and showcases that various actors wanted her to attend. There were also postcard-size headshots in there. There were even more on e-mail, which was the next step. Links to video clips, online photo galleries. It was starting to seem like all actors did all day long was send out postcards and packages and notes to agents who largely didn't want to get postcards and packages and notes. So much hope. So much effort. So many people wanted so much.

"I'm sick of actors," Scarlett said.

"Ah." Mrs. Amberson smiled blindly at the ceiling. "That statement is the first step toward wisdom."

"I can't do this."

"Do what, O'Hara?"

"Deal with Chelsea," Scarlett said. "Or her family."

"Of course you can."

"Chelsea's mom told Max that I'd be spying on him. Remember how I'm *not* doing that? Remember how that was just something that was in her head?"

"It still is," Mrs. Amberson said calmly. "She is the only person who believes it is happening. Don't worry about her. Houses have fallen on nicer people than Miranda Biggs."

"*Max* believes it!"

Mrs. Amberson chose to step over this point.

"Just remember, success when you're very young . . ." she said. "It brings a special kind of strain. It's our job to keep Chelsea sane on her rise to success."

"What about me?" Scarlett asked. "What about *my* sanity?"

"You'll be fine. You have tremendous strength of character."

"No I don't."

"You really need to relax, O'Hara. Do you see this position I'm in? Do you know what it is?"

"Yes. It's called lying down."

"Anatomical zero, O'Hara. This is where you feel the masses and spaces in your body. The head is a mass. The cervical curve of the neck is a space. The shoulders are a mass. The lumbar curve is a space. The pelvis is a mass. The —"

"I get the idea," Scarlett said.

"We are gentle waves, head to foot. That's the point. We are built to ebb and flow. Ebb and flow. You are ebbing, but not flowing. Flow, O'Hara."

She sat up quickly and cocked her head to the side, like her ear was filled with water. Or chi.

"That pose," she said, "is called corpse pose. After you do yoga, you play dead. You let the body absorb what it has learned. Absorbing experience, O'Hara. That is what I believe in. Now tell me, how is your brother? Our first successful booking!"

"He's happier than before," Scarlett said. "I worked with him last night on the script. *Crime and Punishment* is my favorite show."

"Well, it's a good job to have. A few days of work, some SAG points, a very solid résumé builder."

It was strange to hear her talk about it in that way, so casually, as if being in the best show on television wasn't a big deal.

"There's something I need from you," she said. "Tomorrow, I'd like you to have dinner with the Biggses, Miranda invited you. And before you say no . . ."

Scarlett had been forming the word.

"There are rumblings on the Great White Way," she said. "It sounds like *The Flower Girl* might not be with us too much longer. It's time to set Chelsea up with some auditions. We have to walk the walk."

"So I have to have dinner with the Biggses?"

"You were invited."

"Why?"

"Because you have a connection to Max through his school, and because I think Miranda would like Chelsea to have a friend."

"You can't just hire a friend," Scarlett said.

"You would be amazed what people can do," Mrs. Amberson replied. "And I'm not suggesting that you two will become close. But it would provide an invaluable opportunity to know more about this *fascinating* family. Also, if you think about it, it may help convince Max that you aren't spying on him at all. I imagine the most casual dinner conversation will soon reveal the fact that Miranda knows nothing."

"That doesn't make any sense," Scarlett said.

"And I will give you fifty dollars. Cash."

It pained Scarlett that she could be so easily bought, and that the money was so quickly allocated in her mind. Fifty dollars was a month of coffee, or at least four cab rides to or from school in the rain, or a sweater, or a bunch of books. . . . It was a multitude of small life improvements, little kindnesses she could inflict on herself. And, in truth, there was part of her that wanted to see just what life in the Biggses' house was like.

"You know you want to see," Mrs. Amberson said, eerily tuning in on this thought. "You are a student of human nature, O'Hara.

Fifty dollars, when you come back with the details. And they eat very early, so that Chelsea can get to the theater. Four o'clock. So that shouldn't be a problem with your parents."

"Fine," Scarlett said. "But I'm not staying all night. Just dinner. Which is what, an hour?"

"An hour will be enough," Mrs. Amberson said, smiling.

THAT SPECIAL SOMETHING

Scarlett showed up at the appointed time the next day, malice in her heart, and twenty-five of the promised fifty dollars in her pocket. Chelsea lived in an old building in the East Thirties. Not a massive, fancy one like Mrs. Amberson's. A smaller one, with no doorman. The elevator was one of those ridiculously small ones that only held two people. The hall was dark, and there were only three doors. One had been left ajar, and Scarlett pushed it open, feeling it make cushy contact with what must have been a bunch of coats hanging on the wall behind.

"Is that Scarlett?" Mrs. Biggs said. "Come in!"

Scarlett stepped into a tiny hallway, which was halved in size by all the coats. The living room was absolutely packed, every inch of space used to death. There was a full-size sofa, bookshelves, a set of drawers, a crowded console with the television and stereo equipment, stacks of DVDs of musicals, and books on acting. The space around it was taken up by an electronic keyboard, an exercise ball, free weights, and piles of music. It seemed like an excessive amount of activity went on in here — a lot of living.

Mrs. Biggs was sitting at a tiny table over by the kitchen alcove, doing something on a computer. She was wearing the dress that Scarlett had seen Chelsea in when they met. It also fit her perfectly. She and Chelsea were almost identical in size.

"Chelsea will be home in a minute," she said, waving Scarlett to the sofa without even looking up. "Give me just a second. Chelsea got two fan mail letters today. I'm just answering them. Have a seat."

The sofa was crowded at one end with piled blankets and pillows and clothes. There was a strong plug-in air freshener at the end of the sofa — a sickly one that was probably supposed to smell like clean linen but smelled more like sticky, floral bleach. The scent rang a bell in Scarlett's mind. She knew it.

This was Max's *bed*. Max trailed that air freshener smell all day. *That's* what it was.

Scarlett quickly turned herself away from the sofa she was about to sit on and made a circuit around the room instead, pretending to take an interest in the things on the walls. There was a clear theme in the decorating scheme, and that theme was Chelsea. Somewhere in Scarlett's mind, where things she didn't know she was thinking were being thought, this had been expected. It seemed like every inch of wall space was encrusted with a show poster or a photo. There was no sign of Max except for the pile of clothes and bedding. It was like some kind of nature documentary, where you had to hunt for evidence that the animal had a den nearby.

Miranda noticed that Scarlett hadn't sat, then looked over and saw why.

"Oh sorry," she said, nodding at the pile in annoyance. "I tell Max to put his things away when he wakes up, but he never does."

To be fair to Max, which was something Scarlett didn't really feel like being, there didn't seem to be anywhere for his stuff to go. This apartment was full. It would have been a tight fit for one person, or one really close couple. Three people — three people who needed their own space — that was impossible. Living like this would have made her insane.

Scarlett stood there uncomfortably while Mrs. Biggs typed. It was weird enough being invited here — but stranger still to be ignored once she arrived. As someone raised in the hospitality industry, Scarlett disapproved of this.

"There," Miranda said, finishing up and shutting the computer. "So . . . I thought it might be nice for Chelsea to talk to you some more . . . and Max. We're new to the city, so we don't know many . . . Chelsea's busy with the show, and Max doesn't . . ."

None of those sentences were complete, but Scarlett grasped the missing concept. They don't have *friends*. Friends, luckily, were something that Scarlett never felt short of. She might not have studied dance for a dozen years or been in a commercial or a Broadway show . . . but she had people she could call at one in the morning.

"So," Miranda said, getting up and stepping into the kitchen, "was school good?"

When normal adults asked this question, Scarlett would move through a rote response indicating that school was school and the experience had yet to kill her. But Miranda Biggs didn't ask innocent, polite questions. She wanted to know about Max. Of that, Scarlett was sure, and she wasn't going to tell. Scarlett decided that she would talk about absolutely everything else, much more than she wanted to know. She walked Miranda through periods one through seven, everything but Bio. Scarlett listened to the impatient thwack of vegetables being chopped.

"Right," Miranda said, her voice barely concealing her impatience, "but don't you and Max have a class together? Biology?"

"Oh," Scarlett said as if just remembering this. "Yeah."

"And how's that?"

"Fine."

"Fine?"

"Well," Scarlett said, "it's just been a few days."

More dismemberment of vegetables. Scarlett smiled to herself.

There was a jangle of keys, and Chelsea appeared. Her hair was back in two chunky little braids, and she wore a sleek exercise outfit. She was makeup-free, but had flushed little apple cheeks, fresh from a workout of some kind.

"Oh hi!" she chirped. "Just had to meet my trainer for a session."

"Good," Miranda said. "You're here. I have to go out and get more broccoli. Did you do free weights?"

"No. I think I pulled something in my neck. Derrick told me I'd better not push it or I might have trouble during the show tonight."

"I know the muscle mass is making your weight go up a little, but as long as we balance out the rest . . ."

"He's checking every day," Chelsea said. "I've gained five pounds, but I'm obviously leaner."

"As long as he's checking."

On that unpleasant note, Miranda left to get her broccoli, and Chelsea excused herself to take a shower. Scarlett finally took a seat on the sofa and stared at the piles of Max's things.

Chelsea was a quick showerer. She was back in a few minutes, wrapped in a towel.

"One sec," she said, disappearing into what Scarlett presumed was her bedroom to change. It looked like there were two bedrooms in this apartment — one for Chelsea, and one for Chelsea's mom.

"Must be kind of hard," Scarlett said. "All three of you in here."

"Oh, you have *no* idea." Chelsea emerged, dressed in a nearly identical set of exercise clothes. Scarlett had a feeling that if she looked through Chelsea's drawers, she would find a dozen of these uniforms. "Max sleeps in here, which is why his stuff is everywhere. It's a pain for him to be in the living room, but in a way, he has the most space."

She shrugged away his lack of privacy as if it simply could not be helped, and sat down next to Scarlett to put on her sneakers.

"We're supposed to be getting a bigger place sometime," she said. "But we can't afford it right now. Everything here is so insanely expensive! He didn't want to move, and he doesn't need to be here like I do. But my mom was obsessed with getting him into a school in Manhattan."

"We're lab partners now. He sits next to me."

"Be careful," Chelsea said. "He cheats."

"That's what he said. I thought he was kidding."

"It's true. He does. He's really lazy, and he'll try to get you to help him. Don't let him take advantage. I'm not going to mind, *trust* me. I don't even know why my mom dragged him to New York. He should have stayed at home."

"Where is home?"

"Binghamton. A few hours away. Our house is there, and my dad."

"Your parents are still married?" Scarlett asked. Scarlett had assumed that there was no Mr. Biggs, that Mrs. Biggs had divorced and taken her kids to the city. As soon as she said this, though, she realized that sounded kind of bad. But Chelsea just laughed.

"Oh yeah. My parents are just . . . they're fine. I don't think it matters to them if they see each other very often. I think my dad likes having the house all to himself. We live on a golf course. He manages the place. He can just golf whenever he wants now. That's like his *dream*."

Mrs. Biggs returned with a shopping bag and Max in tow. He looked absolutely appalled to see Scarlett in his living room. She would have warned him in advance, but he hadn't shown for Bio that day, which had been a pleasant surprise. A totally Max-free day would have been better still, but life doesn't give you everything you ask for.

"Scarlett's here for dinner," Mrs. Biggs said.

Max grunted what Scarlett assumed was some kind of insult and dropped his bag in the center of the room.

"Not there, Max!" his mom called. "Someone will trip!"

"Who?" he asked, kicking it aside.

"I'm just making chicken and vegetables," she said, ignoring this remark and addressing Scarlett. "I don't like . . . weird food. I don't like spices and things."

What Miranda Biggs didn't like, it seemed, was flavor of any kind. She steamed some broccoli until it was anemic, piled some lettuce with no dressing, and plopped down a baked, dry chicken breast. This was served up at a tiny table really only made for two people. Max sat down at the table without bothering to remove the earbuds from his ears. Sound dribbled from his head.

"I have some low-fat salad dressing spray," Mrs. Biggs said. "Max, turn that off!"

Max couldn't hear her, on account of the earbuds. She pulled one of them loose. Then she reached around to the refrigerator without even getting up and retrieved a spray bottle of low-fat dressing, as promised.

"Your brother went to the High School of Performing Arts, right?" Chelsea asked.

"Right."

"But you don't have the acting bug?"

"No," Scarlett said.

"So what do you *do*?"

Max was clearly paying some kind of attention, because Scarlett saw him looking over at her at this.

"I . . . go to school. . . ."

She was answering this question like a five-year-old. *I go to school.* Genius. What else did she do? She tied her shoes. She liked kittens.

"Yeah," Chelsea said sympathetically, as if she knew this answer was exactly as pathetic as Scarlett feared. "You have to feel it. It has to be in you. And, you're, you know, an agent. Or something."

Max let out an audible sigh, grabbed the salad dressing, and sprayed everything on his plate until it had a high sheen.

"You need to be a special kind of person to be a star," Mrs. Biggs said, slicing her chicken breast with a vigor usually reserved for the severing of human heads from still-struggling bodies. "It doesn't just *happen*. It's about talent, and it's about focus. Chelsea's been working toward her goal all her life. Sure, there are people who work just as hard, but if they don't have the special something, then they aren't going to make it. Chelsea has both."

Max's eyes fluttered slightly closed.

"Max is the academic one," Mrs. Biggs said, remembering her other child at the table. "He gets by on just brains."

"And the blood of virgins . . ." he said, drifting into the conversation.

"Don't use that language at the table," Mrs. Biggs snapped.

"English?"

Mrs. Biggs just looked up tiredly.

"That's *not* what Max gets by on," Chelsea said under her breath.

It was so strange being the outsider to all these little barbs and understandings. Scarlett suddenly had a lot of sympathy for people like . . . well, Eric and Chip . . . who had sat in the middle of six Martins at the dinner table and tried to keep up.

"I have to get home," she said, the moment Mrs. Biggs stood to yank the plates away. "But thanks . . ."

"You should come again!" Chelsea said. "Anytime you want."

Just when Scarlett thought she'd made her escape and was halfway down the steps, she heard a creak above her. Max was following her down.

"So," he called down the stairwell, "you're dating my sister now, huh? Or was that just you being a good lackey?"

"My boss gave me fifty bucks," Scarlett answered honestly. "Next time? I'm going to ask her for double."

For the first time, Scarlett heard Max laugh. If she had been guessing, she would have thought his laugh would sound like a man cackle, or something like the squawk of a dying bird. But it was a full, round sound. Not unlike an actor laugh — from the belly, full of voice. The largeness and humanness seemed to startle them both, and he turned and went back up.

As Scarlett walked back to the Hopewell, she saw Spencer's bike still leaning against the stop sign invitingly. Someone had put a half-eaten hamburger on the seat, but still, no one had made the effort to take it. Upstairs, it was very quiet. The pigeons were cooing and resting on the outside of Scarlett's air conditioner, their tiny feet tapping on the metal. She looked through her homework list — three paragraphs of French, thirty-five Trigonometry problems, five chapters of *Great Expectations* to read, one chapter of Biology with six end-of-chapter questions to answer, and five articles on the government of Pakistan to find, digest, and summarize. She decided the articles were a good place to start, but once she got online, she ended up reading all of her messages and watching Eric's commercial seven times, closing down the window after each viewing and telling herself that she *would not* reopen it. Then she would go looking for articles for five minutes, but find her mind dragging her back to the commercial for one more look.

She slammed the computer shut and faced the silence. And in the silence, a question came. Another creeping question. The question the Biggses had put there: *What was she going to do with her life?* She'd never felt a pressing need to answer this question before now. She was fifteen. She wouldn't have to choose a college or decide on a major for at least two more years. But still . . . there were classes to pick now. There were skills to pick up. Everyone else did things. It wasn't just Chelsea who had trained since she was just a small cellular life-form. Almost all of her friends were developing some kind of special skill. And it wasn't just a question of who she was and how much money they had — after all, Spencer had become an actor. Sure, he was just kind of born that way, but he had also taught himself many, many things. He always had a mission. Marlene had . . . well, cancer. But that had weirdly provided her with a social life and maybe some kind of perspective. And she was eleven, so who cared?

The only other person who didn't really seem to have a definite goal was . . .

The door to the Orchid Suite flew open, and in came Lola, the very person she was thinking of.

Except that Lola didn't look like Lola. Her face was flushed and her eyes were narrowed. She was walking quickly, instead of her usual smooth, graceful step, and her back was hunched. It was like her entire body was trying to curl itself into a fist.

"You okay?" Scarlett asked.

Lola tore off her Bubble T-shirt and threw it at the end of her bed.

"Fine," she said, her jaw set.

This was so obviously a lie that it didn't need to be said. Scarlett just kept looking at her until she decided to explain.

"Do you remember Boonz?" Lola finally said.

"Chip's friend?"

"Well, she's one of his friend's girlfriends. He doesn't like her. Boonz was the one who made fun of me about the dress."

"Oh," Scarlett said, nodding quickly. *"Her."*

Chip had given Lola a beautiful Dior dress. It was a dress Lola had seen in the window of Bergdorf's and coveted deeply, but never even imagined owning. Lola wore the dress everywhere, to everything. It was the best article of clothing she had ever owned — was ever likely to own — and she maintained it with the zeal of a curator. It was her favorite thing until Chip's friend Boonz made a snide comment about the repetitive wearings, questioning whether or not Lola owned any other clothes. The weight of dealing with much wealthier people must have been pressing on Lola for some time, though she had never really shown it. But when Boonz did that, something inside of Lola snapped. She ran away from the party and from Chip, escaping from society types and a competition she could never win.

"I guess I thought that stuff was over," Lola said. "Chip's up in Boston in school. He doesn't see a lot of these people anymore. But she came into the spa this afternoon, she and some other girl. I was restocking some shelves. They followed me around, asking me stupid questions about the products. It was all just to mock me for working there. I even lost a sale, a big sale, because they wouldn't leave me alone. You can't get away when you work there."

Her humiliation was so clear, Scarlett couldn't think of anything that would make it better.

"Sorry," Scarlett said.

"It's fine," Lola said. But she didn't look fine. She reached to her dresser for a shirt. The drawer stuck. She jiggled it once, but it only gave another inch or two. She rattled it even harder until Scarlett heard a tiny crack and the drawer stopped moving completely.

"It's their problem, not yours," Scarlett said. "There's nothing weird about having a job."

Scarlett knew this was a pointless thing to say. It was *true*, but it was pointless.

"They *make* it my problem!" Lola yelled. "I can't get away from them. How do they make me feel so bad . . . about everything? Everything in my life?"

She tried to squeeze her hand into the opening to get a shirt, but she obviously couldn't reach. She grabbed the drawer on either side and pulled it hard.

"Damn it!" Lola mumbled. "Damn it, damn it, *damn it*!"

Each word increased in volume and brought a more fervent shake and pull. The entire front piece of the drawer came off in Lola's hands, leaving the contents exposed. Lola dropped it in disgust, reached into the naked, half-extended shelf and yanked the first shirt from the stack. She sat on the end of her bed and looked at the hole she had just created. It was all too symbolic.

THE TERRIBLE SECRET
OF SPENCER

After the madness of the first few days of school, a week passed in relative quiet. Schoolwork piled up so quickly that Scarlett almost forgot about her heartache for a moment or two. Max annoyed her in Biology every day, then she either hung out at Dakota's with the others to do some homework and talk, or she went to Mrs. Amberson's to work. Then it was home, more homework, an hour or so of convincing herself not to write to Eric, and maybe some TV. This was the grind.

Throughout it all, she didn't see Spencer once. The *Crime and Punishment* schedule went round the clock. Sometimes there was evidence that he'd come home for a few hours for a nap, or some clothes, or a shower. From the messages she got from him, it sounded like they had gone to a twenty-four hour schedule, and he was just sleeping in the makeup trailer whenever he could. When he resurfaced, there was no warning. Scarlett was trying to find three articles online about the German banking system when Spencer burst into her room. He didn't even knock.

"Come here," he said, grabbing her and dragging her down to the

Jazz Suite. He shut the door behind them and locked it. No one ever locked the Jazz Suite door. Scarlett had never even noticed that the door had a lock.

"That locks?" she asked.

"Yeah, I didn't realize that until this one time in high school when I had Suzanna over and . . . never mind. I figured it out under duress. Sit down."

Scarlett sat on the sofa. Spencer reached into his bag and produced a manila envelope, from which he extracted a disk.

"Is that . . ." Scarlett asked.

"Yes," Spencer said, "this is the episode."

"Put it in! Put it in!"

But he didn't put it in.

"This," he said, "is a very, very big secret that I am *not* supposed to have. One of the editors loaned it to me. And I had to swear on my life that I wouldn't show it to anyone, but you don't count . . . I mean, you're special. You have to watch it with me. I'm way too nervous to watch it on my own. But you can't tell anyone what happens. Promise?"

"Promise," Scarlett said. "Plus, I already know, and it's on in three hours."

"No. You *really* have to promise. Like, on your life. On everything. You can't e-mail or talk to anyone about it."

"Spencer, I read the script."

"The script changed," he said.

"Put it in!"

Spencer exhaled deeply a few times and put the disk in the DVD player. He took a seat next to her and picked up the control, but paused before hitting PLAY.

"There are going to be some things that I'm going to have to explain. . . ."

"Shut up and play it!"

He took another breath and hit the button.

The signature credits were missing. There were just a few blue screens with information printed in block letters — the episode name ("Crossfire"), number (391), the airdate. The action started on the street, just as Scarlett had read, with Sonny Lavinski and his partner, Benzo, finding a body in a Dumpster.

"I'm coming up soon," he said. "After this scene."

An apartment building, not unlike Mrs. Amberson's, appeared on the screen.

"Here!" he said. "I guess this is my evil headquarters. I haven't seen the exterior shots before, but this is definitely my part."

Sure enough, the scene shifted inside and there Spencer was, sitting behind a bank of computer screens. They had styled his hair a little differently than normal, forcing it into position with lots of gel. His face was definitely narrower and a lot less smiley and loose than in life.

His character, David Frieze, was smug, answering questions about the murder with false politeness as he typed away on one of a half dozen keyboards. He told the detectives he was busy trying to win an eBay auction for an original Pac-Man arcade machine, which got a wry remark from Sonny before the scene ended.

"You just talked to *Sonny Lavinski*!" Scarlett cried.

"I did," Spencer said, arms folded tight across his chest, his eyes focused on the screen, still taking in his own performance.

Without commercials, the episode went fairly quickly. Benzo was keeping himself busy screwing up the investigation, as was his duty, and then Spencer's character was brought up again in conversation.

"You're about to come back on!" Scarlett said. "They're going to interview you again. Even Benzo's starting to think you did it, which never happens. Not at this point. There must still be twenty minutes to go. Benzo *never* gets it until about fifteen minutes before it all ends. This is weird."

Spencer grabbed the control and paused the show.

"Okay," he said, "just a warning. This part is new. This is where I describe my process for . . ."

"Shhhh!" Scarlett said, elbowing him. "Don't tell me! I want to watch!"

"But you really should know . . ."

"Spencer!"

"Okay . . ." he said, picking up the remote.

Sonny and Benzo appeared at Spencer's apartment again, this time in the living room, where a full view of Central Park could be seen. Spencer was even more annoying this time, playing a hand-held video game throughout the entire questioning. Sonny finally put pressure on him, and he set the game down beside him.

In real life, next to her, Scarlett felt Spencer tense up and put his hand over his face.

"Oh God," he said quietly.

TV Spencer began to deliver a very long monologue on the craft of Internet porn, a long analogy that involved a lot of doughnuts. Cream doughnuts, jam doughnuts, crullers, doughnut holes — all friendly, innocent foods that were now contaminated, utterly filthy and horrible and poisonous. It would have been traumatic hearing this disgusting speech come from anyone's mouth, but this was all coming from *her brother*. Sonny . . . blessed, saintlike Sonny . . . shut him down.

Spencer paused the show, but did not look over.

"That," he said, "is what I like to call the Unified Porn Theory."

Scarlett could barely speak.

"I didn't even know you could say those things on network TV," she finally managed.

"They're putting one of those 'may not be suitable for younger viewers' warnings on it."

"Or the actor's little sister."

"Well, yeah," he said. "I was thinking to myself during filming — *oh my God, this is going to be on television. Everyone is going to hear me say this.* But I tried to make my stress work for me. It makes me more intense, right? They wanted me to really play it up, make him seem like a total sociopath."

"Oh sure," Scarlett said, trying to sound enthusiastic, and failing. "You totally sold it. You seem like a complete perv."

"Thank you."

"So, that's the big secret?" she asked. "Don't worry. I'm not going to tell anyone about that. I'm already trying to forget it."

"There's nothing else like *that*," he said carefully. "But there was another change."

Scarlett didn't notice anything different. They got all the way to the very end, and it followed the script she knew, right through the trial, right through the guilty verdict, the courtroom outburst. . . . As he was being dragged down the courtroom steps in handcuffs, Sonny followed behind, making wisecracks all the way.

"Okay," Spencer said, "um . . ."

"Shhhhhhh!"

Then Spencer did the kind of thing that he did best — he threw himself down the final five steps of the courthouse, tumbling and causing the crowd to scatter. He and Sonny tussled, and Sonny knocked him to the ground. And then Spencer (or David) got Sonny's gun.

And fired.

Sonny slumped to the ground. Spencer (or David) took a crowd member hostage as he made his escape. And then Benzo declared Sonny dead. The episode stopped abruptly.

Spencer shut the television off and gave her a moment to collect her thoughts.

"Did you just . . . did you just *kill Sonny Lavinski?*" Scarlett asked.

"Kind of," he admitted.

"My favorite character? Of all time?"

"Uh . . ."

"He's not dead, right? This is a joke, right?"

Spencer twiddled his thumbs.

"Sorry," he said.

Scarlett punched him in the arm. Hard. Spencer didn't even blink.

"I feel that was deserved," he said. "But it's better than the pervy part, right?"

"No! You killed him! So . . . he's gone?"

"God, you have no idea how weird it was on set that day," he said, leaning back. "What happened was, he showed up drunk that morning, and was yelling at everyone. He was so hard to work with."

"Sonny?" Scarlett said, shocked. "Really?"

"Guy's nasty, Scarlett. Seriously. Always has been, from what I hear. But this was a particularly bad day. Then, right after lunch, he said he was quitting. Just like that, in the middle of the set, announcing it to everyone."

"He quit? Just like that?"

"Yep," Spencer said. "He said he'd stay on set for three more hours, then he was gone. The director and the crew almost went insane. Everyone was on the phone. We were all standing around. No one knew what to do. They got the writers down to the set, and all the people in charge had an emergency meeting in one of the trailers. Next thing I know, they're calling for me. Originally, I was just supposed to yell at him as I was dragged off. Instead, they said I had to make an escape attempt, get the gun from Sonny's belt, and shoot him in the chest. There wasn't even enough time to rehearse it. I made it up on that take. Just threw myself down the steps, shot him, they filmed his dead body, and then he left."

"What . . . what does this mean?"

"I'm a cast member now," he added. "At least for a few weeks, anyway. They said probably until December, maybe even longer. They're working on the story line now. They totally weren't ready for this."

Spencer got up and went to the window. He brushed back the heavy silver curtain and leaned his forehead against the glass, gazing miserably down to the street below.

"My bike's still out there," he mumbled. "God, why doesn't anyone *take* it? It's not that bad. . . ."

"Why aren't you happier?" she asked. "I feel like we should be celebrating, right? Shouldn't we be jumping up and down?"

"I'm nervous," he said.

"You don't even have to *do* anything. You did it already. It's done."

"I calm down when I'm performing. Performing is easy. This is different. This is waiting."

"Waiting for what?" Scarlett asked.

Spencer paced, running his hands through his hair.

"People were so intense," he said, rubbing at his neck. "Half the crew was crying when the scene was shot. And once we did the death scene, people were so weird to me. The craft services girl wouldn't even give me hot coffee. I mean, you love Sonny Lavinski. What are you thinking, right now? About the me you saw on the screen? I can't watch that with Marlene. Or Lola. Or Mom. I don't know how I just watched that with you. I don't think I can watch it. I'm going out. I'll be back later, before the show, but . . ."

He got up, popped out the disk, and stuck it back in the envelope.

"Remember," he said. "You can't tell anyone anything about what you just saw."

When he was gone, the full implication of the news gradually sank into Scarlett's skull. Sonny Lavinski was dead, and she was one of a handful of people who knew it. And his killer was getting on his rickety bike to try to ride off his anxiety.

In a few hours, the world was going to meet Spencer.

ACT III

NEW YORK MOURNS SONNY
The New York Bulletin

Last night, television history was made when Detective Sonny Lavinski (played by Donald Purchase) was shot dead on the season premiere of police drama Crime and Punishment. *Lavinski's death came as a major surprise to millions of viewers who had tuned in for the start of Lavinski's 16th season. What began as a fairly ordinary case involving the murder of an NYU student ended with a shooting at the foot of the courthouse steps, with Lavinski dying in the arms of his partner, Mike Benzo.*

Reaction across the city, the country, and the Internet was immediate. News of Lavinski's murder trumped coverage of real-life murders, instantly becoming one of the top news stories. The headline rippled across news tickers around Manhattan, causing crowds of people in Times Square to stop and point. The Crime and Punishment *online fan site, which boasts more than two hundred thousand members, immediately crashed.*

Sources from the set report that Lavinski's departure was long in

146

planning, and that much work had gone into keeping the story line under wraps.

"It was just time," said one staff writer who asked to go unnamed. "Donald's been great to work with. We were all crushed when he said he had to go. He didn't want it dragged out. He said that would hurt the fans who were really attached to his character. He wanted it to be quick. So that's how we wrote it."

Lavinski's killer, David Frieze, is played by cast newcomer Spencer Martin, 19.

"Yeah," another on-set source confirmed, "that story line is going to be a big part of this season. David Frieze is the new baddie on the street."

Over five hundred dedicated fans had an impromptu candlelight vigil on the steps of the New York Supreme Court, where the death scene was shot.

"I can't stop crying," said Felicia Wills of Brooklyn, as she placed a bouquet of flowers on the steps where Lavinski fell. "It's never going to be the same without Sonny."

Andrew Walsh of Manhattan said he was riding by on his bike when he saw the gathering and asked what happened.

"I was recording the show," he said. "I was about to go home and watch it. I never thought they'd kill Sonny Lavinski. That's like . . . killing television. I'm in shock. I'm honestly in shock."

A larger, more organized event in Central Park is to follow on Saturday.

THE LOVE OF
THE MASSES

The next morning, when Scarlett emerged from her room, she was struck by the sight of Spencer coming out of the bathroom wearing white pants and a white shirt. It was the whitest outfit she had ever seen, broken only by a sliver of dark silver tie.

"Is it Dress Like a Kentucky Colonel Day?" she asked. "I always forget to mark it on my calendar."

Spencer straightened his tie.

"I kind of wanted to get dressed up today, but my only dress pants are my work ones and these. And my good suit, but I didn't feel like wearing that. They're nice, right? They're really nice pants. I should wear them more often."

"They're nice," Scarlett conceded, taking a good look at them as they walked down the hall. "But they do look a little . . . musical-ish."

"That's because they *are* musical-ish," he said, pushing the elevator button, which stuck and clacked back out again. "They were part of my costume for *The Music Man*. I swiped them from the costume room when the show was over. I have the jacket, too, but it doesn't fit right. The arms are too short. Here, read this."

He pulled a copy of the *New York Bulletin* out of his messenger bag and passed it to Scarlett. It was already folded open to a page, and he tapped on an article.

"They're already lying about it," he said. "I am already spinning in the spin machine."

"Why are they saying it was planned?" she asked, scanning the article. "I don't get it. You said he walked off."

"Because it sounds better than, 'Bitter, greedy, slightly drunk guy leaves set with no warning after fifteen years.' Did you see the part about 'cast newcomer Spencer Martin'? That's my favorite part. That's the part where the article really shines. I'm the new baddie on the street!"

The arrow above the elevator pointed to five, and the doors creaked open. Spencer reached over and opened the gate for Scarlett.

"I'm feeling generous this morning," he said. "I feel like treating my favorite sister to an iced coffee."

"You still killed Sonny," Scarlett said. "You can't just buy me off with cold caffeine."

"Did I mention that I'd also treat you to a cab ride to school?"

"It's important to forgive," Scarlett said. "Are you always going to be like this? I like this new you. The old one was okay, but this one is better."

"As long as I'm a fancy, rich television star."

Spencer yanked the gate shut, and the inner doors squawked closed.

"You seem calmer today," she observed.

He shrugged, dismissing the panic of the day before.

"You know," he said, "the more I think about it, the more I'm glad I killed that guy. I'd do it again."

Scarlett smacked him playfully. Rather than reply, he threw himself back against the sunburst and slid down to the elevator floor. The door opened at that moment and the German couple staying in the Sterling Suite looked at him in bafflement. His eyes were closed, so he didn't immediately notice. Scarlett kicked his foot, and he looked up.

"Sorry," he said, getting up and stumbling slightly as he exited the elevator. "I have this inner ear thing and I lose my balance. . . ."

He swayed a bit as he held the gate for Scarlett to exit and the couple to enter. They looked concerned, and a little scared.

"It'll pass," he said as the elevator door slowly closed on them. "It always does. Have a good day!"

"They don't speak English," Lola said from behind the front desk. "Could you not freak them out by pretending to be dead in public spaces?"

"You can't be mad at me today, Lo," he said, leaning over the desk. "Your heart is filled with Spencerlove."

"I'm not mad," she said, smiling. "It's just that I'd like to keep the last guests we have left. Also, you aren't supposed to wear white after Labor Day."

"I'm the bad guy. I break the rules."

"Do you shoot more today?" Lola asked.

"No," Spencer said, checking to make sure he'd put his wallet into his fancy white pants. "It's just a read through. See you later."

As he and Scarlett walked to Third Avenue, a few heads turned in their direction. Spencer glowed with contentment. By the time they reached the coffee and doughnut shop, he had actually started humming to himself, very lightly, under his breath. They took a spot in line behind an older man who was ordering a large box of cream and jam doughnuts and an iced coffee. As he waited for his food, he kept looking over his shoulder at Spencer, each look getting longer and longer until it was an outright and undeniable stare. Spencer wheeled around, turning his back to the man, and leaned down to Scarlett.

"That guy is looking at me," he said in a low voice.

"You're on TV now," she whispered back. "And you just killed Sonny Lavinski. And you're dressed like the ice-cream man."

"I know. I just didn't expect anyone to recognize me. Like, that much."

The man at the counter wasn't the only one. Two women stopped outside the window, pointing inside. Spencer turned back around and put on his most innocent smile, waving at the women.

The man got his box of doughnuts and drink and paid, and only then did he ask, "Aren't you that punk from *Crime and Punishment*?"

"Yeah," Spencer said, slipping the man a sideways smile.

"I thought so."

He made a low sound, not unlike the first, tentative whir of a blender, and stood off to the side while Spencer ordered the iced coffees. While Spencer paid and batted his eyelashes at the woman behind the counter, Scarlett watched the man. There was something in his aspect that suggested that maybe some medication had been forgotten. He didn't eat a doughnut or drink his iced coffee. He just stared at Spencer.

"Here," Spencer said, pressing a massive iced coffee with whipped cream into Scarlett's hand. "Healthy breakfast."

He grabbed his own drink and shoved five dollars into the tip cup. They were just passing the man, and Spencer was just giving him a friendly nod of good-bye, when it started.

"You son of a bitch!" he said in an even, angry voice.

The smile dropped from Spencer's face in an instant.

"Sorry?" he asked.

"You heard me, you *son of a bitch*."

"Okay," Spencer said, quickly giving Scarlett a shove in the direction of the door. "Nice meeting you. Stay classy."

"What is *wrong* with that guy?" Scarlett asked as they stepped out onto the sidewalk. "Don't people know the difference between fantasy and reality?"

"He's just a weirdo," Spencer said, pulling the straw out of his cup and using it to scoop up some whipped cream. "Dime a dozen. You grew up here, you know that."

"I know, but . . ."

Scarlett felt something smack the middle of her back. It wasn't hard, but it was definitely solid. She turned just in time to see the man who had just yelled at them. He was following them with his box of doughnuts in his hand. He removed another one.

"That's the son of a bitch!" he yelled as he got closer. "That's the son of a bitch!"

Spencer turned in time to catch a cream one midchest. He looked down at his shirtfront, where he'd been struck.

"Is he really throwing doughnuts at me?" he asked.

"At us," Scarlett said. "He got me, too."

"What?"

Spencer stopped and changed position just enough to block Scarlett.

"What the hell are you *doing*?" he yelled at their attacker. "You hit my sister with a doughnut!"

"Let's just go," Scarlett said, catching Spencer's shirt and attempting to tug him along. But Spencer would not be moved. Another doughnut took flight. This time, it was jelly, and it made clear, perfect contact with the side of Spencer's head — cutting a streak of powder across his dark hair and exploding into a thick raspberry mess along his ear and neck. Against the white shirt, it looked like blood.

"Son of a bitch!" the man screamed again.

By this point, all the passersby stopped to watch the display. Not all of them knew which particular son of a bitch Spencer was, but a few did. Those few were pointing and whispering the sacred name: *Lavinski*. The rest of the crowd was prepared to accept the spectacle in the spirit in which it was offered — just one of those things that New York occasionally threw in their path to shake things up.

"He's an actor!" Scarlett yelled back, stepping from behind Spencer. "And you're a lunatic!"

The man reached for another doughnut.

"That box holds at least a dozen," Scarlett said. "He's got a lot more to go. Come *on*, Spencer!"

Spencer just maneuvered her back behind him again and held his ground.

"Seriously," he said. "You do know it's just a show, right? Right?"

The cream doughnut that immediately followed didn't rupture in quite the same way as the jelly had. It got him low on the torso, leaving a cream blotch on his hip. The next assault came from behind. A kid, maybe Scarlett's age, decided to take advantage of the open food fight that seemed to be going on and lobbed half a granola bar in their general direction. It glanced off Scarlett's elbow and landed on the sidewalk.

"Okay," Scarlett said, "that was just ineffective."

"A *show*," Spencer was saying, still trying to reason with their primary threat. "Not a real gun. Not a real murder. Not even my idea . . ."

Scarlett saw a cab with its light on stopping to let someone out. She took Spencer by the arm and pulled him toward it. He allowed himself to be moved this time, narrowly missing what looked like a very unstable blueberry jelly doughnut, which exploded on the back of the car.

"One Hundred Fourth and the park," Scarlett said to the driver, who already looked very sad that they were his passengers. "The faster you go, the less messed up your car gets."

Spencer got the door closed right before the man threw his iced coffee at the window. The window was half rolled up, which provided some protection, but not enough. The coffee drenched Spencer, soaking his face and side and pooling in his lap.

"Are you okay?" Spencer asked.

Scarlett's heart was thumping in her chest. She looked down at herself. Tiny spots of powder and jam covered her shirt.

"I'm fine," she said. "Just drop me at Dakota's. I'll borrow a shirt."

There was little point in asking Spencer the same question. The white clothes highlighted the damage. One side of his head and face was soaked with coffee-thinned jam. It dripped from his ear and down his shoulder. The majority of it was pooled in his lap. There were heavy impact marks of jam and cream on his chest and legs, which looked like someone had decided to make an abstract painting, using him as the canvas.

Scarlett dug around in her bag. She had no tissues; paper would have to do. She ripped a few pages from a notebook. Spencer didn't make a move. Figuring he was too stunned by the assault, Scarlett reached over to clean off his ear and cheek. As her hand drew near, he reached up to block her.

"Leave it," he said.

"What?"

"I have to make sure it stays this way until I get to the set."

"You *want* the jam on your head?"

"Not much point in trying to clean up. I can't hide this." He tilted his head in the opposite direction to slow the dripping of the evidence. "It's my one day of fame. Might as well enjoy it."

"I didn't think this is what fame was like."

"Me neither," he said.

The cab stopped at a red light. The driver handed back a pile of napkins, indicating that he would like his backseat cleaned up a little. Spencer took them and mopped up the space around him. Scarlett blotted her shirt. Mostly it just smeared the dots and made it worse. Her hand shook a little.

Scarlett called Dakota to request the shirt, and Dakota was waiting at the curb when they arrived. She was unable to contain her shock at the view inside the cab.

"Breakfast," Spencer said. "I'm a really messy eater."

"We never give him soup," Scarlett added.

Spencer nodded gravely, waved good-bye, and the cab pulled off.

"What. Was. That?" Dakota said. "Tell. Me. Now. What. Was. That?"

"There was an incident," Scarlett said.

She explained the morning's events as they walked up the three flights to Dakota's apartment, where Dakota had already laid out a selection of new T-shirts on her bed. Scarlett picked through them and selected a basic white one, similar to the one that she had on.

"Can you bring your jam-covered brother to my house every morning?" Dakota asked. "Why doesn't he need to take off his shirt? He totally needed a new shirt."

Many moons ago, in sixth grade, Dakota developed a crush on Spencer. It was an obsession that had long faded into a ritual joke that was important for them to perform every once in a while. Or, it was important to Dakota to perform and for Scarlett to nervously tolerate because she loved her friend and sometimes friends do these sorts of things . . . because sometimes friends *think* they are joking when they are not joking at all.

"How much do you think he would charge to take off his shirt?" she went on, to Scarlett's dismay. "I know he's famous and every-thing now, but everyone has a price."

"I don't know," Scarlett said. "A quarter?"

"Really? I like how *cheap* he is."

While Scarlett changed, Dakota fell back on her bed, imagining something Scarlett would undoubtedly find horrible.

"What are you going to do?" she asked. "Your brother just killed Sonny Lavinski."

"Do? I don't do anything. No one knows he's my brother except for you guys. And he's just going to be on the show for a while."

"But you guys got *attacked*," Dakota said.

"Yeah, well, it was just some freak," Scarlett said. "I don't think we're going to have any more problems like that. And who's even going to know?"

"Dissection," Ms. Fitzweld was shouting in eighth period, "is *not the same* as slicing to bits. You are not cutting up a pork chop."

Actually, she wasn't shouting. Ms. Fitzweld just happened to have one of those natural speaking voices that was sharp and pointy and overly loud — like she could see someone off in the distance ramming her car repeatedly with a shopping cart and could do nothing about it except take it out on sophomore Biology students.

"You do as little cutting as possible!" she raged on. "Do you understand me? Now, one person from each station come over here and get your fetal pig. Bring your dissection tray."

Scarlett put on her plastic apron and a pair of goggles and made her way toward the barrel, tray in hand. She winced as her classmates walked past with their little plastic-bagged pigs on trays. The formaldehyde was overwhelming. It smelled like a sterilized headache.

"I see Slax is skipping today," Dakota said, coming up beside her.

True enough, Max's seat was still empty.

"That's sad," Scarlett said. "I feel all dead inside when he's not here."

The pig supply had run low. There were two left, at the very bottom of the barrel. Scarlett adjusted her ill-fitting plastic glove and leaned in, her nose almost touching the rim. She tried to lift a pig by the corner of the bag, but it was too heavy.

"Stop being squeamish," Ms. Fitzweld said. "Pick it up."

Even through two layers of plastic, the heavy wetness of the pig was palpable. Scarlett grabbed it and plopped it on the tray. Back at her seat, she read through the instructions. Task one: sex the pig. She was glad Max wasn't around for this. She quickly examined hers and found it was a boy.

"Sorry, piggy boy," she said quietly. "I really am."

The classroom door opened, and Max sauntered in. Today, he was wearing a striped tie loose around his neck. Scarlett fondly remembered all the ways you could choke someone with a tie.

"Where have you been?" Ms. Fitzweld snapped.

"The bathroom," Max said with a smile.

"Thank you for sharing. Do it again and I'm docking you half a grade on the next exam. Get over to your station."

"Actually, I was reading the Internet," Max said, sitting down and pulling on his gloves. "But I thought saying I was in the bathroom sounded cooler. Guess what I found out. Someone was throwing doughnuts at your brother this morning."

Scarlett stopped what she was doing.

"Where did you see that?" she said.

"It was on *Spies of New York*. I'll read it to you."

He pulled out his phone and held it low, just under the desk.

"Let's see. '*Sonny-Killer Wears White After Labor Day, New York Responds*. On seeing Sonny's killer, one loyal fan responded with a volley of doughnuts that sent him running for a cab in the company of an unidentified blonde' . . . That's you I assume; they probably think you're dating him or something. . . . Then it says, 'After covering Martin in jam and cream, the assailant dumped a cup of iced coffee on him before the cab drove away. We thoroughly applaud this man's civic action and encourage other like-minded citizens to avenge our Sonny.' Guess it was his lucky day for some random nut job to come along with a box of jelly doughnuts."

"There was nothing random about it," Scarlett snapped. "It was because of the show last night. He had to give a speech about doughnuts. That's why the guy was throwing them."

"I know," he said. "I saw it. My mom turned it on because she wanted to see what kinds of jobs your boss is getting for her clients."

"So a crazy person attacked us." She pushed the dissection pan toward him. "Cut the pig."

"Not me," he said. "I'll just screw it up. We'll both fail. I'd hate to drag you down with me."

Scarlett dragged the pan back with a bitter heart. Hers, not the pig's — though the pig couldn't have been happy about it, either.

"Does your brother always wear white?" Max asked as Scarlett began the unpleasant task of the first incision with the scissors. "It's kind of a weird outfit. It's like something you would wear if you wanted a lot of people to look at you."

"He wears, whatever . . . I don't know."

"All I'm saying is that it seems like a good outfit to pick if you knew someone was going to, I don't know, throw jam doughnuts at you. And you wanted it to show up well in pictures."

"I was there," Scarlett said coldly. "It just happened. It wasn't planned."

"Sure," Max said. "There's no way that an actor would lie or pretend or stage something."

"He would have told me."

"Of course he would," Max said. "Whatever you want to think. All actors care about is that you spell their name right. Trust me. I live with one."

"So do I," Scarlett said.

"Fine," Max said, holding up his hands. "Ignore me. I'm wrong. Your brother is different from the rest. It was all a coincidence."

Try as she might, though, Scarlett couldn't ignore it. Max's idea immediately took root in her mind, and soon its tendrils had spread in all directions, crowding out other thoughts. There *was* something wrong about that morning.

"You know I have a point," he said, leaning close. "Bet it drives you crazy."

DECEPTIONS

"You're *here*!" Mrs. Amberson exclaimed when Scarlett arrived after school. "Thank God!"

There had been some kind of note explosion around the apartment — tiny blue papers covered in names and numbers on the sofa, on the tables, on the floor.

"O'Hara, you have no idea what today has been like. I need you to get on that computer right now and find every story, every photograph. I have calls to make. I'll be in my room. Your brother is coming up. He'll be here soon."

Scarlett sat down at the desk. Murray came out from around the sofa to have a look at her. His walk was a little steadier than normal.

"Murray seems calm today," Scarlett said.

"Yes," Mrs. Amberson called from the bedroom. "I got him acupuncture."

Murray looked up at Scarlett with his large black eyes, which seemed to say "help me" in pathetic doggie language.

"Sorry," she said to him.

He gave a little quake, then all of his legs slid in different directions and he landed on his belly.

Scarlett sat down and resigned herself to her job. In truth, she was curious to see exactly what was out there. The answer was: a lot. Thousands of hits. A dozen or more photos from phones repeated over and over again. News sites, blogs, boards . . . the scene was everywhere. The more she looked at the photographs, the more the obvious theatricality of it all became apparent. *"Does your brother always wear white?"* No, he did not. Scarlett had never seen those pants before. What were the chances that Spencer would wear all white and they would *just happen* to find the local lunatic who would *just happen* to throw doughnuts, which *just happened* to be the featured item in the speech Spencer had given on television the night before?

Very slim chances indeed.

But this wasn't the kind of thing Spencer would have set up on his own. Oh no. This had the mark of Amberson all over it.

Scarlett took a deep breath. She wasn't sure what was worse — Spencer and Mrs. Amberson pulling this off without telling her, or Max being right. If it was true.

The door buzzer rang. Mrs. Amberson ran to it while talking on the phone.

". . . classically trained," Scarlett heard her saying. "European style. Oh yes. A natural clown, but clowns always give the most *profound* performances. Quite skilled in musical theater as well, so if you want to discuss any song-and-dance options . . . Hold on one moment while I get the door. . . ."

She picked up the buzzer handset and clapped it to her other ear.

"Yes, yes," she said. "Send him up . . . No, I can't talk about the dog right now, this is not a good time . . . No, that wasn't to you, Carmine, I'm talking to my doorman . . . Murray, I am sorry about that but we'll just have to . . . Oh, that's fine, Carmine, you call me back when you're out of the tunnel . . . He does *not* have rabies, Murray, that drooling issue is completely harmless. Now, I have to go . . . Yes, you too, Carmine. Kiss, kiss . . . No, Murray, that was not to you. Good-bye."

She hung up both phones at once and leaned against the wall with one hand, taking a deep breath.

"O'Hara!" she called. "Your brother is coming up. Order him some food — and for yourself as well. I am sure I have menus somewhere."

A minute or two later, Spencer came in. The splattered white outfit of earlier had been replaced by a very stylish dress shirt and what looked like very expensive jeans. It was practically a Chip outfit.

"My star!" Mrs. Amberson said, embracing him. "Were you molested on your way here?"

"They got me a car to drive me here. They're sending one from now on. The wardrobe woman had mercy on me. That's how I got these clothes. And they put my pants from this morning up on eBay. My *pants* . . . are on *eBay*."

"Wonderful. What's eBay? Never mind. We have much to discuss. . . . But give me just a moment. One more call to make."

She sailed back off to her bedroom.

"What was it like today at work?" Scarlett asked as Spencer started wandering the room.

"Very, very, very weird. People are acting different already, like they respect me. No one respects me."

"I do."

"Yeah, but you have horrible judgment."

"I know," Scarlett said.

He came over to look at the photographs she was pulling up, but stopped short as he approached the desk.

"Rat," he said, backing up. "Rat . . ."

"That's not a rat. That's Murray. Be careful. New people make him tinkle."

Spencer and Murray regarded each other with mutual suspicion.

"Where did he come from?"

"Moo," Scarlett said.

"The moon?"

"No, Moo."

"What the hell is Moo?" he asked.

"It's a person. A friend of Mrs. Amberson's."

"She has a friend named Moo? Who owns this . . . is it a dog?"

"She does," Scarlett said. "Really. I'm not kidding about the tinkling. Don't freak him out."

Spencer backed away from Murray and fell backward onto the sofa.

"This is the weirdest day of my life," he said. "I woke up yesterday, no one knew who I was. I saw my face on the news. Scarlett . . . what the hell is going on?"

His eyes were wide, and he looked extremely wired. The fancy haircut they'd given him for the part, the one they'd spiked up on the show, made his dark hair look much nicer, much shinier and perfect. That combined with the new clothes, the fact that he didn't look sweaty and exhausted from riding around the city on his broken bike . . . Spencer had been gently remade into someone a little more wealthy and professional. But the enthusiasm of earlier sounded a bit more like uncertainty now.

"You're excited, right?" Scarlett asked. "You seemed happy this morning."

"I'm still happy. I'm just . . . my brain . . . It shut off a while ago."

"Is that why you forgot to tell me it was all a fake?"

Spencer cupped his face in his hands.

"I blocked you as best I could," he said guiltily. "You kept trying to step in front of me."

"Because someone was *attacking* you! With . . . food!"

"Sorry about your shirt," he said, taking his hands from his face but keeping his eyes averted. "I'll get you a new one."

"It's not the shirt," Scarlett said. "I don't like it when people keep things from me."

Mrs. Amberson emerged at that moment, clapping her hands together.

"*What* a conversation I just had!" she said, still clapping.

"She knows," Spencer said. "I told you she would figure it out."

There was no sign of regret from her boss. If anything, this news seemed to delight her.

"Well done, O'Hara!" she exclaimed. "Nothing gets past you. Your brother did say that and I didn't doubt him."

Scarlett looked between the two of them, waiting for someone to offer her an explanation.

"When it happened," Spencer began, "the shooting, the change in the script, I had to tell Amy, because she had to take care of signing me up for the next episode. Once she saw that monologue I had to do — she had an idea."

"It was obvious, O'Hara. . . ." Mrs. Amberson drifted across the room and scooped Murray up in her arms. "We had to do something. This is Spencer's moment, and we had to take it. When you have a shot at publicity, you can't be shy."

"And I had to be in this, why?" Scarlett asked.

"Sympathy!" she exclaimed. "Have you *seen* those photos, O'Hara? The actor protecting his younger sister from the assault of the fans. You played a vital role."

"So why didn't anyone tell me if I was so vital?" Scarlett asked.

"You wouldn't have liked it," Spencer said. "You don't like performing."

"Precisely!" Mrs. Amberson chimed in. "This way you didn't have to perform, you just had to react! Acting is reacting, as they say. And I knew that you would want to help your brother and that you wouldn't mind a little sin of omission."

As much as Scarlett didn't want to admit it, Mrs. Amberson was no fool. She had pulled off the perfect media stunt. And Spencer had played it so well that even Scarlett hadn't known that everything going on around her was just part of a show.

"I don't like performing," Scarlett said. "But I like knowing. So . . . this doesn't happen again, right?"

"Of course, O'Hara. Full disclosure from now on."

"Now that we can talk about it," Spencer said, "who was that guy?"

"Oh, just a very strange person I found wandering around. I gave him fifty dollars for the doughnuts, with the promise of an extra hundred if he pulled it off. I was watching from a store window across the street."

"You were there?" Scarlett asked.

"Well, I had to make sure it all went according to plan and to pay the man. He seemed to embrace the task with great zeal."

"He was a little scary," Spencer said, rubbing his eyes wearily. "He threw them kind of hard."

"Also," Mrs. Amberson said, "I ensured that the event was properly photographed. I think I did a very nice job. *Spies of New York* took three of my pictures. I sent them from your e-mail account, O'Hara. I hope you don't mind. Now, the fruit of our labors. You . . ."

She turned to Spencer.

". . . are going to be on *Good Morning, New York!* at six fifteen tomorrow morning. Then we are going uptown so that you can do a quick appearance with the ladies on *The Point* at nine. From there, we go back downtown to have coffee with a reporter from *Entertainment Now*. Then we have an early lunch with someone from the *Bulletin*. And then, you are due on set for the read through of the new episode. Now, is that full-service or what?"

She was clearly proud of herself and stroked Murray with just a touch of smugness. Murray had gone completely limp in acquiescence. Spencer clearly had a little trouble processing this information. He stared blankly.

"A little media training would help, I suppose," Mrs. Amberson said, noting this. "No time like the present. I can coach you as well as anyone. Scarlett, run out and get us some sushi, will you? It's going to be a busy night. Oh, and Murray needs a walk."

Scarlett accepted the gently vibrating mass of dog that was handed to her, along with some cash. As she stepped into the hall, one thought was at the forefront of her mind. Sure, she was excited about all of the things that were happening to Spencer. Yes, she was still a bit shocked at how she had been played. But her main thought was . . . Max had known. It beat away at the back of her mind. He had seen what she had missed, correctly worked out the behaviors of two people she knew very well. The implications of this were grim. If he was right about this, he could be right about other things.

No, she told herself. Everyone is right once in a while. Even the Maxes of the world. Everyone gets lucky.

The next morning, Scarlett and the rest of the Martins watched the first of the interviews before school. More new clothes had been acquired for Spencer. He wore a chocolate-colored shirt that made his deep brown eyes pop for the camera. His hair had been carefully tousled.

"He looks great," Lola said, weighing in with her professional opinion, as photos of Spencer flew by on the teaser before the start of the show. "Whoever dressed him did an amazing job. He should always wear brown. And it almost looks to me like they darkened his hair. Doesn't it look almost black? His hair isn't that dark. It's Mom's color."

"His hair is a little darker than mine," her mom said, stirring her coffee. She had been stirring for five minutes straight, transfixed in anticipation. "You know, I really never doubted he would make it. But this feels very strange, sitting here watching this. I'm trying to figure out whether my mom would be thrilled or horrified."

"Horrified," Scarlett's dad said.

The show started, and the Martins fell silent. The host gave a recap of events, showing clips from the *Crime and Punishment* episode. Then Spencer was seen, lounging in a chair at the studio as if he didn't have a care in the world. Mrs. Amberson must have worked him over well to get him looking so relaxed.

The questions were a little tedious, but Scarlett was rapt. Had he watched the show before? (No. His sister had to walk him through the plot. The name of the sister was not specified, but everyone looked at Scarlett.) Was he a Sonny fan? (Who wasn't? This made no sense given the last answer, but it sounded charming.) What was it like working with such a great actor? (Spencer flat-out lied about that one and said that Donald Purchase was a great guy and very nice, because presumably he would have gotten into major trouble if he'd said otherwise.)

"I'm pretty sure they've tinted his hair," Lola said.

"How about this?" the host asked. "That pair of pants you were photographed in when you were attacked on the street yesterday are being auctioned on eBay. I hear they're up to four hundred dollars."

"Oh right," Spencer said with a laugh, as if he'd already forgotten about that. He hadn't. He had asked Marlene to follow the auction and text him updates every hour. She was sitting there with Scarlett's laptop now.

"Four hundred and sixty," Marlene corrected.

"What do you think about that?" the host asked. "A pair of jam-and-coffee-stained pants selling for that much?"

"Sounds reasonable to me," he said. "Worth every penny. For another four hundred I'll come model them for you, whoever you are."

"Be careful," the host said, laughing. "The way people have been reacting . . ."

"Bring it on," Spencer said.

"Oh God, Spencer," Lola said to the television. "What are you saying?"

Scarlett considered for a moment revealing that the attack was a fake, but stopped herself. *She* should have been told because she was involved. Otherwise, it was probably best to keep that quiet. Too many questions would be asked. And Marlene would tell the entire world if she knew.

"Thanks for coming by," the host said, concluding the piece. "Spencer Martin is David Frieze . . . New York's Most Hated."

A large picture of Sonny appeared behind the two of them, like a looming ghost.

EINE KLEINE SCHADENFREUDE

The call came as Scarlett was walking home through Central Park after school a few days later. The number was unknown, which caused her heart to palpitate. But it was Chelsea, and she did not sound like herself. Her voice was bumpy and broken.

"Sorry to bug you," she said. "It's just, I called Amy and she wasn't answering, and my mom is out, and I didn't know who to call and . . ."

And then she burst into tears. Chelsea's projection, even when weeping, was a little too good, and Scarlett had to hold the phone away from her ear. It sounded like she had gotten a call from a tropical storm.

"Are you . . . ?" Obviously, Chelsea wasn't okay. That was a stupid question to be asking.

"The show," Chelsea managed. "It's closing. We just found out. I'm going to tell Amy in a minute . . . but my mom is out and . . . and I just had to call someone . . . and . . . I was wondering . . . if you could maybe . . . come over?"

There was no point in Scarlett wondering why she had gotten

this call — there was no one else. You can't say no in situations like that.

"I'll be right there," she said.

Chelsea was waiting by the door when Scarlett arrived. The living room was even more of a mess than before. There were shoes and clothes all around, covering the sofa and coffee table.

"Sorry," Chelsea said. "Come into my room."

Chelsea's bedroom was probably the biggest in the apartment, but it was just large enough to hold a twin bed, a dresser, and a small elliptical machine. Given the limited space and the fact that Chelsea went to the gym all the time and danced six days a week, the machine seemed like overkill. But that was a stupid point to make. Of course there was an elliptical machine.

Scarlett had expected Chelsea's room to be absolutely pristine and neat, set up entirely for efficiency. This was only partially the case. Her exercise and dance shoes were lined up neatly, her bed was made up snugly with a buttery-colored bedspread and accent pillows. But the walls were totally covered with taped up bits of paper. One entire wall was covered end to end at eye-level height with lists, lists written in silver or blue marker on colored pieces of paper, cataloging songs to learn, things to do, names of people, movies, books. . . . The other walls were mostly covered with pictures from magazines of actors, old Playbill covers, show advertisements, and quotes.

One card was prominently displayed right above Chelsea's bed, as if it was designed to communicate its message to her as she slept. It read: "ACTORS WORK AND SLAVE AND IT IS THE COLOR OF YOUR HAIR THAT CAN DETERMINE YOUR FATE IN THE END." — HELEN HAYES.

Chelsea sat on her floor, squashed between her row of dance and workout shoes and her nightstand. She reached up and turned on her little bedside lamp. It was so light and chintzy that it almost toppled from the pressure of a single finger.

"My mom is out looking at houses in Brooklyn and I didn't want to tell her over the phone," she said. "We won't even *need* the apartment now. We probably won't even be staying."

She looked like she was going to start crying again, but was trying hard to stop herself — squinting her eyes, balling her fists, rubbing her cheeks with her fingertips. Chelsea was sincere, Scarlett was sure, but there was something very precise and theatrical about her actions. Scarlett reached her hand down and put it on Chelsea's shoulder. The outside-Scarlett was all sympathy. Meanwhile, the evil, inside-Scarlett was filled with a strange delight. Something had gone wrong for Chelsea. All the striving to be perfect, all the training, the star-material mind-set . . . none of it helped her now. Now Chelsea was almost down on Scarlett's level.

Scarlett was sort of appalled that this was the way she thought. Chelsea had never done anything to her. And now she was curled up on the floor, sitting on her own shoes, asking Scarlett for help. Scarlett doubled her shoulder-patting efforts, but could think of nothing to say.

"Know what I really want?" Chelsea asked, sniffing. "A milk shake."

This was good. This was nice and concrete. Scarlett knew where to get milk shakes.

"So let's get a milk shake," Scarlett said.

"I can't get a *milk shake*."

"Yes you can. You just go to a place that sells milk shakes, and you ask for one, and you give them some money."

Chelsea gave her a look that said, "If it was that easy, everyone would be doing it."

"Any flavor you want," Scarlett said, pulling on Chelsea's arms to get her on her feet. "The best milk shakes in town are just a few blocks from here. Shake Shack. It'll take us fifteen minutes to walk there. Come on."

Chelsea resisted the pulling. She was stronger than Scarlett, her powerful legs locked into place, and her toned arms resisted.

"I haven't had a milk shake since . . ." She considered for a moment. "I don't know. Since I was ten?"

"You are *way* overdue," Scarlett said, pulling harder. "At least walk over there. See for yourself the creamy goodness. If you ever deserved one, it's today."

On the word *deserved*, Chelsea perked up.

"I guess . . . I guess I do deserve it. Right? I work hard. It's not my fault the show closed, right? It's not all my fault."

Scarlett took advantage of the break in resistance to get Chelsea moving. Once up, Chelsea moved quickly, allowing Scarlett to guide her down the street. The Shake Shack was in Madison Square Park, a tiny plot of grass in the middle of a busy restaurant-and-shopping district.

"You order," Chelsea said, pressing the money into Scarlett's hand. "I can't do it."

"What flavor?"

"I don't know." Chelsea wrung her hands and looked away. "You pick."

Scarlett ordered two large black and whites. They were her favorite.

"That cheeseburger looks good," Chelsea said, watching someone go by with a brimming cardboard tray of burgers and fries.

"And a cheeseburger," Scarlett added, without waiting to consult Chelsea. "*And* fries."

They sat down on a bench in the park with their box of food. Chelsea looked at it fearfully for a moment, then took one of the shakes.

"It's so heavy," she said, examining the cup. "I don't remember them weighing this much."

Scarlett decided not to explain that these shakes were made from a thick custardy base. That was something Chelsea did not need to hear.

Chelsea poked in a straw and hesitated before putting her lips on it, easing herself down slowly, until she worked up the courage to take the first sip. It took a major effort to get these shakes up the straw. Her cheeks sank in and she had to draw a second breath to get there, but once she did, her eyes registered surprise.

"It's good, right?" Scarlett said.

The experience of so much fat and sugar rendered Chelsea speechless. She nodded and continued to drink away like a champion, vacuuming up half the milk shake faster than anyone Scarlett had ever seen. Chelsea had been hungry for a long time.

"It closes in a couple weeks, maybe sooner," she said, when she paused for breath. "They're still figuring out the dates."

She churned the straw a few times through the hole in the top of the cup, making a loud straw-squawk. Then she pulled the lid off and drew out some shake on the straw, watching it drip thickly back into the cup. The viscosity of the drink fascinated her. Scarlett offered her the box with the cheeseburger and the fries. Chelsea tentatively took one of the latter.

"Dip the fry in the milk shake," Scarlett advised.

"Are you serious?"

Scarlett guided the fry hand to Chelsea's shake to dip. Chelsea laughed, and nervously took a bite.

"Why is that so *good*?" she asked.

"Because it is made of . . ."

Scarlett stopped before she said the word *fat*. Delicious, life-sustaining fat.

". . . all natural ingredients. Organic. All made fresh."

Chelsea was already dipping a second fry.

"I don't know what I'm going to do without the show," she said. "It's only been three weeks, but I feel like my whole life was shaped around it."

Scarlett knew that feeling, and she hadn't even been *in* the show.

"Yeah, but . . ." She took a fry for herself. ". . . you can do other stuff. You have school, and you can audition."

"My show pays for most of that apartment," Chelsea said.

Scarlett had no idea what to say to that. She had never been responsible for the rent. She let Chelsea eat — and Chelsea was eating. She cleared out the fries, got the cheeseburger down, and polished off her shake.

"You know what I would like?" Chelsea said, poking around at the bottom of her cup, trying to get whatever was left at the bottom. "I'd like to go on a date. I've never been on one. I don't get to meet a lot of people, except through work. And I don't have any time. Do you have a boyfriend?"

The question was so out of the blue that Scarlett coughed on her shake.

"I . . . no. Not a . . . no. Not . . . no."

"But you've at least been on a date," Chelsea said with certainty.

Had she ever been on a real date? No, come to think of it. Not a planned one. She'd had . . . encounters. That was the word she would assign to whatever the hell it was that she had ever done. Encounters with Josh. Encounters with Eric. Weird, unformed, exciting, anxiety-causing encounters in dusty places, and in small rooms, and in front of televisions. Never scheduled. Never defined. Maybe they were dates. Who could define a date?

"Sure," Scarlett said.

"God," Chelsea said, hanging her head a bit. "I'm so pathetic."

"But . . ." Scarlett couldn't just smack Chelsea when she was down. ". . . they kind of sucked."

"They did?"

"They make you crazy."

Chelsea smiled a little. She ate another fry and drained the rest of the milk shake.

"My mom's going to know I ate this," she said, staring mournfully at the empty cup and paper burger container.

"How?"

"She'll just know," Chelsea said. "I'll come home with no job, and fat."

She threw the remainder of the fries in the trash without asking Scarlett if she wanted them.

The entire walk back, Chelsea clutched at her stomach, mumbling things about how heavy and ill she felt, and how maybe she could get right to the gym and get her metabolism going.

Back at the Biggses, Max was home. He had the television at an extremely loud volume, all the while keeping his earbuds in. There was no way he could be listening to both. It must have been auditory nonsense. On seeing them, he yanked on the cord at his neck and plucked out the earbuds, looking extremely disturbed, almost guilty.

"You'll be thrilled," Chelsea said. "The show is closing."

Max cocked his head to the side and examined Chelsea's face. Her tears had long dried, but her eyes were still watery, her expression set on "distraught."

"So there is a God," he said.

"I hate you," Chelsea mumbled, flouncing into her room. Scarlett heard her banging around in there. She stayed in the living room and faced Max, silently challenging him. It didn't matter that she didn't like Chelsea very much, or that she, too, was delighted to hear the news . . . there are some things you don't do. Like kick your sister when she's down. Max stared right back at her.

"When's it done?" he called to Chelsea casually, like he was asking what time they were eating dinner.

"Shut up and die," Chelsea responded.

Max smiled at Scarlett, as if to say, "See?"

Chelsea reemerged with her bag.

"I have to go to the theater. Here, Scarlett." She placed a small bundle of theater tickets, bound together with rubber bands, into Scarlett's hand. "These are stubs, for comp tickets. If you know anyone who wants to go to the show for free, just give them one of these and have them call the number on the front and give them my name. I won't need these anymore, and we have lots of empty seats to fill."

Chelsea started to walk to the door, but Scarlett stayed where she was.

"I have to ask Max something about Bio," she said.

"Oh . . . okay. Well. Thanks for coming. Thanks for not leaving me *alone*."

Max waved her good-bye, and she slammed the door.

"What the hell is wrong with you?" Scarlett asked.

"Did you stay here to lecture me? Because that's not going to work."

"It doesn't matter that the show sucks," Scarlett said. "She's your *sister*."

"She'll be fine. It's not like something *actually bad* happened."

"It's bad to her," Scarlett snapped. "She's upset."

"Notice how she has no actual friends to call when something happens? She has to call you, and you don't even like her."

This was kind of a good point, which made it all the more infuriating for him to say. But she *tried* at least.

"You have no actual friends," Scarlett said. "What's your excuse?"

"I'm picky. And you're just pretending to care about this. What's worse? Not caring, or faking?"

Also, annoyingly, a fair question.

Scarlett brought herself to really look at Max. If his personality could be removed and replaced, he would be attractive. Not like Eric, who was attractive in every conventional sense — but striking. Hard-looking.

"Do you know *why* she has no actual friends?" he went on. "You think that show has done anyone any good? It's closing. Let's have a party. Maybe we can go home."

"Go home?"

"Nobody asked me if I wanted to move here," he said. "I'm not here by choice."

"You had to take a test to get into Perkins," she said. "It's hard. They don't take many people, especially in sophomore year. There are only about ten spaces. So you had to make *some* kind of effort to be here."

On that, Max seemed to shut down. He turned back to the television.

"This is a really boring discussion," Max replied. "You should go. I only get to watch porn when the place is empty."

Lola's little rolling suitcase was open on the floor of the Orchid Suite when Scarlett got home, and there was a brand-new red dress draped on her blue bedspread. Lola was leaning on her bureau and having a low conversation on the phone that could only have been with Chip. She had just returned from the trip to Boston, to Chip's dance.

"New dress," Scarlett said when she hung up.

"Oh." Lola put her hands on her hips and looked at it, as if admiring a moose she had shot, stuffed, and mounted herself. "It's from Chip. Kind of a little gesture to replace the old dress."

"And the dance?"

"Oh, I sort of skipped the dancing part. Spencer showed me one, but I think I could only do it because he knows how to lead. Chip doesn't really dance, either."

Scarlett set herself up on her bed and dumped out the contents of her bag, piling her textbooks to one side, sorting through the detritus of notes and scribblings of the day. Lola watched her, almost sadly.

"You look like you want to do my homework," Scarlett said, offering her a dog-eared school library copy of *The Scarlet Letter*.

"That's okay," Lola said. "I think you'll do a better job. English was never really my thing. I don't think any subject was really my thing."

Scarlett stuck her pen in her mouth in preparation for doing triage. She would do the Trig first, get that out of the way. The French was long — two pages to write. She was supposed to have gone to the Met to look at twelve paintings and take notes on them, but she hadn't done that yet. Bio was one very long chapter to read, with questions to answer to hand in.

Lola drifted around the room all the while, putting her dirty clothes in the clothes hamper, examining the drawer she had broken the other week.

"Boston is really pretty," she said. "I went to Harvard to see Carly. You remember my friend Carly? And my freshman-year boyfriend, Dev, he goes to MIT now. And Darcy goes to Wellesley, so I got to see her. I saw a lot of people. I just kept running into people I knew. It seems like *everyone* is in Boston. I always wanted to go to school in Massachusetts. That's where I always saw myself ending up. It looks just like I pictured it — lots of brick buildings and trees, and people wearing cute little sweaters and scarves and meeting in coffee places. . . ."

"So why don't you go?" Scarlett asked. "It's fall. This is when you apply."

"I know," she said. "It just felt weird, being up there. Being the only one who didn't do it. You know, apply. Get in. Go away. I felt like there was something wrong with me. And all the stuff they were studying . . . I don't know. School always came easy to you. Not to me."

Scarlett looked up from the mess of books and notes on her bed to see if Lola was actually pointing and laughing as she said this. She was not. She appeared to be completely serious.

"What are you talking about?"

"It's true," Lola said. "I had to work to get through school. Really hard. I put in more hours than anyone. I still got B's and C's. I got two D's in math. I've seen you. You read through stuff once, and you get it. When you sit there doing math, you actually solve the problems. I would just sit there and stare until my eyes went dry. I'd get them wrong. Every paper I wrote for English, I'd break my back trying to make it good and every time they'd say I just summarized the story. Sometimes not even correctly. That *Hamlet* stuff this summer? I saw the play, what, twenty times? I still don't understand it. You helped work on it. Spencer was in it . . . it was no trouble for him. I can speak well and dress myself, but I'm not really good at anything. I was good at selling makeup. That's it."

This wasn't like Lola at all. Lola was quiet and confident and secure, and she did things well. In Scarlett's memory, Lola always got good grades, probably straight A's. She'd never seen Lola's report card, but Lola always did the work. She always studied for hours on end. And her parents never seemed upset.

"You were visiting really hard schools," Scarlett said. "Harvard, and MIT, and . . . wherever Chip goes. It just looks intimidating.

You should start looking at some places you want to go to. Get the applications."

Lola shook her head and smiled, dismissing everything she had just said. "All I mean is," she said, "when it's your turn to go to college, I don't think you should wait. You shouldn't be like me. Well, you're already not like me."

"You're going to apply somewhere, right?"

"We'll figure that out later," Lola said. "Spencer's going to be on *Tinsel Talk* at seven thirty."

THE DOOR THAT'S ALWAYS OPEN

During the next three weeks, there was an unpleasant development at the Hopewell. Lola appeared to regress many years in age, her voice becoming a babyish coo. She spent every waking moment talking to Chip on the phone — soft, intimate conversations. She talked to him while she cleaned, while she sat at the front desk, while she walked down the street. At night, for privacy, she would go into the bathroom and take long baths, annoying the others, who were forced to use guest bathrooms on other floors while she was in there. Scarlett would try to read or work or sleep to the mumbles and gentle splooshes of water echoing off the tiles and the tub. Scarlett was just waiting for her to drop the phone in the tub and short out this torment. She was *pretty* sure a cell phone in the tub wasn't lethal.

On the weekends, Chip came back to New York. Sometimes, if he could bail on a class early enough in the day, he would drive the four or five hours in the middle of the afternoon, and Scarlett would come home to find him milling around the lobby as Lola did ineffectual things with a dust cloth.

He was able to do this without too much worry, because Spencer was almost never home. The studio sent a car for him early in the day, and he would reappear very late and sink into bed. If he was awake enough, he would try to explain to Scarlett what was going on: the confusion on the set, the constantly changing scripts and story lines, the sudden relocations, the occasional flinging of doughnuts. But overall, he was extremely happy about everything, and might not even have been that bothered by Chip's presence.

At first, Scarlett felt a kind of elation, as she made it through day after day without talking to Eric. It felt like she had done something hard, and succeeded. But with time, it occurred to her that there was less and less of a buzz, and more just a big gaping hole in her life where he used to be. Even missing him and being obsessive felt better than just having nothing, so she ranged around miserably, going from home to school to Mrs. Amberson's. The dark came sooner and the homework became more sadistic.

It was on a Saturday that Scarlett agreed to sit at the front desk out of sheer boredom, bringing down all her books and piling them around her. She had no real intention of doing any work, but having them around made her look purposeful and academic and solemn. What she was really going to do was aimlessly surf the Internet until she got bored, and then she was going to go to Dakota's and sit through a movie with her and Josh, and then she was going to come home and sleep. Tomorrow she would plod along in the same way, maybe trying to attempt some of the homework that she had stacked around herself now, but she wasn't prepared to make any commitments about that.

But then she got a surprise. Someone had been at the computer before her and folded down a browser page. It was a blog with a very interesting title.

"'*Diary of a Powerkid*'?" Scarlett read aloud.

It turned out that Marlene had been keeping said blog since her return from camp, detailing all the Powerkid outings she had been on. The Marlene writing this blog was a gentle, grateful creature:

September 5
We went to the Central Park Zoo today and got to go around with the zookeeper while she fed some of the animals. I really love animals and this was awesome to get to see. I feel bad for some of them being in cages because they look so bored. I was bored sometimes when I was in the hospital. But it was really good and I got to throw some fish to the seals!!!

September 17
Today we went to the ice-cream plant where you can see ice cream being made. When I was sick, ice cream was one of the only things I could eat without throwing up and it's one of my favorite foods. So I was really happy to get to go here and see how it is made. We got to put in whatever we wanted so I put in marshmallows and peanut butter chips. It was so good!!!!! ☺

September 24
We are going to see the New York Liberty play today, which is the women's basketball team. I am really excited because we are going to get to meet the players and we will all get a signed ball. They are all really nice to us.

Scarlett remembered all of these. Marlene thought the zoo trip was stupid because it was five minutes from their house, she thought the ice cream "tasted like feet," and she hated basketball. So what was this for? Who was reading it? There were comments on some of the entries from some other Powerkids, but always just general nods of agreement.

"What are you doing?" Scarlett whispered to the screen.

She read through all of them entirely. There was nothing about the other Martins. Nothing about school or life in general. Marlene wrote only about Powerkids.

The front doorbell rang, and Scarlett hit the buzzer to open it. They only had two rooms full — two couples from Spain who had been bumped to the Hopewell when the Holiday Inn was over-booked. They looked unhappy every time Scarlett passed them.

She was greatly startled to find herself facing Eric, who was approaching her almost sheepishly.

"Sorry to drop in unannounced," he said. "I was in the neighborhood, and I know your door is always open. Hope that's okay. . . ."

You might have thought that fifteen years of living at a hotel would have prepared Scarlett for people coming in unannounced, and that she might have coped better than most when confronted in the lobby with the sole object of her obsessions — but this would be incorrect. Her heart stopped like a dropped clock. She remained utterly still for a moment, taking stock of her position, her expression, her body. She was wearing an old pair of Lola's yoga pants and a T-shirt, just passable enough to be seen from the waist up. She hadn't touched her hair since waking, so who knew what it was doing. No makeup. Hopefully no food on her face.

"Is this a bad time?" he asked.

"Uh . . . no?"

"Actually," he said, "I'm here because I need your help. I'm in a showcase next week and . . . I'm totally screwed. I have no idea what to do for my scene. I've been making myself crazy for days, and I remembered how much you helped with *Hamlet*. I know it's kind of rude, but . . . I have to present tomorrow. And I'm desperate. Could you help me?"

"What are you doing?" she managed to ask.

"*The Seagull*. Chekhov."

He pulled out a copy of the play and passed it over to her.

"I'm Trigorin. I'm this famous writer, and I'm here at this estate with my girlfriend, who's a famous actress. But she's older, and kind of has a complex about her age, about not being the ingénue anymore. And there's this beautiful young girl, Nina, who comes and tells me about her dreams of being on the stage and asks me to talk about what it's like to be a famous writer. And then I have to talk for two pages straight. It's a really long monologue. I have no idea what to do with it."

As luck would have it, *The Seagull* had been on their reading list the year before. Scarlett had read it, thought it was boring, and wondered why Russian people went to the country and hung out if it made them so suicidal.

"I sort of know it," she said. "But I'd have to . . . look at it."

"Do you mind?" he asked. "Seriously. You'd be saving me. But you look busy."

"I'm just sitting here," Scarlett said honestly. "No one's around. I could."

"You can?" He beamed hugely. "If you could just read that section . . . I'll treat you to a coffee. I'll just go and get one, and then I'll come back?"

"Sure," Scarlett said.

The moment he was gone, Scarlett had the attack. She almost broke the desk drawer getting out the mirror Lola stashed in there. Face, face, face . . . nothing could be done with the face. Hair? Big, as usual. Clothes? There was no time to change anything. That would require going upstairs. No. She would have to make do. She would have to rely on being useful, and that meant digesting the contents of the play *instantly*. She flew over the pages, tripping on long Russian names and the long speeches. Incomprehensible.

Flip, flip, flip ahead to the page that Eric had marked. This looked somewhat familiar. She got through it three times.

Then she thought about calling Dakota. Dakota would have a thing or two to say about this. The dreaded actor, coming back to see the girl who worked for the agent.

No, she would not call Dakota. And besides, Eric was at the door again. This was all going much too fast. Weeks of silence followed by this?

The buzzer went off again, and she whacked the button.

"All set," he said, holding up the two coffees triumphantly. "Can we talk in here, or . . ."

"We should probably go in there," Scarlett said, pointing at the open doors of the dining room.

Eric looked around at the space that he had spent so much time in that summer.

"It's so empty," he said, sitting down in one of the creaky chairs. "It doesn't even look like the same room. And Spencer, huh? He's kind of famous now. It never stops with you guys, does it? And that doughnut thing? What was that?"

"I know," Scarlett said nervously. "Living with us is kind of like living with circus folk."

He laughed and rocked back and forth for a moment until they both seemed to come to the conclusion that they should immediately start working on the scene.

"Okay," Scarlett said. "You're older and famous and successful, and your books are popular and your face is everywhere. And Nina's kind of a . . . fan girl. She wants to be like you. She wants to be a famous artist. She tells him how lucky he is."

"I blow her off," Eric said. "I'm talking about candy, telling her she's young."

"But you're *listening*," she said. "You're looking for an excuse to talk about yourself."

"You think?"

"You talk for ten minutes or something after that," Scarlett said. "Who can talk about themselves for ten minutes if they really think they're that boring?" She flipped the page, skimming the speech. "And you're saying that being a famous writer makes you insecure. How you don't react to things like a normal person. You're sort of telling her the truth, but you're also kind of lying. You're trying to impress her by talking down about what you do."

"I see what you're saying," Eric replied. "I do get together with her later in the play. I'm flirting."

It would have been a much more awkward and horrible moment if a car alarm hadn't immediately started going off just outside.

"You're in charge of this scene," Scarlett said. "You know she's hanging on your every word. Why don't you . . . um . . . try it?"

They did it four times, with Scarlett offering suggestions on different tones of voice, or things to do with his hands. Nothing helped. All she could think about was that she was making Eric move. He was here. He was talking. He was just a few feet away. But she was nervous, and he was frustrated. She had to do *something*.

Off in the corner of the room, by the kitchen door, was a midsize silver trash can. No one ever used it, so it sat there purposeless and empty most of the time. She grabbed it and held it out.

"Well, uh . . . why don't you do it standing in this?"

Eric stared at the trash can.

"Just an idea," Scarlett said quickly. "Because . . . Trigorin is really showing that he's in charge and that he can have whatever he wants, but he's *saying* he feels insecure and strange and embarrassed, so if you stood in a trash can, you might . . ."

There was a moment of pure panic as Scarlett released the complete insanity of what she had just said, and braced herself for the inevitable reaction. But to her amazement, Eric was nodding.

"It's a good one," he said, accepting the trash can. "It's a really good one. This is why I needed you. You have good ideas."

"All the time," Scarlett said, looking away as he stepped in. It came up just past his knees. The metal bottom made creaky, unhappy noises from the weight.

"I hope I don't break this," he said, looking down.

"Don't worry," Scarlett said. "Just . . . think you're awesome, but every once in a while, just look down and remember . . ."

"I'm standing in a trash can," he said.

He tried the scene again, and this time, there was real improvement. Maybe it was the effort to hold still in the slightly unstable trash can, maybe sheer stupidity just works . . . but what came out was markedly different. And when he did the speech this time, he didn't just do it *at* Scarlett, he did it *to* her. Scarlett had been trying to keep still and look like the director from *Hamlet* always looked, interested, but distant, or even a little bored. But now, they were locked in eye contact, and the outside sounds fell away, and it was just Eric and Scarlett back like it was before, he the magnet and she the metal getting pulled closer and closer.

Which is probably why her mom looked so very weirded out when she appeared at the door with a basket of laundry.

"Oh," she said. Scarlett could tell that she was trying not to look too confused. Her mom had learned some grace in the face of finding people doing weird things in her house.

"It's a scene," Scarlett said quickly.

"I thought it might be. Scarlett, did the people from the Sterling Suite . . . ?"

"They're still out," Scarlett said.

"Well, then, how about I just shut these doors?"

"We won't be long," Eric said, keeping as dignified as possible when you're discovered giving speeches from a trash can. "I should probably be going anyway. I have another rehearsal this afternoon."

Scarlett wanted to tell him he didn't have to go. That he couldn't go. But he was already stepping out of the trash as soon as the doors were closed.

"I have to rehearse all the time," he said. "I'm in three different projects right now. Thanks for helping me out. It really made a difference. I think I have some ideas now."

"No problem," Scarlett said, mournfully watching him pick up his bag. "Let me know how it goes?"

"Oh, sure," he said. "I'll let you know."

Her mom was sitting at the front desk and gave him a cheerful good-bye. He talked with her for a moment, as was his way. Southern. Polite to everyone.

"He just dropped by?" her mom asked when he was gone.

"Yup." Scarlett tried to keep her face as expressionless as possible. Finding that hard, she busied herself with some dust on the detail of the wood paneling.

Scarlett's mom had never officially acknowledged knowing anything about her and Eric, but someone had undoubtedly told her. Probably Lola. Her mom was another one of those never-been-broken-up-with types. Her parents had met at eighteen (her mom) and nineteen (her dad). Her mom fled the wilds of Ohio to go to Hunter College. Her dad was a part-time photography student and full-time ska band member. The Martins were tolerant of his ways, but the Reynoldses were not impressed with their daughter's new boyfriend. They were really not impressed when they married four years later in the Hopewell dining room. They lived out in Ohio and had never once made the trip to the hotel. Since it was hard to move four kids and leave an empty hotel, visits were rare. Her mom had essentially been cut off, and Scarlett's grandparents only sent cards and gifts to the kids. They were distant, miserable people.

Given that history, Scarlett expected that her mom was looking at her situation with a sympathetic eye. She may not have understood breaking up, but she understood going out on a limb for love . . . or whatever it was Scarlett was in.

"Why don't you just tell me what's going on and make this easier?" she asked.

"Nothing is going on," Scarlett said. "He came by because he needed help. We were working on a scene."

Funny how incredibly lame "working on a scene" sounded when you said it out loud.

"Are you being honest with me?"

"Yes," Scarlett said, and she was.

"Good," her mom said with a little sigh. She got up and returned the desk to Scarlett. "Because I would hate to make Spencer beat him again."

Apparently, her mom knew all. And she *also* didn't like Eric. Wonderful.

"It's nothing," Scarlett said again, as solidly as she could. She took her seat and when her mom was gone, she buried her face in her hands. She was infected again, every sense inflamed with Eric.

THE VISITOR

There was a collection of Martin family photos on the hallway wall right next to the Jazz Suite, covering the life histories of all four Martin siblings. There were the usual baby and school photos, but there were also a few signature candids. There was one of Spencer as a sophomore dressed in a gangster suit with a fake mustache for *Guys and Dolls*. There was Lola looking demure and lovely in her Easter dress when she was ten. There was six-year-old Scarlett riding her bike out on the sidewalk, her expression unreadable under the cloudlike mass of blonde curls that covered her head like a weather pattern. There was Marlene, aged eight, in the playroom at the hospital giving a rare smile.

In the center of the collection was one group photo that, if you studied it closely enough, would tell you all you needed to know about the Martin siblings. At the time the picture was taken, Marlene had just gotten out of the hospital. The chemotherapy had caused her hair to fall out, and a reddish fuzz was just growing in. She was making a sun-in-the-eyes scowl. Lola stood behind her, her arms clasped around her shoulders, a radiant smile on her face.

Spencer had just hit the same height as their dad, and he seemed to tower over them all.

Scarlett was on the edge of the picture. It was taken just before she realized that, for her, longer hair just meant bigger hair and that there was a secret point just below the nape of her neck — the magical line past which her hair became a nightmare.

So she looked a bit wild in the picture, longish blonde curls blowing in all directions. Her braces had recently been removed, and her teeth still felt huge and strange in her mouth. She was wearing one of Lola's old dresses (some things never changed), which was just a little too long on her. She was the only one not looking at the camera. She was turned halfway back toward the hotel, and the expression on her face clearly said, "Am I the only one seeing this?"

Because in the background, a man could plainly be seen stealing the lid of their trash can.

After the photo was taken, Scarlett reported the theft of the lid to her dad, who said, "It must have just gotten knocked off. No one steals trash can lids." Which was a reasonable enough assumption, except that it was false — a fact he admitted when he saw the picture and said, "Oh yeah. I guess you were right." They still had that trash can, and it still had no lid.

This photo used to hang proudly with the dozen or so others behind the front desk downstairs (the Martins liked photos), but Marlene had requested that it be taken down. She didn't like people seeing her "bald pictures." So it had been moved here, to the fifth floor. Scarlett didn't think this was a crazy request. She had never liked having the picture downstairs, advertising to the world that you could steal stuff from the Hopewell, get your picture taken doing it, and almost be celebrated for your accomplishment.

What disturbed Scarlett about the photograph now, however, was the strange woman who was staring at it when she got home from school. She wasn't a guest — they only had five right now, and all of them were male, in town for a business meeting about popcorn franchises. This woman was maybe about fifty and carried a small plastic bag from Macy's in one hand, and a clump of tissues in the other. Scarlett had already had a painfully long week, and this wasn't the kind of thing you wanted to find on a Friday afternoon.

"Can I help you?" Scarlett asked nervously.

"He killed Sonny," the woman said, poking at Spencer's photo with the tissues.

Scarlett did a quick mental inventory. She could tell from the quiet that she was the only Martin on the floor. The woman was three doors away, past the bathroom and Marlene's room and the Jazz Suite. Three doors was ample running room, and chances were, the woman had no idea which door the stairs were hidden behind. She could make it, easy. Escape, very possible.

Just to be safe, she did a second inventory, looking for any possible weapon she had that could fend off an attacker, but the only thing in sight was a pair of Marlene's sneakers, which she had left in the hall by her door. Marlene's sneakers were small and from Payless. Scarlett had a similar pair, and she had once tried to kill a roach with them and, after beating said roach with one, the roach quite literally shook itself off and walked away, almost with an audible laugh. The only other option was a pile of newspapers that someone, possibly her, was supposed to take down for recycling. Newspaper is a terrible weapon.

The woman turned to Scarlett with a genuinely confused expression.

"Why did he do it?" she asked. "Kill Sonny?"

"Because that's what the script said?" Scarlett replied.

The woman sighed. She was clearly not going to cause any harm, but still. It is never good to find someone crying in your hall, poking your brother's picture with tissues.

"How did you get up here?" Scarlett asked.

"One of the men downstairs let me in," she said. "No one was around. I just walked around until I got up here and saw this picture. I read about this place online. . . ."

"We live up here," Scarlett said. "This is our house, this part."

"Oh!" The woman looked genuinely contrite. "I didn't know. It doesn't say."

"It usually doesn't come up," Scarlett said.

"This young man . . . is your brother?"

"Yes," Scarlett said. "My older brother. And he's nice. Not, you know, a killer. Just an actor."

"I'm sure he is," she said, though not very convincingly. "I just wanted to see him and ask him, and I found this hotel online, and I just wanted to ask him why. I loved Sonny. I've loved Sonny for fifteen years."

"The guy is fine," Scarlett said. "He just moved to LA."

"Guy?"

"The actor," Scarlett said.

The woman cocked her head in bafflement.

"The *actor* who played *Sonny*," Scarlett said.

"I just want to know why. . . ."

She started crying again.

"I was sick for a long time," the woman said, dabbing her eyes. "I couldn't do much. I used to watch *Crime and Punishment* a lot."

"My sister used to be really sick, too," Scarlett said, trying to show the woman she understood, even though she didn't. "She used to watch a lot of TV. And I loved Sonny, too."

"I felt like Sonny was always there. I could always depend on him. Now I don't know what to do."

"The spin-off is pretty good," Scarlett said. "*Crime and Punishment: First Degree?*"

"I tried that," she said, crying harder. "It's not the show. It's Sonny. I just don't understand. I need to understand. Who would do this? What kind of person?"

Her intensity was making the hair on Scarlett's arms stand on end.

"Let me show you something," Scarlett said. "Wait right there. . . ."

"How did you get rid of her?" Spencer asked.

He was the last to arrive and hadn't quite gotten the full story as he was ushered into the living room for a family conference about the stranger. He sat on the floor on the side of the room, eating a container of Chinese food. Scarlett sat in the middle of the sofa, the others gathered around her. She was the witness. The unharmed victim.

"I showed her a picture of you in a dress from . . . whatever show that was where you had to wear a dress," Scarlett said. "She didn't think you were scary after that, and I convinced her that Sonny would want her to go."

"I think I looked nice in the dress," Spencer said, nodding. "I had really good hair, too."

"You did," Scarlett said. "But you also looked a little cheap."

"I resent that. It was the fake boobs, right? I kind of couldn't *help* that. I'm not exactly blessed in that department. Don't judge me. And I could have gone bigger, but I said no. . . ."

"Enough," her dad said tiredly. "This is serious. There are a lot of weirdos out there, and they've clearly figured out where you live."

Spencer fell silent and poked at the noodles, looking unhappily puzzled by whatever he saw in the depths of the container. Outside, the pigeons on the window ledge cooed soothingly.

"Sorry," Spencer said. "They must have just traced it back to the articles about the show. And I talked to a reporter in the lobby the other day, but that article's not out. . . ."

"It's not your fault," their mom said. "We just need to rethink how we do things. It's obviously not enough to lock the lobby door when no one's at the desk. We'll either have to make sure someone is sitting there around the clock . . ."

Scarlett heard her father groan lightly.

". . . or we stop giving keys to guests. We have the buzzer wired up to this floor. We do something to keep people out."

"But this is a hotel," Lola said, stating the obvious. "We let people in for a living."

"People who pay to stay here."

"How do we know they won't start coming just to see him?" Lola said, flicking a hand in Spencer's direction.

"You say that like having guests is a bad thing," Spencer said.

"It is if they're *insane*."

"Insane people have credit cards."

"Why won't you take anything seriously?" she snapped.

And then she left the room, followed closely by Marlene. Spencer sighed, pushed his chopsticks into the noodles, and set the container on the floor next to him as if he was setting down a great burden.

"It's not your fault," their mom said again. "We'll figure something out. Lola's just . . ."

"I know what Lola is."

"Don't start," Scarlett's dad said. "Okay? This isn't the time."

Spencer shook his head, picked up his food, and left the room without another word.

"The two of them," her dad said tiredly. "What is it with the two of them? Always going after each other. I thought they'd stop doing that when they grew up."

"They still have a little ways to go on the growing up thing," her mom said. "Give them time."

"They're both technically adults now, scary as that is." He shook his head and looked over at Scarlett. "When do you think they'll stop fighting?"

"I'd give it until they're forty," Scarlett said.

The three Martin sisters were all in the Orchid Suite a half hour later — Scarlett attempting to do her homework while Lola tried to braid Marlene's hair. Marlene was speculating a mile a minute about the freaks and psychos that were theoretically coming for them now, and all the things they might do to the hotel. They would try to burn it down. They would leave poisonous chemicals in the lobby. They would check in under assumed names and sneak around the hotel at night, killing them all, one by one. On the non-lethal side, she also thought they would release rats or pigeons into the hotel (or, as Scarlett thought, *more* rats and pigeons), they would leave bad reviews online (*more* bad reviews), and they would destroy the furniture (again, a redundant gesture). Lola listened, tight-lipped and silent. She would work the braids halfway, give up, and undo them and start over. Scarlett read the same passage from *The Sun Also Rises* six times, but it never sunk in.

Spencer waited about an hour before he knocked on the door and let himself in. Scarlett knew he would come eventually. He could never leave an argument with Lola hanging. He dropped himself down on Scarlett's bed, next to her. He gave Lola a defiant look.

"You think this is my fault," he said. This was a more tempered response than he normally gave, which made Scarlett think that he probably was blaming himself.

"This *is* your fault."

"You can't blame me for getting a job," he replied.

"Yes, a *normal* job. But everything you do makes things crazy here. Crazy people wandering the fifth floor are bad. Your little sister getting hurt is bad."

"No one hurt me," Scarlett said. "Notice how I'm fine?"

"You think I'm okay with people hurting you guys?" Spencer asked, ignoring this.

"No. I just don't think you think about consequences."

"I don't know what you want from me, Lo," he said.

"I want something to be simple," Lola said. "I want there not to be a problem. Your face is everywhere now. People know you live here."

"Want me to move?" he said with a wry smile.

"I just want you to take some responsibility! We can't change everything just because you want to be an actor."

Marlene shifted forward, pulling her half-formed braids from

Lola's hands, her eyes round with anticipation. When Spencer and Lola fought, it happened fast.

"Guys," Scarlett said quickly. "Don't do this."

"I don't want to do this," Lola said, her voice shaking. "Trust me. I'm sick of doing this."

"So don't," Spencer replied with a shrug. "Lola, what's your problem?"

"My problem is that your problems follow us everywhere! You get crazy people coming after you on the street, and Scarlett got caught in that. Now they come home, to work . . ."

"Those people who bothered you at work had nothing to do with Spencer," Scarlett said. "They were Chip's friends."

Spencer had been fairly restrained up until that point, processing all the accusations that were flying in his direction. At the sound of the name *Chip*, however, a look of furious understanding passed over his face, and his calmness was gone.

"Oh," he said. "Chip's friends. Chip's friends bother you and it's *my* fault. It's not your fault for dating someone like Chip. Who could blame you for dating a *great guy* like that?"

Scarlett had seen them fight before — plenty of times — but there was something about the way this particular fight was going that scared her. The barometric pressure in the room dropped suddenly. Marlene sensed it, too. She didn't seem so eager to watch anymore.

"Lola," Scarlett said, "it's not that bad. That first day with the doughnuts wasn't even . . ."

But Lola didn't want to know what it wasn't.

"Don't!" she yelled. "You *always* side with him!"

"She's not *siding* with me," Spencer shot back. "What gets you mad is that I'm actually doing something I like, and you have no idea what you want to do. You always act a martyr because you gave up going to college. No one asked you to. You didn't even try. But for some reason it's *my* fault that you have no plan — I mean, aside from dating rich people."

Spencer must have hit a nerve. Lola clutched at her phone and, for a second, Scarlett thought she was going to throw it at the wall, or even at Spencer. Instead, she just left the room.

"She's going to run out of rooms to storm out of," Spencer said. "We only have about fifteen more."

The next morning, Scarlett was vaguely aware that Lola was moving around at a slightly earlier hour than normal, but these were not things she cared about much at five A.M. She rolled toward the wall and continued sleeping. When she woke, she found a note sitting on her alarm clock. She picked it up and squinted at it in the half light. It read:

> *I just need to take a few days away to think things over. I'm taking the early bus to Boston. (I'll call Mom and Dad from the bus — don't worry, you don't have to tell them.) Not sure when I'll be back. Keep an eye on Marlene for me, okay?*
> *Love, Lo*

Scarlett jumped out of bed and pushed open Lola's closet door. Her little wheeled suitcase was gone. She immediately ran to Spencer's room, because this sort of thing — a brazen, dumb move — was his department. It took a few knocks to rouse him, tousled, unshaven, and confused.

"Lola's gone," she said. "She went to Boston."

Spencer left the door hanging open as an invitation to let her come in, then walked back to his bed and dropped himself on it face-first, bouncing as he hit.

"Uh-huh," he mumbled from the pillow.

"She ran off in the middle of the night," Scarlett said, standing over him shaking his shoulder. "She . . . *ran away.*"

Seeing that he wasn't going to be able to escape this conversation, Spencer reluctantly pushed himself up and rubbed his eyes.

"It's not a big deal," he said. "She's eighteen. She can handle a little road trip."

"But this is *Lola*," Scarlett said. "Lola doesn't run away. And what about her job?"

"Let her go blow off some steam for a few days, lose another retail job. It's not the end of the world. It'll be fine."

But Scarlett didn't feel fine. She felt queasy. Lola wasn't a creature of clockwork predictability, but there was a soothing rhythm to her actions, like a loose, flowing embroidery made of even, careful stitches.

"I don't like it," Scarlett said, shaking her head at the note. "I think there's something wrong with her."

"Look," Spencer said, "everyone rebels. Lola's way overdue. Going to Boston is nothing. I did way stupider things than that. One time, I went to Jersey to see a girl I'd never even met in person."

"Jersey is a lot closer," Scarlett said.

"Not when you go by bike. I didn't have the twenty bucks for the train and it looked a lot closer on the map. FYI, it's not close. Can you trust me on this one? She'll be back in a few days to obsess about the towels and yell at me for whatever. This is actually a good thing. It shows she's normal."

"You're sure?" Scarlett asked.

He flipped over on his side, toward the wall.

"Have I ever been wrong?" he replied.

TEMPTATION

For Scarlett, watching her parents' reactions for the next two days was like watching the Supreme Court work out the legal technicalities of a difficult and fascinating case — the verdict of which would have massive implications on the ground rules of life.

There was the basic issue: Lola took off in the middle of the night to hang out with her boyfriend. On the face of it, very bad. But then again, it was Lola. Who was eighteen and sensible. Who gave selflessly to help the family. Who was staying at a known location with a known person, and visiting other known high school friends who had also gone to school in Boston. Who was checking in every day by phone. She was in no immediate danger. So, in a way, it was like a strange, extended "get to know college life!" visit. And clearly her parents felt guilty and in some way responsible for the fact that Lola wasn't going to college, even though, as Spencer had pointed out, this was her choice.

Scarlett's life, however, got more difficult. Between the stranger in the house and Lola's vanishing act — neither of which was her fault — Scarlett's parents felt it was time to set up a lot of new rules.

Being the younger sibling meant inheriting the punishments of those who came before.

Up until now, anything Scarlett had to do until six thirty was fine. She could go to work, or study with friends, or whatever she needed. Anything after six thirty had to be phoned in and approved, but this was generally pretty easy. She had been taking the subway by herself since she was Marlene's age, and movements up until around ten o'clock (which she rarely asked for) were usually okay. If she went to a show with Mrs. Amberson, she would come home in the cab, and when she had worked on *Hamlet* downtown, she always came home with Spencer if it was late.

This easy schedule was history. Scarlett had to clock in and clock out with regularity, and her parents often made Spencer come by and bring her home in the chauffeured car provided by the studio. Which, as Scarlett had pointed out to them several times, was worse . . . as he was generally the target anyway. This argument was dismissed.

So, when the text from Eric came, she instantly sensed trouble.

Hey, it read, *Thanks for all the help with the scene. The showcase is on Thursday at eight. Hope you can come.*

Scarlett had to wait until eighth period to show Dakota and get her inevitable berating and admonition not to go. That was the fire she had to walk through to earn her passage. She waited by the door, her phone concealed inside of her notebook.

"Look at this," she said, thrusting it at Dakota as she approached.

Dakota peered into the notebook and looked aghast.

"Oh for God's sake," she said. "And you're going to go, right? Right. Of course you are."

"There's a problem," Scarlett said. "My parents have gotten crazy with the being out thing. If I tell them I want to go to this, they're probably going to make Spencer come and get me and bring me home."

"Yeah," Dakota said. "Does he even know that you've been seeing Eric? I'm sure he would love that. He would think that was *great*."

"It hasn't come up," Scarlett said. "And I haven't been seeing him. I *saw* him. He came to me. To my house. You cannot blame me for this."

As they spoke, Max came along. Scarlett grabbed Dakota by the elbow and started moving her forward into the lab.

"And now he wants you to go to his show. Why's that again? Because you *work for an agent*. And Eric is an actor. We have been through this."

She leaned forward and tapped Scarlett on the forehead, emphasizing those words. Scarlett grabbed her finger.

"It's one show," Scarlett said. "And you have to help me cover. I'm going to say I'm working at your house. . . ."

"No you aren't."

There was no doubt that Max was listening now, but the bell was about to ring, and Scarlett wanted to finish her thought. "I'm going to say that I'm studying at your house, and then I'm going to have Spencer bring his car to *your house*."

There was just enough temptation in this to make Dakota waver. Scarlett hated using the Spencer card, but she needed the heavy artillery.

"I can't stop you, can I?" Dakota said. "If I don't agree, you're just going to do something else, also stupid, right?"

"Right."

Dakota bit her upper lip with her bottom teeth.

"Fine," she said. "Lie. Use me. Fine. But this is a bad idea."

Max was suspiciously still all period. It started to rain, a massive, punishing downpour, and it kept going through the end of the school day. Frances Perkins was always very *loud* in the rain. Maybe it was because the spacious, curvy building that was made to make sure that the TB patients had good, circulating air also functioned like a drum. When the rain hit the windows or the glass skylights on the top floor, the sound bounced around, floor to high ceiling.

The tower rooms were particularly bad on rainy days, and the Biology lab was a tower room, one very noisy circle of hell. All during the period, Ms. Fitzweld was up at the front of the room, attempting to communicate something about the parasympathetic nervous system in her shouty voice. The violence of the noise around them made Max's actions, or lack of them, even more alarming. He slid off his stool at the end of the period and slipped off without a backward glance. Scarlett was almost offended. If you're going to bother someone every day of the year, you at least owe them a sneer or something as you go.

"Freak," she said to herself.

Scarlett's locker was right by a group of music practice rooms, and she entered and exited each day to the sound of music of varying quality. Today, someone was playing the piano and singing, and doing a really good job. And she knew the song. It took her a moment to place it, but she realized it was "Pick Me." It was an odd, slowed-down version, and the person singing it was male.

She backed up a few steps and peeked through the window into the room. Max sat at one of the pianos, staring at the window, as if knowing that she would be looking in. He stopped playing and waved her in, his hand curling slowly, as if it was a dare. Scarlett opened the door.

"Stop following me," he said.

Even though he had distorted his voice to sing in a high register, one fact had been made perfectly clear — Max could sing, easily as well as Chelsea. He could also play the piano. Also quite well. It was a complete shock to Scarlett's system, like opening a door and finding a cat talking on a phone or a cluster of butterflies performing open-heart surgery.

"Who's Eric?" he asked. "You keep talking about him. You and your evil friend."

"None of your business."

"It is kind of my business since you keep talking about him in front of me," Max replied.

"You play piano," Scarlett said. "And you sing."

"You noticed that?" Max said, looking at her incredulously. "What tipped you off? Was it *the piano*?"

"I thought you didn't like performers," Scarlett said. She stayed close to the door, her hand on it at all times, ready to bolt. It wasn't like she thought Max would leap across the room and pin her to the wall or anything, but being alone with him made her uneasy.

"I don't perform," he said. "I just play for myself. So when you make your report, don't tell my mom you saw me play."

"I told you, I don't report," Scarlett said. "But why wouldn't you tell her?"

"You figure it out," he said, putting his hands on the keys. He held them there, waiting for her to make a move, so she backed up and out. As she shut the door, Scarlett heard the music start up again — and she had a funny but very definite feeling that everything that had just happened had been prearranged, like she had unwittingly had a part in a play and had walked in exactly on cue.

Scarlett set everything up. The show would go from eight until probably nine thirty or ten, giving her plenty of time to get up to Dakota's, where Spencer would pick her up at eleven. She headed down to NYU a full hour earlier than she needed to and walked around until quarter of, when she went to the building. She felt out of place from the moment she stepped in the door. She had come alone to an NYU show, the only person who seemed to be without a companion — at least the only one who clearly wasn't a student. As she sat on the folding bleachers in the black box theater, she was the only one not engaged in a conversation, not saying hello to everyone else, not sharing a joke. She had no purpose here.

And then, she heard the girl in front of her talking about Eric. It didn't sound like they were dating or anything. She was just pointing to his name in the program and talking about something the two of them did in some kind of workshop, which was apparently *hilarious*.

Scarlett instantly felt small and irrelevant. She stared at the two wooden tables and the three gaudily painted gold café chairs that constituted the set and quietly wished someone would kill her. Eric didn't want her here. He had just said that to be polite. So here she was, freaky and young and alone. At least she would get to see the parade of attractive girls in Eric's class. That would do wonders for her ego and mental state.

Someone, Scarlett guessed one of the instructors, came out to give an introduction to the play, what class it was for. The parts were split up, so Eric would only be playing his role for one scene. As soon as the lights went down, Scarlett immediately felt at ease. She loved sitting under the blanket of darkness, watching the show. And, amazingly, she was able to watch the whole thing — not just Eric. There were numerous things she found herself wanting to change. The second girl playing Nina would have been much better as Masha, for a start. The play-within-a-play at the beginning was set up all wrong.

Eric was by far the best at his part. He completely erased his Southern accent and deepened his speech. Scarlett could see him doing what they'd discussed. She followed all the turns in the speech. A few things had been changed, smart changes.

When the lights came up, the actors bowed and walked to the audience, who were only five feet away anyway. There was a melee of hugs and congratulations and spontaneous discussions on the play itself. A girl jettisoned out of her seat and went to Eric, monopolizing him. Scarlett waited for a minute or two, then just couldn't take it anymore. They were clearly together. She left the room, jogged up the stairs, and out of the building.

"Hey!" someone said.

Eric was standing at the bottom of the steps, looking up in confusion.

"You didn't even say hi," he said.

"Oh sorry. I just . . . I kind of have to get back."

"I'll walk you to the subway, at least," he said, coming up the steps. "I know you hate being walked places. I know you don't *need* it because you're a tough city girl, but I can't help it. It's a Southern thing."

Scarlett couldn't tell if he wanted to walk her or just suffered from some strange sense of obligation, but she was prepared to accept the offer.

"What is this *South* like, anyway?" Scarlett said.

"Oh, you know," he said. "Pickup trucks. Jug bands."

"Taking your cousin to the prom?"

"In a pickup truck," he clarified.

"Don't you need your jacket?"

"I'll be okay," he said.

They walked across Washington Square Park, which was sparsely populated. A few NYU skaters hung out in the center, and a few homeless people rested on the benches. Most of the light came from the Washington Arch, the massive white stone doorway to the park, illuminated with spotlights.

For the first time in a long time, she felt like she could simply make conversation with Eric. Like a normal person.

"The first Nina was good," she said. "The second one was playing the wrong part. She should have played Masha."

"That's funny," Eric said. "That's exactly what she told me. She felt like she would have been better at that."

"The guy who played the doctor was amazing."

"He's also a total pain in the ass and hates me."

"Why?" Scarlett asked, even though almost everyone she knew hated Eric. At least they had reasons.

"He thought he should have done my scene," Eric said. "Like it's my fault he didn't get it."

"No," Scarlett said assuredly. "You were in the right part, and so was he."

"Was it the worst show you've ever seen?" he asked. "You can tell me."

"No," Scarlett replied. "I can show you the worst thing I've ever seen."

They were just passing under the arch. Eric stopped and leaned against the white stone, watching her with an amused smile. She fumbled around in the front pocket of her bag and found the pile of tickets for *The Flower Girl*. She wiggled a few loose from the rubber band and handed them to him.

"This," she said, "is the worst show in the world. And it's closing soon, so see it while you can."

"That's what I like about you," he said, examining the tickets. "You always have a stack of Broadway tickets on you, ready to pass around to anyone who wants them."

There was a playfulness in his tone that Scarlett hadn't heard for a long time.

"I *dare* you to go to that show," she said.

"You *dare* me?"

"Yeah," she said, managing a smile. "I dare you."

"When?"

"Whenever you want. Tomorrow, even —"

Scarlett's phone started to ring. It was Spencer.

"Oh no," she said. It was only ten twenty-five.

"Something wrong?" Eric asked.

"No," Scarlett said. "I just have to take this. I . . ."

"Right," he said. "I'll let you go. You need to . . ."

And with one final smile, he backed off. Scarlett answered the phone on what was probably the last ring.

"Where are you?" Spencer asked. "I'm sitting in front of Dakota's. I just buzzed, and she says she's coming down. Because you apparently aren't here?"

"I had to go see a show. And Mom and Dad were being so weird, I didn't think they'd let me go by myself."

"You should have told me," he said, sighing. "Where are you? Midtown?"

Nope. Standing here at NYU, watching Eric walk away. If she said NYU, he would know. He would guess. They had fought before over something just like this — she had gone somewhere with Eric without telling him and had put him in an awkward position. He would be furious. She had promised never to lie to Spencer again, especially about Eric. But she could continue to evade the truth as long as possible by being nonspecific.

In the background, she heard Dakota giving Spencer an overly cheery hello. She shivered.

"Can you meet me in front of the *Flower Girl* theater?" she asked.

Not a lie — she would meet him there. Technically, she was still on solid ground.

"Where's that, Forty-seventh?"

"Yes," she said. "And can I talk to Dakota for a second?"

There was a shuffling sound as the phone was passed over.

"Hellooooooooo?" Dakota said.

"I need to get to Broadway," Scarlett said quietly. "Can you buy me ten minutes?"

"Can I . . . oh . . . yeah. Um . . ."

Much fake, nervous laughter.

"He can't know I'm down here," Scarlett said, lowering her voice. "You know why. So I have to get to midtown. Can you just . . . just talk to him for a few minutes? He's my brother. He doesn't bite. Just ask him about the show or something. Tell him you like it. Tell him whatever you want."

Dakota laughed in a way that suggested that she was going to make Scarlett pay for this at some point, but Scarlett knew she was more than willing to take on the task. Besides, what was one more debt? Scarlett was always writing social checks she couldn't cover, and the only hope was that if she kept moving fast enough, no one would ever take a look at her accounts. Some people, if they're fast enough, never have to pay.

STRANGE GAMES

The next day, Scarlett got superpowers. Her brain bounced quickly along, remembering details of articles read long before in International Politics, and an obscure verb she didn't even remember learning in French. It allowed her to make a comment so intelligent in English that it concluded a fifteen-minute discussion. For a few hours, she wondered if she just might be a genius.

That there was a possibility that she might be seeing Eric, that he might call at any point, well, perhaps that had something to do with the pulse and the charge. It didn't slow as the day went on, and by Biology, with no call or message, it was so high and frantic that she couldn't even listen or concentrate enough to be annoyed by Max or take any notes. Her brain was burning.

When she emerged at the end of the day, the air was sticky and the sky had a greenish tint. There was an inescapable promise of a storm, something ugly and massive that would wash out the streets and flood the subways. She hurried in the direction of Mrs. Amberson's to walk Murray, her brain giving her the vague warning that this was not something she wanted to be caught in. Dakota, however, was positively glowing. She had done her job so well the night before that Scarlett was left waiting at the theater for almost a half hour. She accompanied Scarlett on her walk across Central Park to Mrs. Amberson's, detailing everything she and Spencer had talked about. She wasn't even making her usual effort to sound unexcited.

"Didn't he . . . didn't you say there was some girl he liked all summer, someone from the show?"

"Stephanie," Scarlett said absently. She was clotheslined at ankle level by a dog leash because she was busy looking at her phone. And she could only get away with this behavior because Dakota was so consumed in her awkward questions about Spencer. They were mutually guilty.

"Oh right, yeah. Whatever happened with her?"

"Nothing," Scarlett replied.

"Stop looking at that phone," Dakota said. "Stop looking at that phone or I'll eat it."

Scarlett sighed, and shoved it in her pocket.

"He thinks I'm pressuring him," she heard herself say. "I shouldn't have given him the ticket. But he looked like he wanted to go. He was laughing."

Dakota stepped ahead and stretched out her arm to prevent Scarlett from going any farther.

"I say this as someone who loves you. It's going to keep happening. So either you stop dealing with him, or you stop talking about it. But this has to be done. You're making me crazy."

"I just felt like something was going to happen today," Scarlett said. "Something huge. I can't explain it."

"It's been two months now," Dakota replied. "I need the old you to come back. I need to have a different conversation. I have to . . . I have to go meet Andy."

"Who's Andy?" Scarlett asked.

"Some grad student my parents found for me to work on French conversation with. I have to meet him up on One Hundred Eleventh Street in a half an hour."

"Oh," Scarlett said. Had Dakota told her this before? Had she just tuned it out? It seemed like something she should have heard about. "I'm going to try harder, I promise."

"Yeah," Dakota said sadly. "I know you are."

When she got home, the door to the Jazz Suite was shut tightly, and she could hear low voices from inside.

"In here," Marlene called.

Scarlett cautiously peered around the doorway into Marlene's room.

"Do you want to sit down?" she asked, somewhat formally.

Scarlett didn't know if she wanted to sit down. She had never been asked to come and sit on Marlene's bed. It seemed unwise to say no.

Like Spencer, Marlene had her own room. Hers was the only one in the hotel that had truly been redecorated. The walls had been redone in light yellow, because that was her favorite color. Marlene was propped up by her massive supply of pillows and stuffed animals. Scarlett was never really clear where all the pillows had come from, but the stuffed animals were a byproduct of her illness; they are just *what people bring* when they visit a kid in a hospital. She had well over a hundred. Most of them were in a box in the attic. She kept the choicest ones in her room to form her strange little throne. Scarlett stared at the little monkeys, bears, fish, tigers, and other strange creatures that were smooshed under her weight, yet still looked happy to give their stuffing to support their queen. She was holding a large biography of Princess Diana, one thick with glossy photos.

"Lola's home."

"Oh," Scarlett said, nodding in the direction of the Jazz Suite. "That's what's going on."

Marlene nodded sagely.

"They've been in there for an hour. She's in trouble."

"Yeah," Scarlett said, "I figured."

They both ran out of things to say at this point, and a tense silence fell.

"So," Scarlett said. "Princess Diana, huh? Is that for school?"

"I bet if Princess Diana had been alive when I was little, I could have met her," she said. "She went to a lot of hospitals all over the world. She was always going to hospitals."

"Maybe," Scarlett said. "I think she went to a lot of hospitals in England."

"She went to hospitals everywhere," Marlene said firmly.

"You're the one reading the book," Scarlett quickly conceded.

"And she touched people with AIDS when a lot of people were afraid to. She showed people it was okay."

"That's . . . great?"

"Prince Charles never loved her. I think he just married her because she was pretty and his mom said he had to get married. He cheated on her with that woman he married . . ."

"Camilla," Scarlett said.

"Right, so she made her whole life about charity because she knew she would never be happy. So she made everyone else happy."

"Oh. Right."

Marlene played with the book a bit, opening it a bit wider until the spine creaked.

"When I was sick," Marlene went on, "I could always tell the people who really wanted to be there visiting us, or giving us stuff, and the people who didn't. A lot of celebrities do it just to get their picture taken. They're nice and all, but you can tell they only want to get it over with. The ones who mean it, you can always tell. I think she really meant it." With that, she slammed the book shut and set it aside.

"I have to go. We're going to a Yankees game. They're letting us catch balls with the players before it starts. What are you doing tonight . . . nothing?"

"Homework," Scarlett said rigidly. She held out her very heavy bag to prove her point. It was important to remind Marlene that she was older and a sophomore at a very hard school and at least try to give the impression that she had a lot to do, at all times. Otherwise, Marlene would quickly get out of control. If she was making these kinds of remarks at eleven, she would only get more dangerous as time went on.

Of course, when Scarlett got back to her room, she dropped the heavy bag to the floor and promptly ignored it in favor of getting out her computer and checking to make sure Eric hadn't sent her a message, and to generally track his whereabouts online. There was no message, though. She pushed the computer aside. Dakota was right. She was going to drive everyone away from her if she couldn't find a way to stop. Of course, that sounded good on paper. It sounded like something you should just be able to do — just not care anymore. Just forget.

Still, there was something in Dakota's manner today that Scarlett had never seen before, and it alarmed her. She had pressed her friends a bit too far. She quickly texted Dakota an apology, and a response of forgiveness came right back. No major damage there.

There was a bang at the end of the hall, the sound of the elevator gate being pushed back with extreme force. The only person this could be was Spencer, but he wasn't normally home this early, and he wouldn't normally slam the gate in that manner. He appeared at her open door a moment later. There was some kind of substance slicking down his hair and glossing his face on one side. Whatever it was, it had run down his shoulder and arm in a long pinkish stain on his shirt.

"Ask me about my day," he said. "Go on. Ask me."

"How . . . was your day?"

"My day was *fine* up until about ten minutes ago. They let me go early, so I thought it was a nice day out. Had a couple errands I wanted to do. Thought I'd walk, you know, get some exercise, save the environment. I had my sunglasses on. I figured no one would recognize me. Guess I was wrong."

He dropped his bag to the floor. It was also covered in the substance.

"I was just a few blocks away, I was on Park, and some guy came along in a Hummer and stopped at the red light. He opened the window and asked me if I was David Frieze, and before I could even answer, he tossed a milk shake on me. He just reached out and dumped it over my head. Would have been a good day to have my bike, which has still not been stolen. That was my day. How was yours?"

"Lola's home. She's getting yelled at. We think."

This calmed him a little. He leaned backward out the door to have a look. He seemed contented by the fact that Lola was being dealt some justice.

"I guess I should shower," he said. "But all these flies are following me, and they think I'm their god. I feel responsible."

"Power corrupts," Scarlett said.

He was about to leave, but then remembered something and stepped back inside.

"You have to help me learn some pages. Script's in the bag. Let's do the jail scene, the one where I'm locked to the chair. It's in the middle."

He dropped the bag and went off. Scarlett went over and carefully extracted the script. The next episode was a very confusing one. The writers were clearly struggling to work fast and fill some space until they figured out what to do next. The entire episode was just scenes of the police mourning Sonny in their own ways — excessive drinking, emotional outbursts, making bad decisions and smacking people around — and David Frieze sneaking around the city doing suspicious-looking things until they caught him. There was a scene at Columbia, which took place in a lab. He was stealing chemicals when the police burst in and took him off to the station.

"Why are you stealing this stuff?" Scarlett asked when Spencer returned.

"I think I'm building a bomb or something." He dropped to the floor and ran his hands through his clean, wet hair. "It doesn't really make any sense."

"And why is Benzo always so stupid?" she asked. "He punches you in the face while you're handcuffed to a chair at the station?"

"Yup."

"Won't that, like, ruin the trial? Beating up the defendant?"

"I do what they tell me," Spencer said. "I'm just the actor. I think they're just writing that in because people want to see me get hit."

He reached around and felt the back of his neck, as if the sensation of the milk shake running down it was still with him.

"Okay." He rubbed his hands together. "I was looking at these earlier. I think I have them. Let's try it."

They had gotten through the scene four times when the door opened slightly and Lola poked her head inside.

"Hey," she said. "We, um, need you guys for a second."

"Need us for what?" Spencer asked. "How was Boston? Did Chip show you all the coloring projects he made in school?"

"We didn't stay in Boston," Lola said.

"No?"

"No. We went to Vegas."

For once, Spencer looked like he might actually approve of a Chip and Lola adventure.

"Trip to Vegas," he said, nodding. "I respect that. You did it right. Finally, Chip did something worth doing with that credit card of his. You totally beat anything I ever did. From now on, you are master."

"Vegas?" Scarlett said. "That's kind of . . . far."

"It's not that long of a flight," Lola replied. "We did it on the spur of the moment."

"I like it when you get crazy," Spencer added. "Pretty soon you'll be putting unironed sheets on the beds and forgetting to moisturize."

"Spencer . . ."

"I mean it," he said. "I think that's great. It's good for you. You need a wild phase. So what did you do? Did you get one of those rooms with a champagne-glass hot tub? Did you get one of those old-timey photos? Or one where you're dressed like you're in *Star Trek*? I love those. Chip would look so good dressed as a Klingon. I can see it now. . . ."

"You should come down," she said, and vanished.

Spencer and Scarlett looked at each other in bafflement.

"My trials were never public," he said, shrugging. "Maybe we're the jury?"

There was an air of manufactured calm in the Jazz Suite. Scarlett's parents were sitting side by side in a stiff tableau. Lola was on one of the sagging armchairs that used to be in the Sterling Suite.

"Shut the door and sit down," Scarlett's dad said. "We all need to talk."

"This is kind of awesome," Spencer said in a low voice. "I never got this."

"Lola?" Scarlett's mom's eyes were a bit red, and it sounded like keeping an even tone took effort. "Why don't you go ahead?"

"We already know," Spencer said. "You two are back together. We've accepted it. All I want to know is . . . does this change the being-nice-to-Chip rule? Because I think that was just when you two were broken up."

"She didn't say that," Scarlett said.

"Traitor."

"Guys," their dad said.

"I think it was pretty clear," Scarlett cut in.

"We're on the same side here."

"Guys!" he said again, more firmly.

"Come on, Lo," Spencer said. "What's the ruling? Be kind, for the sake of my sanity. I had a really bad day."

"You have to be nice," Lola said. "All the time. Because . . ."

"*All* the time?" Spencer said in disgust.

Lola looked to their parents helplessly, as if she needed assistance thinking up a comeback to her brother. Scarlett's mom raised her hand in a gentle "go on" motion.

"Because," Lola repeated, "he's my husband."

LOLA MAKES
A JOKE

There was a yawning silence for several moments, during which Scarlett became profoundly aware of a blood vessel right behind her ear. It pounded away, thumping on the inside of her head.

"Don't take this the wrong way, Lo," Spencer said, "but there's a reason I do the jokes around here."

Scarlett looked from Lola to her father to her mother. None of them acknowledged any joke. Lola sucked on her lower lip, then she held out her left hand she had been trying to conceal, revealing a small diamond ring. At least, it looked like a diamond. It seemed to be on the finger wedding rings were usually on.

"Look," Spencer said, sighing, "if Ninety-eight bought you a diamond, it would be as big as a doorknob. That much, I know."

It was a good point. A *very* good point. Scarlett felt herself nodding at the logic.

"There wasn't a lot of choice," Lola replied. "We bought it in one of the hotel gift shops."

This also, disturbingly, made a kind of sense.

"I get it," Spencer said. "This is some kind of payback. It was good. You actually terrified me for a second back there. I have to learn some lines, okay?"

"She's not kidding," her mom said.

The blood vessel thrummed harder. Scarlett could hear cars on the street outside, some kids screaming and laughing as they went down the street — but they almost sounded like they were underwater. Her pulse had gotten so rapid that she almost felt elated. She clutched at Spencer's arm.

Spencer just shook his head and looked up at the ceiling, as if he simply could not believe that such a bad act was allowed to continue.

"I . . . we . . . we wanted to," Lola said. "I love him, and . . . we knew it was what we wanted. And we were there, so we just . . . we did it."

Lola rambled on for another minute, maybe more, explaining how quickly it had all happened. About going to one of Vegas's many all-night wedding chapels in a rented limo, using the rent-a-witnesses . . .

By this point, Scarlett knew it was true. Every word of it. Scarlett felt the acceptance hit Spencer. He melted a bit against the wall, sliding down a few inches. The pipes creaked and pinged a bit as they recovered from Spencer's recent shower. It sounded as if the Hopewell itself was reacting to the news.

"This is a surprise, for all of us," Scarlett's mom said. "But we need to . . ."

Her parents looked like they were going to be sick. Both of them. But what could they say? They were a couple that got together as teenagers — her mom's family violently opposed to the marriage.

This wasn't the kind of thing they would want to judge, especially since it was done. But they were judging it. Clearly.

"Maybe it's not legal?" Scarlett heard herself saying.

"It's completely legal," Lola replied.

"You can't do this," Scarlett said. "You can't. You're eighteen. You don't even like him that much."

"Scarlett . . ."

"It's Vegas," Scarlett said, going on. "They have to have some kind of 'we were drunk and insane' clause in Vegas. Chip's family is all lawyered up. A few phone calls from them and the whole thing could go away, right?"

"We weren't drunk."

"You can *fix* it," Scarlett said. She was losing control of the volume of her voice. "It just happened. You can do something about it now. You have to be able to fix it. I could go look it up right now."

"I'm sorry."

"Don't be sorry. Do something!"

"Scarlett," her mom said. It was a warning, not a yell.

"So that's it?" Scarlett said, refusing to give up. "This is just . . . okay?"

"It's here," her dad said diplomatically. "We've dealt with big things before."

"Yeah, when Marlene got *cancer*. That wasn't a choice."

Lola's phone started to ring. She checked to see who was calling.

"Chip," she said, holding it up. She conversed with him quietly, but Scarlett wasn't paying attention.

"Chip's parents want to know if they can meet with you guys," she said. "Like, a parent-to-parent thing."

Scarlett's mom blinked and rubbed her face hard with her hands.

"I'll get changed," she said, getting up.

Scarlett heard her dad talking to Spencer about being there when Marlene got home and ordering some dinner. She heard her dad trying to talk to her and asking her if she was okay, and she said yes, just to say something.

When their parents had gone, Lola, Spencer, and Scarlett sat in the Jazz Suite for a long while, saying nothing to one another. Spencer planted himself on the sofa and turned on the television, switching channels until he found wrestling, which he watched with grim determination. Scarlett sat next to him and stared at the wall. Lola just waited expectantly, ready to talk to anyone who would talk to her. But no one did. The storm rushed outside the windows and poured down into the streets. This was how Marlene found them when she got home about a half hour later.

"It rained," she said, pointing out the obvious. "What's going on?"

No one spoke.

"What is going *on*?"

"You tell her," Spencer said. "I'm not."

Scarlett put her head on her knees as Lola went through her hesitant speech all over again, this time in a more general version, suitable for eleven-year-olds who probably don't care about rent-a-witnesses.

And then there was silence.

And then there was screaming. Happy screaming. Ecstasy. Scarlett lifted her head to see Marlene leaping around and jumping on top of Lola.

"I knew it!" she screamed. "I knew it!" Of course, there was no possible way she could have known. Spencer said something under his breath, but Scarlett couldn't make it out. Marlene had gone utterly manic.

"Where's Chip?" she called. "Where is he, where is he?"

"Mom and Dad are talking to his parents, and then I'll go and see him later, when I'm done here."

"I want to go with *you*," Marlene said, wrapping herself around Lola's waist. "I want to see Chip!"

"You'll see him later," Lola said. "We need to talk now."

"I want to *go*."

Lola and Marlene had one side of the room for their strange joy — Spencer and Scarlett had the other, silent, disbelieving. Lola glanced over at them fearfully.

"So," Spencer asked dryly, "when do you leave?"

"Leave?" Lola repeated.

In all the commotion Scarlett hadn't had time to do this basic math. Lola getting married meant *Lola moving in with Chip*. This question also got Marlene's attention. She immediately stopped dancing around and backed away a bit.

"What do you mean *leave*?" she said accusingly. "Where are you going?"

"People live together when they get married," Spencer said. "So, Lola's going to go live with Chip. Is that going to be in Boston or here, Lo? Maybe you guys can get places in both, take the boat back and forth."

"Why are you moving?" Marlene said. "You could stay here. There's lots of space."

"Or here." Spencer nodded. "You guys could live here."

"It doesn't work that way, Marlene," Lola said quietly.

"*Why?*"

"When people get married," Lola said, "they form a new family. So they live together."

"But . . ."

Scarlett could see Marlene struggling with the concept. *They* were Lola's family. And she was right. They were Lola's family — the only one she had until recently. There was no need for another. Marlene had gone a dangerous shade of red and looked like she had started to sweat.

"You don't have to," she said so forcefully that a fine mist of spit came out with the words. "You don't have to move. You don't have to."

Lola looked to Spencer for help, but he simply folded his arms over his chest. He wasn't going to throw her a lifeline. Scarlett's expression must have told her the same thing. Marlene's chest heaved violently as she waited for Lola to say something.

"It probably won't be far," Lola tried again. "And you'll come over, and we can go on the boat, and we can do everything we usually do, and . . ."

Lola cut herself off. She reached for Marlene, but Marlene smacked her hand away.

"I hate you," Marlene said. "I am always going to hate you if you leave! *Tell me you aren't going to leave!*"

In the past, she was known to flail and scratch from time to time. Scarlett had thought that phase was long over, but Marlene looked like she was capable of just about anything at the moment. Lola didn't move to defend herself; she waited for Marlene to do whatever she was about to do. Spencer, however, seemed less willing to let this happen. He got up and caught both of Marlene's arms from behind, pulling her back toward the sofa. Marlene struggled, but he had a firm hold on her, locking her between his knees. Overwhelmed and trapped, Marlene gave up. She flung herself against his chest, breaking into screaming sobs. He held her, stroking her back, and looked at Lola over the top of her head.

"Go on," he said. "Tell me how I'm the one who screws things up around here."

ACT IV

Gothammag.com
THE MOST HATED MAN IN NEW YORK

When I meet Spencer Martin in the lobby of his family's small Upper East Side hotel, he's doing a handstand. A slightly younger girl with wild blonde curls stands next to him. From upside-down, he asks me to wait just a moment over by the desk.

"Remember," he says to the girl, "go slow."

The girl lifts her foot, and pauses.

"You've got it," he says, shifting his weight from arm to arm, steadying himself. "Don't worry. What's the worst that can happen?"

I'm about to ask what's going on when the girl swings her leg back and appears to kick Martin directly in the face. I'm not sure what to do — call for help, call the police, or join her. Right now, a lot of people around New York think kicking Spencer Martin in the face is a very, very good idea.

Martin comes crashing to the floor, landing with a loud smack, sprawled in all directions. I've just decided that the correct thing to do is come to his aid, when he sits up.

"I think that works," he says, getting off the floor, completely uninjured. He puts an arm around the girl's shoulders. "This is Scarlett. She's my sister. She's still mad at me for shooting Sonny."

This is all the explanation I get for the scene I've just witnessed.

Unlike the intense, sneering character he plays on television, Martin is the picture of affability. On screen, he looks gaunt, with piercing eyes. In person, he is tall and slender, his eyes bright and friendly. Martin, 19, is a recent graduate of the High School of Performing Arts. Right before he was cast on Crime and Punishment, he was your typical young New York actor — working a day job as a waiter, doing small productions at night. He is eager to please, maybe to offset the negative reaction many people have had to his character.

Though he lives in a hotel, Martin is quick to point out that he isn't exactly a Hilton — his getting a part on television has nothing to do with privilege. A quick look around the lobby, where we sit down to talk, confirms his story. There are threadbare patches on the arms of the chairs and the floorboards are uneven. The phone never rings, and no one comes through the front door. No, the Hiltons they are not.

"I spent most of the summer doing Hamlet in that room right there," Martin says, pointing at the dining room. "On a unicycle."

A unicycle? Hamlet? In the hotel?

"It was kind of a carnival, old movie setting," he explains. "We had to do the show here because . . . well, that's a long story. But we were sort of the goofballs of the show. I've run into that dining room door head-first more times than I can count."

Martin explains that his part on Crime and Punishment was supposed to be a small one — a one-off episode. But when the script was changed to accommodate the departure of Donald Purchase, he found himself thrust into the spotlight.

So, how does it feel to be the most hated man in New York?

"I don't know," he says. "Kind of weird? Very weird? I like doing this part, but . . . people seem really upset about what happened. It's just a show. . . ."

But for many, Crime and Punishment *isn't just a show — and the characters aren't just people on TV. They're old friends. And Sonny Lavinski was the oldest friend of all. I've read enough reports of people attacking Martin in the street, throwing food at him, to know this must be an ongoing issue for him. Would he still take the part, even knowing what would happen?*

"Sure," he says, without hesitation. "I'm an actor. I have to take work when I can get it."

Does he worry that he'll be typecast? That he might not work again because people will always associate him with this odious role? That maybe he's done a little too well?

For the first time since I've met him, Martin's features cloud over, his cheeks hollow a bit, and I see just the smallest hint of the darkness of his character.

"You think?" he asks.

THE WORST
OF TIMES

All of the rooms in the Hopewell Hotel were called suites, even though they were single rooms, and a suite by definition is a series of rooms. It had always been this way. When the hotel was given its very expensive makeover in 1929, this lie was physically manifested in the form of a hand-engraved brass sign on every door, edged in a Deco lightning-bolt motif.

No one ever complained about the non-suiteness of a Hopewell room. They complained about other things, like broken televisions, or squeaky old bed frames, or the damp in the walls. Or incidents like that time two years ago when a pigeon got into the Sterling Suite when it had been vacant for a while and the window was left open to air the room. The pigeon nested in one of the wall sconces, a fact that remained undiscovered until the guest turned on the light and the enraged pigeon flew out, much like the proverbial bat from hell, and started flapping around the room. Smoke started billowing out of the wall. Within seconds, the Sterling Suite was a scene from a horror film.

When those are your problems, no one gets crazy about semantics.

Everything over the next few days had a similar air of hazy definition and disaster. Whatever had happened was *called* a wedding, but it didn't feel like one. Not that Scarlett had any real frame of reference for how weddings were supposed to be. She had never attended one, never developed any particular fascination for them, harbored no particular like or dislike of any kind. But she didn't think they were supposed to be like this. They weren't supposed to be secret, unseen events where the aftermath looks a lot like the before except everyone is gloomy and tense all the time, like they've just heard that there's been an outbreak of plague in the town upstream.

Chip and Lola took up temporary residence in the swanky Peninsula Hotel. They made a brief appearance on Sunday afternoon, during which they both looked very stressed-out. Monday arrived just like it always did, creeping in during the night like the neighbor's cat, come to illicitly drop dead mice by the bedside. Scarlett opened her eyes and saw Lola's empty bed, instantly remembering what a few hours of sleep had blanked away. She looked at the clock. Six A.M. She had another half hour of sleep to go, but something had woken her.

It was a hand, shaking her very gently. Lola's hand, specifically. Lola was sitting on the other side of Scarlett's bed, facing the windows. She had pulled her hair up into a twist so severely that it was pulling at the skin around her face.

"When did you get here?" Scarlett asked groggily.

"A few minutes ago. But we're all having breakfast together."

"What, now?"

"Half an hour. You get ready for school. I have to go wake up Marlene."

An unpleasant breakfast of burned bacon and undercooked pancakes was spread out over two of the small dining room tables. It looked like no one had slept well, and the sight in front of them wasn't helping. Spencer slumped in his seat, his hair still soaking wet from his shower, a faint trace of stubble around his jaw. Scarlett's father was wearing one of his thrift store cowboy shirts again — a subdued black one with white piping — but he had misbuttoned it. Scarlett's mom's curls were as frazzled as her own for once, and she was furiously passing around the wet pancakes, trying to nudge Marlene into eating.

"What brought you back?" Spencer asked. "Aren't you supposed to be on your honeymoon or something?"

"I'm back to work," Lola said. "Towels don't fold themselves. No honeymoon, at least for a while. There's a lot going on."

Spencer laughed mirthlessly to himself and shoved a piece of badly burned bacon into his mouth.

"How long are you staying at the Peninsula?" Scarlett asked.

"A few more days," Lola replied. "Just while we get everything . . . settled. Then Chip has to go back to school. He's already missed a lot of classes."

"You can always come and stay here," her dad said a bit hesitantly. "You can have the Empire Suite."

"I think we need . . . some space."

"You mean there's no way in hell Chip is going to come and stay here," Spencer said. "It's not really his standard of living."

"Chip would be very happy to stay here," Lola replied. "But I didn't think you would appreciate having to live with him."

"Good call," Spencer said. He pushed himself away from the

table. "Scarlett, if you want a ride, the car will be here in five minutes."

"It's okay," Scarlett said, looking out at the gray sky. "I'll walk."

Scarlett cut across Central Park and made her meandering, diagonal way up the forty blocks past the joggers and the dog walkers and the moms with the big strollers. She had dressed carelessly, throwing on a pink shirt and an old blue skirt of Lola's that didn't really fit her right. It was a horrible day, too. Cloudy, but refusing to rain. Just gray, gray, gray. The leaves were just starting to shrivel and detach apathetically from the trees. Somewhere in the back of her mind, she knew she was late.

Scarlett stopped at the park gate and looked across the street. Frances Perkins looked like the big red loony bin more than ever. Today would be terrible. She would tank on her International Politics quiz. Her French homework was half-baked.

What she needed to do . . . was skip. Just walk away from school. You can't lose if you don't play.

But skipping — that wasn't in her. She was programmed to obey. Scarlett staggered into the building. The computer screens in the hall seemed too bright, and had too much information on them — this activity was being moved to a new room, this class had completed such and such a project, the jazz band was performing at fourth period lunch if anyone wanted to go. The day went every bit as badly as Scarlett suspected, and she developed a massive headache in third period that never went away. But Biology brought the worst news of all. She blinked and stared in front of her, at the word EXAM written on the board.

"If you've had a good look at the syllabus," Ms. Fitzweld said, "you'll see that your grade is based on five exams over the course of the year, and the first of these will be next Monday."

"I hope you study," Max said, leaning close. "I always try to sit next to a winner. There's no point in cheating otherwise."

"Max," Scarlett said calmly, "I swear to God, I'll kill you if you don't shut up right now. I will kill you dead."

"You just violated the no-tolerance violence policy in a huge way."

"It'll be worse when I put my pen in your eye."

Surprisingly, he backed off. But she could feel him watching her the whole period.

"Oh, Martin," Dakota said, putting a hand on her shoulder after class. "You are structurally unsound right now. I have some of those big chocolate chip cookies from Fairway. Here."

It was like she was six years old all of a sudden. But Dakota was right. This is what she needed. She took a big bite of the cookie, feeling the warm chocolate smudge around her mouth.

"Married," she said, spitting crumbs by accident as she walked down the hall. "Married? What does that even mean?"

"Some people get married at eighteen," Dakota offered. "I mean, no one I know, but people do. People used to do it all the time."

"She doesn't even like him that much! She broke up with him a few months ago. She's just bored. You don't get married when you're eighteen because you're *bored*."

Scarlett ate the rest of the cookie in three angry bites.

"She can undo it," Dakota said after a moment. "It's not like it's forever."

"It's *kind* of forever," Scarlett replied. "She said she's not going to, you know, get divorced."

"She's saying that now. She's only been married for five minutes. Once they realize what they've done . . ."

"Once they realize what they've done, Lola will be rich. She probably already is."

Scarlett said it without even meaning to. It just came out of her mouth, a total surprise, like a frog had just sprung forth.

"There is that," Dakota said quietly. "Do you think that . . . that Lola . . ."

"Married for the money?" Scarlett said unhappily. The words hurt. She didn't even want them out in the universe. "No, but . . . I can't think of why *else* she'd do it, either."

Being a good friend, Dakota just left that alone. But it was there, the only possibility left standing in Scarlett's mind.

"Well," Scarlett said, leaning against her locker, feeling the metal give gently against her weight, "at least you'll be happy about one thing. I almost went to Chelsea's show with Eric. But then all this happened, and I never called him."

"You're right. That is a good thing."

"And I guess it makes me seem all aloof and over it, right?" Scarlett added, trying to smile. "That's supposed to make you more attractive to guys, when you don't seem to care. They like a little abuse."

"We love it. We need a spanking."

That was from Max, who was heading for his usual music room by Scarlett's locker. He had stopped a few feet off to unabashedly listen to the conversation. Dakota reeled around on him.

"Do you mind?" she asked.

"Don't ask him that," Scarlett said. "He doesn't mind."

"What she said." Max nodded at Scarlett.

"Go. Away," Dakota told him. "I am not kidding. She is not okay right now."

Max obeyed this time, perhaps a little too quickly.

"See?" Dakota said. "You just need to use a little force with him. Now come to my house. We're going to watch TV."

"I'm not always going to be like this," Scarlett said. "I've been useful to you, right?"

"Many times," Dakota said, leading her along. "Sometimes, we all get a little broken."

A little broken. Scarlett wondered about that. At what point do you get so broken that it's time to just get thrown away? She had a feeling she was going to find out.

THE DOTTED LINE

Mrs. Amberson had told Scarlett she didn't have to come in that week, but going there was better than sitting around at home. She preferred going through the submissions and organizing the file of theater reviews to the yawning silences of the fifth floor. She decided to stop in on the way home from Dakota's. The intense reporting of her movements had loosened slightly in the last few days. It was a minor benefit in an otherwise untenable situation.

Murray the doorman was in extra fine form, poised at his station, eating one of the biggest sandwiches Scarlett had ever seen.

"Hey!" he said. "That dog of yours made a mess again down here today!"

"I told you," Scarlett said, "he is *not my dog.*"

"You gotta do something about . . ."

Scarlett felt like every capillary in her face had just gotten the go code. She could actually feel the blood filtering into her skin. Someone had to be punished today, and that person was going to be Murray the doorman.

"What part of *not my dog* do you not understand?" she asked. "What's the stumbling block? Is it the *not*? Is it the *dog*? Is it the sentence? The dog does not belong to me. He doesn't even belong to my boss. He's a borrowed dog, and he has *issues*!"

Murray made a disapproving sound, slapped down his sandwich, and picked up the receiver to tell Mrs. Amberson that her psychotic assistant was on the way up. Scarlett felt bad enough to stalk away with her head down, not looking back as she turned the corner to go to the elevator bank. She rested her head against the mirrored tiles above the buttons and looked at her face in extreme close-up. Her pores looked huge, her eyes red, and her hair broken and crazy. She didn't like mirror-Scarlett. She didn't like the Scarlett she was in, either. Or anyone else, for that matter.

"Did you just yell at the gatekeeper?" Mrs. Amberson asked, curious, when Scarlett let herself in. She was sitting on one of the white sofas, sucking on a piece of dried mango and scanning a copy of *Variety*. "He called up here sounding very hurt. Remind me to give you a raise."

"He keeps asking about the dog," Scarlett said, walking past her and going right to her desk.

"Are you all right, O'Hara?" Mrs. Amberson said, looking over in interest.

"It's nothing," Scarlett said. She grabbed for the first of the pile of envelopes to be opened and sorted. She tore it viciously, ripping the headshot contained inside. Some actress. Another starry stare and whitened, eager-to-please smile. The world was full of them.

"O'Hara . . ."

Scarlett clawed the next envelope from the stack. Where did they all come from, these idiots who wanted to work with them? There had to be a hundred more today.

"O'Hara. Leave those for a moment. Come sit over here."

246

"I need to get these done."

"They can wait."

Scarlett dropped the envelopes and came and sat opposite Mrs. Amberson, sinking deep into the plush sofa.

"You're having a hard day," Mrs. Amberson said. "You didn't have to come in today, you know. I know it's not the easiest time right now."

"I'm fine," Scarlett said, staring at the carpet.

"Lies are a tremendous karmic setback. Keep it up and you'll come back in the next life as something without a spine. You're not fine. And you don't have to be fine. This move of your sister's . . . it's a shock."

"I don't understand anyone," Scarlett mumbled. She felt her eyes filling up, but blotted any tears away with her thumbs.

Mrs. Amberson thought for a moment before speaking, which was a little bit frightening.

"O'Hara," she finally said, "I speak from long experience — when it comes to romance, all bets are off. I like to think that I'm a sensible person, but I've done some extraordinary things for love. And even the things that didn't work out, I don't regret."

"Are you actually married?" Scarlett asked.

"Oh, let's not tell folktales right now," Mrs. Amberson said. "My point is, the only way we learn anything is by taking chances. I can't really explain what Lola's done, or why, or say if it's a good idea or bad. Nothing in this world is black or white."

"What do I do?" Scarlett asked.

"Well," Mrs. Amberson said. "You can't control other people. They're going to do things you don't like, that you don't agree with, that you don't understand. But, by the same token, they cannot control you. You're stuck in this situation. You have to decide what outcome you want. What do you want, right now?"

"I want my sister," she said. "I don't want to . . . lose my sister."

"How could you lose her?"

"She's gone," Scarlett said. "She's living at the Peninsula, and I don't even know what's going on with her or what she's going to do, and . . ."

"Do you think your sister wants to lose you?" Mrs. Amberson asked.

"No."

"Have you spoken to her? Called her?"

No, Scarlett had not called her. She'd been too angry.

"The answer seems simple enough," Mrs. Amberson said. "I know you are more than capable of being direct. Go to your sister and tell her you do not want to lose her. Find out what is going on. Go do it now. Get to the bottom of it before it becomes a much bigger problem. And I know Lola. She undoubtedly wants to talk to *you*."

Murray came along the edge of the sofa, sniffing a trail on the floor. He wriggled his pencil-thin stump of a tail nervously at her, in a little show of encouragement.

Lola answered on the first ring.

"Are you talking to me?" she asked.

"I called."

"I'm at work right now," she said. "But can we talk? Or meet?"

"You're at *work*?" Scarlett asked.

"I work on Wednesdays. But I get a break soon. Can we meet at the park? Southeast corner, by the book stands? In an hour?"

Lola appeared right on time, wearing a little black skirt and blue Bubble Spa T-shirt. She approached Scarlett cautiously.

"You're still working?" Scarlett asked. "Even after . . ."

"Sure," Lola said. "I had to cover for those few days, though. I had the flu, remember?"

It was so odd. Scarlett and Lola had shared a room all their lives. Lola's presence was just something she took for granted. This looked like Lola as usual, in her black skirt and blue Bubble Spa T-shirt, her fine blonde hair looped back in an attractive knot. But everything had changed. There was a space between them that was hard to cross.

"I'm glad you're still talking to me," Lola said. "You're the only one."

Scarlett could only shrug.

"Marlene was doing so much better," Lola continued. "And Spencer . . . I know that a lot of times it seems like we don't get along, but it's just . . . I don't know. He frustrates me sometimes. We're just so different. But I'm so proud of him. Spencer's on TV. My big brother. I always thought that was impossible, but there he is. And he's so good."

That was maybe the biggest compliment Lola had ever paid Spencer, and he was nowhere around to hear it.

"I didn't think it would be like this," Lola said. "I knew people would be a little shocked, but I didn't expect Marlene to react like that. Or even Spencer. Mom and Dad look heartbroken. I don't want everyone to be upset because of me. I'm going to make it up to everyone. It's going to be fine."

"I need to know something," Scarlett said. "I need you to tell me the truth."

Lola looked over cautiously, but she nodded. She guided Scarlett to a bench and they both sat down. Scarlett had to take a deep breath before asking the question.

"I need to know if you married him for the money. Because you thought we needed it, or . . . just to be . . . secure."

"That's what everyone thinks?" Lola asked quietly.

"I don't know what anyone thinks. I don't even know what I think. I mean, you get married, you move into one of the most expensive hotels in the city . . ."

Lola flipped over the edge of her skirt and examined the hem.

"Let me tell you something about the money," she said. "But I don't want anyone else to know. You have to keep this a secret. Do you promise?"

Scarlett nodded.

"The Sutcliffes aren't paying for the hotel," she said.

"Then who is?" Scarlett asked.

"A friend of their family. The Sutcliffes . . . cut Chip off. All of his money has been locked up. His credit cards have been stopped. Even his tuition bill won't be paid. Right now, we have nothing."

Scarlett just shook her head in confusion. The idea of Chip not having money was . . . well, that idea didn't compute. Chip *was* money. There seemed little else to look at.

"The only way we can fix it," Lola said, "is if I sign a postnuptial agreement that says I have no claim to any of the Sutcliffe money. They brought in a lawyer and everything. If I sign it, they'll recognize the marriage by throwing us a party and announcing it. And they set up an account for me. Mrs. Sutcliffe keeps calling it a 'household account.' A credit card and a few thousand a month for whatever I need, plus credit at shops for buying things for our new apartment."

"You mean, like an allowance?" Scarlett asked. "A really big allowance?"

"I didn't ask for it," Lola said. "The lawyer just read it off as part of the deal. I told them I didn't want that, but they just said it was all part of the package. What they really mean is if I'm going to be their daughter-in-law I have to live up to a certain standard. They're afraid I'm using him, but I'm not. I didn't do this for money."

"Why *did* you marry him?" Scarlett asked.

"It wasn't . . . enough." Lola's voice wobbled uncertainly. "I just needed . . . I wanted something real. Something that worked. And I know you don't believe this, but Chip and I work. I know I'm young, I know all of that. It doesn't mean I don't know what I want. You have to understand, the money is just a side benefit."

"You're telling me that if Chip wasn't Chip Sutcliffe you'd marry him anyway? If he didn't live in a huge apartment on Park Avenue? If he didn't have a car and a driver, if he couldn't buy you expensive stuff?"

"It's all part of who he is," Lola said, shrugging. "He can't help that. That's not why I like him."

"So then sign the paper," Scarlett said, shrugging.

On this, Lola got very animated.

"I wanted to! I said I would sign it. I had the pen in my hand. Chip stopped me."

"Why?"

"Because he didn't want me to feel second-rate," Lola said. "He wants his family to accept me, totally. And if they don't, he's prepared, you know . . . for what comes. He's prepared to let them take it all away. He's for real, Scarlett."

That did sound genuine. Scarlett had never doubted Chip's intentions. She had only doubted Lola's.

"Yeah, but . . ." Scarlett hated doing this to Lola, but it had to be said. "He hasn't felt it yet. He still has lots of nice stuff. He hasn't been kicked out of school yet. So, he can say now that he's fine with it, but how is that really going to *be* for him, when he has no money?"

"I know," Lola said. "I thought about that. The worst part wouldn't be the money, but his parents rejecting us. He feels rejected a lot. Like by Spencer. And, well, kind of by you. You don't get it, Scarlett. His family is a mess. He's always been jealous of *us*. We all get along, more or less. We all like each other. He's never had that. He'd love to be a part of it, but no one will let him in. Except Marlene, and I think she just likes the boat."

This was all too big for Scarlett. They sat in silence for a moment, watching the squirrels run by, and the owners getting tugged along by their dogs, and the nannies pushing the strollers. It was getting cold. Scarlett shivered. She should have been wearing her coat, but she had gone out in a thin jacket. Cold and confused.

"So what do I do?" Lola asked. "Do I do what Chip wants? If I refuse to sign, everyone's just going to think I want money. Or do I just go and sign it? Chip will be mad, but at least everyone else will be happy, and things might actually go back to something like normal. I don't know what to do."

"What's more important?" Scarlett heard herself say. "Taking this stand that just makes you look like you're after money, or proving that you're not?"

"I want to prove that I'm not," Lola said.

"So go and sign the paper."

"He'd be *really* upset, Scarlett."

"Do you have to tell him?" Scarlett asked. "You could sign and you could tell them not to tell Chip. That way, they see you don't care about money, and Chip thinks they just changed their minds."

Lola cocked her head. Obviously, this option had not occurred to her. Lola was just too fundamentally and plainly honest. Unlike Scarlett, apparently.

"You mean lie to him?" Lola asked.

"No, not lie. Just don't tell . . ." Scarlett stopped herself. She had been down this road before and knew better. "Yes, lie."

"But this is . . . the foundation of our marriage."

"No it isn't. It's something dumb the Sutcliffes are doing, and Chip is just mad. Tell him later, when everything has calmed down. Everyone is just *freaking out* right now. Someone . . . has to be calm."

She had no idea what she was saying now. Words were just coming out of her mouth. But Lola seemed interested in the words. She was nodding.

"You're right," she said. "Everyone's too upset right now. Someone has to do something sensible. Chip probably won't even care in a few months. I could just go and sign the paper, and everyone would calm down."

"If you want," Scarlett said, backtracking a little. "I mean, I have no idea about any of this. I'm an idiot."

The idea, now seeded, had quickly taken root in Lola's mind.

"I have to show them that I'm not after the money," she said, mostly to herself. "Chip needs to go back to school. You're right . . . I didn't even think of it, but you're right."

The more she was told that she was right, the more Scarlett wanted to distance herself from the idea. All she'd really said was, "People are crazy. Why don't you lie to them?"

"I need to prove it to everyone," Lola said, turning to look at Scarlett straight on. "Especially you. This isn't about money. You're the only one who knows the specifics, but . . . I'm glad you know."

She took Scarlett's hand and squeezed it. "Do you hate me?" she asked.

"What? No. I . . . No."

Scarlett's eyes were welling up, and so were Lola's.

"I'll always remember you did this for me," Lola said. "Always."

And there was such a moment of sisterly bonding, such genuine gladness that she was there with Lola and they clearly loved each other, that Scarlett decided not to think about the fact that this was probably true. Lola would never forget, and Scarlett had absolutely no idea what she had just done.

OUTRAGEOUS FORTUNE

When Scarlett got home the next afternoon, the lobby was full of bags — shopping bags, garment bags. She hadn't seen so much stuff since the day Mrs. Amberson moved in. There was no one at the front desk, but the door to the dining room was partway open and there were voices coming from inside. Scarlett slid it open the rest of the way, revealing a small gathering — her parents and Lola.

"We're having a kind of family meeting," Lola said chirpily. "To talk about the party."

"Party?" Scarlett repeated.

The party, Scarlett quickly gathered, was going to be a pretty epic affair. It was going to be held at a place called Point Manhattan, a private club on the roof of a building in midtown. The view, Lola assured them, was stunning, and the Sutcliffes pulled a few strings. A fabulous swing band had been hired. Menus were going to be finalized in the morning. The florists were already hard at work getting in the orders from all the flower markets. Scarlett watched her parents valiantly making efforts to argue that the party should be at the Hopewell, but clearly a massive engine had been set in motion, an engine that could be stopped by no one. Lola was hyper, chattering like a monkey.

"Come on," Lola said, pulling Scarlett a little too roughly from her chair, "I have things to show you!"

In the lobby, Lola started grabbing bags. When she could carry no more, she shoved one of the shopping bags along the parqueted floor with her foot. Scarlett picked up what was left.

"What *is* this?" Scarlett asked, looking around.

"Just a few things for the wedding party."

"Does this mean . . ."

"Wait until we get upstairs," Lola said under her breath.

They managed to get it all in the elevator by propping open the gate and piling the bags around them. Once the elevator had creaked and moaned them up to the fifth floor, they pushed out the bags and got everything down the hall to the Orchid Suite. Within five minutes, there was an explosion of pastel tissue paper, box lids, ribbons, and wrappers. Five garment bags weighed down the closet doors. Lola gave them each a quick squeeze, seemingly able to divine their contents by the way they scrunched.

"You signed it," Scarlett said.

She pushed aside some of the packages to make enough room to sit down. All of these lovely things looked so strange in the Orchid Suite — strange and right. At some point in history, people who wore lovely things were here all the time. That's why the hotel was filled with dressing tables with many secret drawers and large carved wardrobes and silk-cushioned chairs to sit on while you applied your makeup.

These were the things that came from the Sutcliffes — small tokens of their much vaster wealth. And all Lola had had to do to earn them was sign a piece of paper saying that she wasn't really equal to them. Yesterday, Scarlett didn't see what the big deal was, and if Lola wanted to sign, she should sign. But now, seeing this, she started to change her mind. Maybe . . . *Chip* was right. Maybe she should have held out, just ignored the Sutcliffes entirely.

Of course, she couldn't say this to Lola now.

"But how did all of that party stuff get planned *today*?" Scarlett said, looking around at the mass of things piled around them.

"It didn't," Lola said. "I think they knew I was going to sign, so Mrs. Sutcliffe — Anna — hired someone earlier in the week to start setting things up on the sly. She has friends everywhere, and she does a lot of society and charity events, so she has the number of every good florist, caterer, bakery in town. She picked out the *cake*." The word *cake* came out with the kind of inflection used for words like *taxes* or *dumped*.

"What's wrong with the cake?"

"The cake," Lola said slowly, "is shaped like an enormous boat. Specifically, their boat. I *hate boats*."

"So why . . ."

"Because," Lola said, waving her arms helplessly, "they love their boat. And they seem convinced that the boat is what brought us back together. Chip must have told her we went for a ride on it, you know, the night of the show. And she knows we took a ride on the boat before he left for school. They went out to the slip yesterday to take photos. This bakery's claim to fame is that they can make anything — and it's all edible. No posts or supports or plastic bits. It's one big . . ."

"Boat cake."

"Right," Lola said.

"Just like every girl dreams of," Scarlett said.

"It's awful. And it's going to cost about ten thousand dollars."

On hearing that figure, Scarlett was struck silent. Lola went through the bags, trying to calm herself down.

"This isn't a party for me," Lola said. "It's a party for them to show off and make it all official. All I have to do is be gracious. *I* picked these clothes out, though. Now look at this. It's for you."

She went over to one of the garment bags and unzipped it, revealing a dress. Even at a first glance, it was clear that it was perfect for Scarlett. It was midnight blue silk, with a fitted bodice and a full skirt, with a wide swath of steel-silver silk at the waist that wrapped around and tied at the front. At the very bottom, there was a fringe of silvery-gray tulle.

"It's very Grace Kelly. And it will be amazing with your hair. And here are the shoes . . . and the purse. . . ." Lola was already fishing around in a bag, producing silver shoes and a bag. "Now, if you don't like this, it can go back, but I think you will . . . or I hope you will . . . and I have a seamstress who can do all alterations in twenty-four hours, and you don't even have to go anywhere, she'll come here, but I know your size so this should fit, but . . . ."

"It's amazing," Scarlett said.

"And this is to go with it," she said, handing Scarlett a small blue jewelry box from a shop on Madison Avenue that she had passed a million times but never been in. Scarlett took the box a bit warily and opened it. Inside, there was a heart-shaped platinum necklace set with a large blue stone.

"It's a sapphire," Lola said. "Take it out, look at it in the light. Go on!"

The chain of the necklace was very delicate, so Scarlett carefully removed it from the small velvet bindings that kept it in place. She held the heart up to the window, allowing the light to shine through it.

"Isn't it pretty?" Lola asked eagerly. "I thought you would love it. If you don't, they have loads of others, but I thought . . ."

"How much did this cost?" Scarlett asked.

"Don't worry about that. Do you like it?"

"Yeah, but . . . I thought you just had a little allowance . . ."

"This is different. Try on the dress! Try it on!"

Lola pulled a tiny shopping bag out of a larger one, and then extracted from that a pink tissue-wrapped bundle.

"New bra to go with it," she said, unrolling the paper.

Scarlett accepted the bra and changed into it, while Lola lifted the dress off its hanger. She lowered it down over Scarlett's head, trapping her in a world of blue satin with occasional scraps of tulle. Lola tugged it down firmly, adjusting it over her hips, tugging at the back, zipping and hooking everything into place.

Scarlett looked in the slightly dusty mirror. For a moment, she tried to fight loving the dress, but it was simply impossible. It was the most beautiful thing she had ever seen, and she could barely believe it was hers. *This* is what it meant for something to fit well. *This* is what people meant by real artistry in clothing. This was the feeling of silk nestled against her skin, forming a shape around her that was graceful and elegant, making her into a new kind of person — a beautiful person. A more confident person. A more together person. A . . .

A richer person.

"Oh my God, Scarlett," Lola said, putting her hand over her mouth. "I knew it would be good on you but . . . oh my God. You're so beautiful."

Scarlett smoothed her hands over the fabric of the skirt.

"I hope they all turn out this good!" Lola squealed. She fussed around Scarlett for a moment, tugging material this way and that, feeling around the waist, examining the hemline from the floor, checking the shoulders, and finally studying the strain of the material around the chest.

"You're bustier than I realized," Lola said, checking to see if there was any material to spare. "We're going to have to have this let out a little. But that's an easy fix. This is the only thing we need to do for yours."

She got out a big notebook covered in light blue leather, flipped through a few pages of scrawled notes and swatches of fabric, and wrote something down.

"It's just a party," she said, mostly to herself. "It's just a party."

"You obviously don't want the party," Scarlett said. "So why don't you just tell them no?"

Lola looked up from the book and sighed.

"Mom and Dad said the same thing, but . . . the Sutcliffes have to make a statement in order to be happy. They have to spend a bunch of money and have the right people see that Chip didn't just run off with his girlfriend, that it's all approved of and correct. It has to look right. It's like a show, and I just have to be in it, and then we'll have peace."

"What makes you think they'll be any different after the party?"

That, Lola was not prepared to answer. She closed the book decisively and reached for another bag.

"Now," she said. "Where's Spencer? I have to see him in this suit. I'm almost positive this will be a great fit. I mean, I know his general size and his pants measurements were up on eBay anyway. Look!"

She unzippered another Bergdorf bag. There was a sharp, gray pin-striped suit inside.

"And these go with it," she said, indicating various bags. "Shirt, shoes, cuff links. It's the perfect suit. I mean, if you were going to have one suit in your whole life, this should be that suit. And he can carry a suit so well, you know, because he's got the height going for him. We might have to take the trousers up a half inch or so, and I had to guess on the shirt since he has long arms, so I just bought three and we'll see which one works."

"I don't think he's here," Scarlett said.

"Okay, well . . . let's show Marlene her dress!"

The clothes seemed to make Lola manic — giving her focus, something she could understand. Something she could share. She plucked up Marlene's garment bag and hurried down the hall, forgetting that Marlene still wasn't very happy with her.

Marlene was on her bed, yet another biography of Princess Diana open in front of her, but it didn't seem like she was reading.

"You really like Princess Diana," Scarlett said.

Marlene gave Scarlett a look that suggested that another pointless conversational remark about Princess Diana might result in a Princess Diana biography making contact with her face. At least she was acting kind of normal.

"I got you a dress," Lola said.

"I don't care."

Lola ignored this and hung the bag on the closet door. She

unzipped it, revealing what looked like a rose-colored ballerina out-fit. Marlene stared at it, then turned right back to her book.

"Well?" Lola said hopefully.

"Looks expensive," she said. "I guess you're rich now."

They left her alone. Lola insisted on waiting for Spencer to get home, and got a similar reaction — he stared at the suit on his bed, asked who died, and shut his door. Lola never once stopped smiling.

"Tomorrow," Lola said as she prepared to go. "I scheduled your fitting with the seamstress at four. And get Spencer to try on his suit, please? You're the only one on my side."

She reached out and grabbed Scarlett's hand for support.

"Sure," Scarlett said. "I'll try."

THE VIOLENT
IMPULSE

It was Max who finally completed the circuit — finally, after all that had happened that week, brought Scarlett to the edge and tipped her over so easily. And he did it with two words.

"Who's Eric?" he asked, sitting down in Bio the next day.

"What?" Scarlett snapped.

"You've been talking about him for weeks. But who is he?"

"He's an actor," Scarlett said. Max didn't need more than that.

"Oh great," he replied. "Just what I need. Another actor tool around."

"What do you mean *around*?"

"He went out with Chelsea last night."

On that bombshell, Ms. Fitzweld turned out the lights and started screaming about some presentation they were going to watch. There was a roar in Scarlett's ears. Chelsea, Eric, Chelsea, Eric . . . How did these two intersect?

Scarlett had learned her deductive technique from Sonny Lavinski. Sonny worked backward, very specifically, using the chain of evidence. She tried to do the same. The last time she had seen Eric, she had given him the ticket to the show, one of Chelsea's passes. That was the starting point. So . . . if he had used one of the passes, gone without Scarlett . . . chances are Chelsea might have heard that someone in the audience was using one of her comps. They'd probably met at the show. Met, fell for each other instantly as fellow *artistes* . . .

Max was moving closer again.

"Why do I feel that this is a problem for you?" he asked.

Scarlett felt her last bit of restraint give. Without a moment's hesitation, she jerked herself sideways, using her shoulder to dump him right off the stool.

Scarlett had some experience now in knowing how people were supposed to fall. There were ways of throwing yourself off a stool or a bench or a table. But Max had none of this training, instinct, or preparation. It was the first time he actually looked surprised by something she'd done. His eyes widened and he teetered, clutching for the edge of the lab station ineffectually. He fell, landing hard on the floor.

It was so simple, so satisfying. Scarlett coughed out a laugh of pure, unbridled relief. The laugh went around the room, and died quickly, snuffed out in a second. And then the silence, as the class waited to see what would happen next, each person judging Scarlett in his or her mind.

"Are you all right?" she asked.

Max got up stiffly. It seemed to Scarlett that he was acting a lot more injured than he probably was.

"Outside," Ms. Fitzweld said. "Both of you."

Her stool seemed higher than normal — so far from the ground. And the walk to the door so long, with so much silence behind it, so many eyes on her. And behind her, her executioner limped along. Once out in the hall, Ms. Fitzweld turned on them both.

"What just happened?" she said quietly. "Please tell me you didn't just knock him off the stool. Because that means assault policy. That's a mandatory three-day suspension and a disciplinary review, and all kinds of bad stuff I don't really want to bring down on you."

This was it. Scarlett had just lost her mind and clocked Max and everyone saw it.

"It was kind of mutual," Max said.

Scarlett did a literal double take, snapping around twice, unable to comprehend what had just been said.

"What does that mean?" Ms. Fitzweld asked.

"We were screwing around, and I fell," he said. "I was trying to push her, she was trying to push me. She won."

Ms. Fitzweld knew as well as Scarlett that this was a lie. Max was handing her a way out — and that scared Scarlett more than anything. He glared at her and widened his eyes a little, daring her to contradict him.

"All right," Ms. Fitzweld said, reaching up and rubbing the back of her neck. "Here's what's going to happen. You, Biggs, are going to the nurse's office to get checked out. Then you're coming back to class. I have to stay here today for a few hours to prepare the exam. You two are going to keep me company, as long as it takes. I think a few hours together on a Friday afternoon will be punishment enough for both of you."

The class was very mumbly when they returned, full of that odd, sudden bloodlust that comes from thinking that someone you only kind of know is about to be handed a huge punishment. All but Dakota seemed a bit disappointed when Max and Scarlett just took their seats again and the class resumed. Dakota came right over when class ended, but Ms. Fitzweld waved her out.

"Because I'm feeling very merciful today," Ms. Fitzweld said, "I won't call your homes personally. I'll give you five minutes to do that. Right here. Right now. Then I'm taking the phones until we're done here."

"I'm good," Max said breezily.

They both looked to Scarlett as she called Lola.

"Hey," she said. "I'm not going to be able to make that fitting . . ."

"What?"

"I have detention," she said, lowering her voice. (Which was dumb. It wasn't like Ms. Fitzweld and Max didn't know that.)

"You what?" Lola said. "Detention?"

"It's a long story. I'll be there as soon as I can."

"What time will that be?"

"I don't know," Scarlett said, looking to Ms. Fitzweld for clues. "Six, or seven?"

Ms. Fitzweld nodded, not looking up.

"But the seamstress will be gone by then!"

"Lola," Scarlett said, "there is literally nothing I can do about it."

"Okay," Lola said nervously. "The bust is fine, I guess. Did it seem like you were bursting out?"

"I can't really have this discussion right now," Scarlett said, looking over at Max. Her phone was kind of loud, and from the way he suddenly turned, she got the sense that he might have heard part of that comment. "It's fine. Don't worry."

She got off the phone and handed it over.

"Okay," Ms. Fitzweld said. "Now that you're both here, you have an opportunity to study for the exam. I'm going to be in and out. There's a hall monitor just outside who'll look in when I'm not here, so if you're not sitting there working, things will be bad for you. Nice and simple. Understood? I'm going to go to the teachers' lounge for a minute. Remember, I've already been nice to you."

"Hey," Max said conversationally, when she was gone, "you know who would probably like to know about this? *Spies of New York*. That's some good reading right there. The sister of Sonny Lavinski's murderer going around *assaulting* people. They're obsessed with *Crime and Punishment*."

Scarlett put her head down on the cool, hard surface of the lab station she was sitting at, not really knowing or caring how well they got cleaned. She was out of comebacks. Out of anger. She was going to start crying right here and right now, and that had to be prevented.

Scarlett heard Max's stool slide back and could tell he was walking in her direction. He sat down next to her.

"Leave me alone," she croaked.

The longer he sat there, though, the more Scarlett got the sense that he wasn't about to torment her. When she finally lifted her head, a curl embedded in her forehead, he was just regarding her curiously. He picked up her pen and started drawing on his arm, a little series of dark stars, right at the wrist.

"What the hell is the matter with you?" he asked casually.

He continued to draw, occasionally looking down at her from the tangle of wild, ostensibly rock-star hair he was cultivating.

She could tell he had attempted to brush out and straighten the waves. Fool.

Scarlett decided to take an unusual course — she would simply tell him the truth. Not the whole truth. Not the part about Eric. But the big truth. At this point, what could it hurt?

"My sister ran off to Vegas and got married to her boyfriend," she said. "She's *eighteen*. She doesn't love him. That's what the hell is wrong with me."

He stopped drawing and put the pen down.

"She pregnant?" he asked.

Was she? No. She would have said. Lola was the type who would have said.

"No," Scarlett said.

"So why did she do it?"

"I don't know. I think she was scared."

"Of what?" he asked.

"Life."

At this, he nodded and started casually tempting fate by poking his fingernail into the opening of the electric socket.

"I know what it's like when your family sucks," he said. "And you know what? There's nothing you can do about it."

"My family doesn't suck," Scarlett said.

There were voices just outside the door, and Max got up and sauntered back, sitting down at his stool just moments before Ms. Fitzweld came back in carrying a large coffee and a few thick folders of paperwork. She looked at Max suspiciously, sensing recent movement.

"How's it coming?" she asked.

Max waggled his notebook in her direction and went back to drawing on his wrist.

They were released at six thirty. Scarlett rarely left school when it was dark — or at least almost dark. The sky was rippled with color, a bright orange bolt over the park and the buildings. And it had gotten colder. Scarlett tightened her coat around her chest. It was a little too late to make the trek across the park by herself. She and Max fell into step beside each other.

"Where are you walking?" he asked, not sounding like he cared in the slightest.

"Down to Eighty-sixth. I'll get the bus across."

One good thing about Max — he didn't feel the need to talk just to fill the air. They just *walked*. She had no idea how far he planned on going with her, and it didn't seem to matter. It was just them and the steady beat of their footsteps on the sidewalk, past apartment buildings along the upper edge of the park, and doormen, and people hurrying around to get ready for a Friday night in the early autumn.

After several blocks of harmonious quiet, Scarlett got the feeling that it would probably be okay if she felt like venting a little more. Complaining about your family — that was like food for Max.

"Her new . . . *in-laws* . . . are having a party tomorrow," she said. "At some fancy place called Point Manhattan. I have to go and pretend to be happy because I'm the only one still talking to her."

"Why don't you skip it?"

"I can't do that," Scarlett said automatically.

"Why not?"

"Because . . . I can't."

"Who are you taking?"

"Taking?" She laughed. In all of this mess, the last thing she would ever have thought of was taking someone to Lola's party. "I don't have anyone to take. Not now, since your sister is . . ."

She decided not to finish the sentence.

"Take me," he said conversationally. "I love watching other people being miserable. I'm *exactly* the person you need."

That actually made Scarlett laugh. Max had a point. He would be the perfect person to take. She had learned in history that people used to hire mourners to wail and look really sad for them at funerals. Max could be her hired misery. And it would serve the Sutcliffes right.

"Sure," she said. "You'd fit right in. You seem like the kind of person who loves Society."

They were approaching Eighty-sixth, and a bus was just pulling up to the stop. Scarlett sprinted to catch it. When she turned around to see if Max had followed, she saw that he had stopped at the place where she had started to run. He raised a lazy hand of good-bye. Scarlett did the same. As the bus pulled away, he was still standing there, staring distractedly at the sidewalk. In those few seconds, he seemed a little lost, like maybe he didn't quite know how to get himself home.

PARTY AT POINT MANHATTAN

Scarlett lay on her bed, staring at the yellowing spot on the ceiling that seemed like it was more over her bed than it ever was Lola's. She could move to Lola's bed now, if she wanted. Get out from under the spot.

No. It would always be Lola's bed. Her spot was here, by the window. That was the way the world was, and how it should remain.

Next door, someone was taking a long shower. Lola would be here soon to dress. She was out at a salon getting her hair, nails, and makeup done. Scarlett had been offered an invitation — a whole morning at one of the nicest spas in town, eating mini brownies and having people apply things to her. She had turned it down to wallow in her bed and stare at the spot on the ceiling.

It occurred to her that she should probably go down the hall and make sure Marlene was dressed. She knew her mom would have already done this, but it seemed big sisterly, and now she was kind of the big sister of the house. That was an unwelcome promotion, a fancy new title with no benefits, just more work.

Marlene was sitting on her bed. She had already stuffed herself into her dress, even though they had about two hours before they had to go. She was stabbing at her hair with a brush.

"It's pretty," Scarlett said.

It was very pretty. It also made Marlene look very demure, which she probably hated. Ideally, Marlene probably wanted an outfit that had a special holder for a gun.

"It itches" was all she said.

"Do you need help?"

"Does it *look* it?"

"With your *hair*?" Scarlett countered.

"No."

Scarlett returned to the Orchid Suite, noticing that the bathroom was now free. Spencer must have been getting ready. Now it was her turn. Mercifully, there was some hot water left for her, and she used it all, until it ran to freezing, probably a half hour. When she returned to her room wrapped in a huge towel, Lola was there. Even on the worst of days, Lola looked better than 90 percent of the population. Today, her hair was exquisite, but her makeup was too heavy, and it made her look much older than she was. She was removing it with a cloth. Lola had been one of the best makeup artists at Henri Bendel. Scarlett was surprised she'd let anyone else touch her face.

"I should have known better," she said. "I'm just going to take it all off and improvise. Can I use your makeup? I don't have mine with me."

Scarlett silently passed the bag over from her dresser.

"How are you?" Lola asked, working at her cheek in slow, careful circles.

Scarlett shrugged.

"Your phone was ringing while you were in the shower."

Scarlett picked it up and read the display. One new call. She had removed Eric's name from her contact list, but she still knew the number as soon as she saw it. One voice mail. She turned away from Lola as she listened.

"Hey . . ." Eric began. "It's me. I was just wondering if we could talk, so if you get this, could you give me a call back?"

Scarlett almost laughed. So this was when he had chosen to call and tell her the news about Chelsea. The timing was impeccable. She shoved the phone under her covers and watched Lola get into her dress. For herself, Lola had chosen a cream-colored gown with a deep V-neck, with very fine light blue detailing. It draped her frame and brushed the floor in a kind of Greek-goddess way. It looked like a wedding dress. Now Scarlett had seen it. Now the truth was in front of her.

"Come on," Lola said. "Let me help you."

Scarlett allowed herself to be dressed, allowed Lola to fuss with her hair and makeup.

"Look," Lola said, her eyes glistening. "Just look at yourself."

She turned Scarlett to their slightly warped, silvering mirror. The blue had been so carefully picked for her — it made her hair look golden. And she had curves in this dress that she didn't seem to have in her other clothes. The material hugged them. In this moment, with the dust-filled light coming in through the window, on what was otherwise the strangest and emptiest of afternoons, she felt good. She wished Eric could see her now. He would be sorry.

"We should get going," Lola said.

Scarlett reached for the silver purse. She didn't know what to put in it. She didn't need money or keys. She shoved in a lipstick and reached for her phone, then stopped. She left it on her bed. Its services would not be required.

A stretch limo had been sent for the six Martins.

"Tacky," Spencer said as it pulled up. The suit Lola had chosen for him was a perfect fit. Lola really did have the eye for these things.

"Says the TV star," his dad replied.

"Hey, I like tacky," he replied. "I'm just surprised they sent something like this. Guess this was the only thing big enough to fit Lola's hillbilly family."

"They could have sent a van," Scarlett said. "Or a little bus."

The ride was short, less than five minutes. The building was right over by Rockefeller Center, and almost as tall and equally as imposing. In the lobby, they were greeted by a line of extremely cranky-looking people in front of a roped-off section of elevators, shaking guests down for their coats and checking them off a list. Scarlett vaguely recognized a few of the people being checked in. They were all dressed a bit like Chip . . . well, except for the girls. But you could practically see the price tags.

Lola stepped ahead to lead the Martin party. With a word from her, the velvet rope was moved aside and they were allowed into the private elevator bank where Chip's friends still stood waiting. The elevator attendant ushered Lola, Scarlett, and Spencer in, but there wasn't quite enough room for anyone else.

"We'll take the next one," her dad said. "You go up first."

The doors closed, and a soothing but overly loud recorded voice welcomed them to the elevator ride up to Point Manhattan. The main light in the elevator went dim, and greenish light came on overhead. Scarlett looked up to see that the ceiling of the elevator was entirely made of glass, so they could watch as they shot up the endless, dark channel into the air, cables and floors flying past. The voice continued to tell them about all of the wonderful things they would be able to see when they reached the top. Scarlett looked into the pinstripes of Spencer's jacket and concentrated on not being sick. This was a little too much elevator for her, even though it was probably safer than the one they had at home.

"Hey, Lola . . ." someone said, her voice tinged with sarcasm. "Nice *dress*."

"Thanks, Boonz," Lola replied coolly.

Boonz, Lola's archenemy, was somewhere in this elevator with them. Scarlett wanted to look for her, but that would require turning away from her study of the jacket fabric.

"Can't believe you guys actually got *married*," Boonz went on.

"Well, believe it," Lola replied.

One of the guys started to snicker. Why, Scarlett had no idea. She saw Spencer turn to look to see what was going on behind him. It messed up her calming view.

"Hey," another girl said, her voice thick with sarcasm, "aren't you the guy from . . ."

"Yes," Spencer said flatly.

"Married," Boonz said again. "I'm going to have to get you guys a really nice present."

"Just having you here is enough," Lola said sweetly.

"Oh, I know. And I guess you won't need anything now, right? You're *set*."

It was a good thing that the elevator slowed and jerked to a soft halt at that moment, giving Scarlett the quick dizzy spell that reminded her that they were dangling from a cable hundreds and hundreds of feet above the ground. She wanted to get off as quickly as possible, but she was behind Lola, who was moving at a dignified, leisurely pace. Lola stepped off to the side to make some adjustment to her dress, and Boonz and her party drifted past, barely containing their laughter.

"I'm going to take a wild guess," Spencer said in a low voice. "I'm going to say those are Chip's friends."

Scarlett was clinging to his sleeve for balance as her head caught up with her altitude.

"It could have been worse," she managed to reply. "Lola could have married one of *them*."

Lola finished her imaginary alterations and pasted a serene smile on her face.

"Let's just wait for Mom, Dad, and Marlene," she said. Scarlett could tell that she was nervous, that the encounter on the elevator had rattled her a bit, but she was doing everything she could to hide the fact.

One of the other elevator doors opened a moment later, and Marlene and Scarlett's parents were deposited. All six Martins made their way down the hall. In front of them, there was a wall made entirely of crystal, illuminated by the rosy glow of untold numbers of candles just beyond it. The room it guarded stretched out and around the building, so its size couldn't really be determined except to say that it was Very Large. There were dozens and dozens of tables topped with what looked like thousands of candles and creamy white flowers. The windows were floor to ceiling, with views directly out to the tops of other skyscrapers. On one side, there was a glass wall that led to a rooftop garden . . . but not like the one Naked Rooftop Lady had next door to their house. This was a mini Versailles-worthy affair. Next to that, there was a stage where a swing band was poised and ready to play, and a massive dance floor. An army of waiters and waitresses buzzed around with pastel-colored cocktails and ornate snacks that Scarlett couldn't even identify. Only a handful of people had arrived.

"Lola!"

A couple approached them. Even though she had never met the Sutcliffes before, Scarlett could have easily picked them out of a lineup. Mrs. Sutcliffe had smoky-brown hair cut into a severe mid-length bob and a surprisingly friendly face, even though her skin didn't look like it quite fit her skull. It was like a too-small piece was stretched over her features and maybe attached by a piece of elastic in the back. She wore a beautifully cut, very simple black dress and a large necklace of white beads, each one the size of a gum ball. Mr. Sutcliffe was a bit of a silver fox in a gray suit with deeply tan skin that looked as hard as shoe leather. Neither of them actually looked at all like Chip.

"My goodness, you are *stunning!*" Mrs. Sutcliffe said, examining her new daughter-in-law like she was looking over a horse she was considering buying. If you were just looking for good genes and someone to take to parties, you could do far worse than Lola, and her expression reflected that. Also, her voice was *deep*. If Scarlett had heard her over the phone, she would have mistaken her for a man. A man with a *beard*.

"Chip is in the smoking lounge waiting for you so you can make your entrance," Mr. Sutcliffe said. He also sounded manly. And a little drunk. Not a lot drunk, but a slow, easy, expensive whiskey or two drunk. He probably wasn't. He was just so rich that Scarlett expected he *always* sounded like that. He offered Lola an arm, and she was taken away.

"Come see the *cake*," Mrs. Sutcliffe said in her manly way.

In the middle of the room, right on the edge of the dance floor, was what appeared to be a large model boat. It was long and black, perfect in every detail, right down to the life preservers. And it was deeply, repulsively ugly.

Spencer ran his tongue over his teeth, but made no comment.

"It's a boat," Scarlett's mom said. "How unique."

"Yes. It's our boat. We know how much it means to them."

Scarlett's parents no doubt recognized the boat. They quickly clasped their hands together for support. They were always doing lovey-dovey things like that. It was usually gross, but today it spoke of frustration.

"Your table is right over here," Mrs. Sutcliffe added, guiding them to a table that couldn't really be defined as central. It was sort of off in the corner, near the sushi station. They were deposited there and left alone. They watched as more suited and stiffly dressed people drifted in and right over to the Sutcliffes.

"Everyone here is old," Marlene said.

A few minutes later, Mrs. Amberson appeared in a stunning floor-length gold dress and sashayed over to them. Scarlett's mom made a polite, approving remark about it. It was nice to have another member of their tiny team.

"Do you like it?" she said, smoothing her hands over her hips. "I wasn't sure if it made me look like an Oscar, but Billy said it was divine, and he doesn't offer compliments lightly. It's important to have a few truly honest friends, not just ones who tell you what you want to hear. Oh, speaking of friends . . . O'Hara, I found one of your friends downstairs being hassled by the staff about an invitation. I brought him up with me."

"One of my . . . ?"

He was walking across the room with the same expression he wore every day in Bio. He hadn't attempted to tame his wavy curls, and they floated around his head with a kind of rock-star-halo effect. Max. In a suit and poorly tied tie and sneakers. He strode right up to the Martin table.

"Here I am," he said, stating the obvious.

Scarlett couldn't blurt out "Why are you here?" in front of everyone, so she just attempted to smile. Max, however, was prepared to do the explaining.

"She invited me after detention yesterday," he added.

What? *What?* She'd done no such thing. She'd sort of made a friendly joke as she was leaving. A *sort of* friendly joke is not an *actual* invitation to an *actual* wedding party.

On the word *detention*, all the other Martins gave her a look. But since Lola had trumped them all for surprises, the matter was let go, to be discussed at some future point.

"Are you going to introduce us?" Scarlett's mom asked.

"This is Max," she said. "Max Biggs."

"That girl's brother?" Spencer asked. "The other client . . ."

"Chelsea." Mrs. Amberson stepped in. "Yes, indeed."

"Marlene," her dad said, "move over so Max can sit next to Scarlett."

Normally, Marlene would have balked at a request like that, but Max fascinated her, showing up out of nowhere with tales of Scarlett in detention. Sensing a kindred spirit, she quickly shuffled over and fixed an unblinking gaze on him. A quick round of introductions was made.

"So," her mom began, "you go to school with Scarlett?"

"I'm her lab partner," Max said, taking the napkin from his place and dropping it on his lap. "We do science together."

"What were you in detention for?" Marlene asked. "Cheating?"

"No," Max said. "Physical violence."

Mrs. Amberson laughed. Spencer gave Max a quick sideways examination, and looked uneasy with his findings.

"You're going to explain that later, right?" Scarlett's mom asked, trying to remain calm. Her nerves were already so tattered.

"I can explain it now," Max said, leaning back to make way for the appetizer, which the waiter said was some kind of salad with "ash-rolled" goat cheese. "She knocked me off my chair."

"Shut up," Marlene said.

Scarlett's dad put a hand over his forehead. It sort of looked like he was trying to wipe his eyebrows off.

"It was an accident," Scarlett said.

"Yeah," Max said, grabbing his fork and tucking in. "It was. But it was really loud, so we both got detention."

Once again, he was letting her off the hook. Her parents seemed to believe this, or at least pretended to . . . but Spencer and Marlene clearly did not. They were all capable of knocking people over. They knew their own blood.

"I understand from your mother that you're also in the performing arts?" Mrs. Amberson said. "You're a musician?"

"Nope," he said plainly, eating away.

And that was it from Max for a while. Mrs. Amberson took the cue to start talking and never stop.

There was a dinner of seven perfect, tiny courses, with lots of glass-switching and wine-pairing and utensil-updating. The food was intimidating: roasted pigeon with braised lettuce, halibut with poached quail eggs, baffling combinations of violet artichokes and lardons and foie gras and pickled shallots... every dish containing a velouté, confit, or foam of some kind or other. Two dedicated servers hovered around them, moving things whenever Scarlett least expected it. It almost seemed like their entire function was to confuse, making the diners doubt their every move and keep them on edge. The band droned on in the background, running through low-key standards and old Sinatra songs.

"This sucks," Marlene said.

"Language," her mom said, halfheartedly.

Under the table, Max's leg casually bumped Scarlett's. It looked like an accident, something he just did while he was shifting, but Scarlett felt it was intentional. Especially when it happened a second time. Had he come just to exact revenge for the stool-tipping by starting a leg war with her at Lola's party? Because she would win that. She slipped a fork under the table in her napkin and had it ready for the next time he moved. Max showed no signs of the impact in his expression, but from the way he pulled back quickly, she knew she had gotten him well. Not enough to cause damage, but enough to get the message.

Spencer picked up on the fact that something strange was going on and gave her a "What are you doing?" look. She just shook her head.

The band started to slip into a faster dancing mood by playing a weird swing version of "Cabaret."

"Actually," Mrs. Amberson was saying, "this reminds me of one night at Studio 54. Liza Minnelli had just taken off her . . ."

The Martins were a lonely little island in a sea of strangers.

They were guests at this party, surrounded by socialites, bankers, politicians . . . all important people who had things to say to one another. Across the room, in full view of everyone, Chip and Lola sat at a table of their own. Chip's friends kept coming over to talk. Lola stared over the room, landing most of her looks on her family's table, catching Scarlett's eye and trying to smile.

". . . and I said that yes, I was pretty sure we could get the horse in there. Not in the bathroom *stalls*, but certainly over by the sinks and . . ."

The waiters came over to threaten them one last time with over-size pineapple ravioli with mint au jus. The band changed gears, signaling that the time for dancing had begun. Scarlett saw one of the servers grab another by the sleeve, point at Spencer, and whisper. There was quiet talk, nodding, surreptitious glances.

"You've got fans," Max said to Spencer in a low voice, while prodding his ravioli with a fork.

Spencer looked over. The servers looked panicked, then busied themselves with stacking some plates on a tray.

"It's not just them," Max went on. "Those people behind you have been staring at you the whole time and taking pictures of the back of your head with their phones. Price of fame, huh?"

"I have to go . . . somewhere," Spencer said, getting up. People must have been talking about the fact that David Frieze had been sitting in their midst, because Scarlett saw many heads turn as Spencer passed through the room and out into the lobby.

"Sorry," Max said when he was gone.

"Not your fault," Scarlett's mom said.

"I think I know that man over there," Mrs. Amberson said, pointing to some random older guy in a suit, one of many random older guys in suits. "It's going to bother me if I don't find out from where. Excuse me."

The Sutcliffes came over as they began their post-dinner circuit of the room and asked Scarlett's parents to accompany them.

"You guys all right here for a minute?" Scarlett's dad asked.

"Sure," Scarlett said, speaking as the remaining senior Martin child.

"It totally wasn't an accident," Marlene said when they were gone. "When she hit you, right?"

"No," Max admitted, sitting back in his chair like he owned the place. "She knocked me down."

"What did you do?"

"Nothing," he said.

"He's lying," Scarlett said.

"I had cancer," Marlene said.

"What kind?"

"Leukemia."

"Still have it?" he replied.

"No," she said, playing with her mint leaves. "Were you lying about the thing about performing, too?"

"Yep," Max said.

"Do you guys want some privacy?" Scarlett asked. This was mostly to Max, and was intended as a slight, but Marlene nodded.

"Why don't you go find Spencer or something?" Marlene said.

"Fine," Scarlett said, getting up, booted from her one place of safety in this whole room. "You two have a good time."

"We will," Max said. "I have lots of things to tell your sister."

Marlene's eyes glistened. She was in love. Scarlett's night was complete.

DANSE MACABRE

She found Spencer in the far corner, at one of the small bars that had been set up all around the room. He had clearly chosen this spot for being the darkest and least noticeable location. In front of him, there was an entire wineglass full of nothing but alarmingly red maraschino cherry stems. He was working away on a small pile, dropping the stems in one by one as he ate them.

"Who the hell is that dude?" he asked as Scarlett approached. "Your *date*."

"He's Max. I didn't invite him."

The barman came over and reached for the glass of stems, but Spencer put his hand over those.

"These are mine," he said. "My trophies. Don't take them away. Bring me some more cherries, actually."

"Very good, sir."

Spencer popped another three cherries in his mouth as the barman went away to do his bidding.

"What are you doing?" Scarlett asked.

"I'm going to eat all the cherries," he said. "All of them. I think they have some big jars of them under the bar, but I know I can do it. And if I run out of cherries, I'll eat all the little paper umbrellas."

The cherries were produced. Spencer reached into his pocket, pulled out his wallet, and stuffed a twenty into the tip jar.

"This is what you're going to do all night?" Scarlett asked as he popped three more cherries into his mouth.

"What else am I supposed to do?"

Something was happening out on the dance floor. People were murmuring in anticipation. Mrs. Sutcliffe was . . . not dragging Lola . . . but definitely forcefully guiding her to the dance floor. Lola was clearly trying to stop this through smiles and politeness, but there was going to be a dance.

"Oh no," Scarlett said.

The band obligingly shifted right into a slowed-down swing band version of "You Are the Sunshine of My Life." Chip and Lola had now been deposited in the center of the floor. Lola gripped Chip, and they shuffled awkwardly to the music. It was really astonishing to see Lola in action — she *really* couldn't move to music. Scarlett saw Chip's friends snickering into their napkins.

"I thought you taught her?" Scarlett said.

"I tried."

"She's dying out there."

Spencer craned his neck to look, then shook his head.

"I can't watch this," Scarlett said. "I have to do something."

"What?"

"You could dance with Lola," Scarlett said.

"That's not *you* doing something, that's *me* doing something."

"We have to help her!"

"I showed up," Spencer said in a low voice. "But I'm not talking to

Chip, or his family, or his friends, and I'm not going to pretend like I want to be here. I'm not going to sit around making dumb-ass small talk about Sonny Lavinski. And I'm not going to dance just because I'm the only one who knows how."

"One dance doesn't mean you approve. She's miserable. Look at that stupid cake! Do you think she wanted that? Does this look like Lola's event to you? It'll take three minutes, and it will make her night."

"I didn't make her miserable," he said. "She brought this on herself."

"These people don't care about her. They're laughing at her."

Spencer didn't reply. He just looked down at his cherries, plucking them from the glass.

"Fine," she said. "Or don't."

Scarlett strode toward the dance floor, having no idea what to do. She couldn't cut in on the first dance, no matter how horrible it was. The band responded to Lola's plight by drawing the song to a close, but the torment wasn't over. Chip's friends, refusing to let this stop, got on the floor and made a circle around them. Some of them got Chip and moved him off to the side. Boonz and another girl had Lola pinned in place, and Lola was struggling. To an outsider, it would have just looked like confusion, but Scarlett saw that it was an assault — an embarrassment. Another attack on Lola's dignity.

"Those guys," Marlene said in a low voice. She was by Scarlett's side now, watching the disaster unfolding on the floor. Even in her rose-colored ballerina dress, Marlene looked like she meant business. She strode forward, and Scarlett had a very bad feeling about what she planned on doing. Marlene's mouth was silently forming words. Very, very bad words that Scarlett hadn't really been aware that Marlene knew.

Scarlett caught her in what she hoped looked like a goofy sisterly embrace, but what was really a stranglehold, with her hand over Marlene's mouth. Marlene bit it and tried to wriggle free. There was only so long that this could be contained. Meanwhile, Boonz was bouncing all around Lola, goading her into going faster. Lola looked like she might start crying.

This is when Spencer appeared on the other side of the floor. He forced his way into the group. He got hold of Lola, putting her in a dance position, one arm secured firmly behind her back, hands clasped on the other side. Lola stumbled a bit even at that, but he tightened his grip until it looked like he was almost entirely holding her up. He whispered what must have been some instructions into her ear. She rearranged herself a bit.

And then, they were dancing.

In reality, Scarlett knew that Spencer had her in such a firm grip that he was either dragging or carrying her, but the effect was the same. Lola had relaxed, and she looked radiant. With his lead, she moved gracefully across the floor. Everyone at the party began to notice. An approving crowd had gathered around the edge of the floor to watch the bride and her brother dance.

"I hope he doesn't drop her," Marlene said once Scarlett had removed her hand.

As the song drew to a close and a new, faster one started up, Spencer swung around and released Lola in their direction, spinning her out the length of his arm. Scarlett and Marlene caught her, and Lola burst out in happy laughter, triggering some good-natured applause from the room. The photographer dropped in front of them and caught a picture of the sisterly bliss.

Spencer loosened his tie a little and removed his jacket, throwing it against the bandstand.

"What's he doing?" Lola asked, still laughing and out of breath.

"You wanted him to dance," Scarlett said. "I think he's dancing."

He was. Spencer cued the crowd on the sides of the floor to start clapping in time with the beat, and they were happy to oblige. The band, too, was happy to provide some support. The drummer hit the bass to back up the claps. Spencer tapped his foot for a few seconds, following the beat, looking around the room to calculate all of those impossible little elements in that arithmetic that only he could do — working out the slipperiness of the floor, the tempo of the music. Then he took over the center of the floor. He began with a series of Fred Astaire–type flourishes. Everyone moved to give him even more room. It was a welcome jolt of entertainment in an otherwise staid evening. The people who clearly liked the swing music and knew the dances well nodded their heads and swayed along, ready to join in. As the song reached its peak and the trumpet player tilted his head back for his big solo, Spencer launched into a series of spins, which accelerated rapidly.

Too rapidly. It looked like he was losing control.

It was in that moment that Scarlett knew exactly what he was doing. There was no time to voice any kind of reaction, only to move. Instinctively, she stepped in front of Lola and pressed her back toward the wall. Spencer pulled his oldest move: a stagger, a trip, a brief flight through the air, his trajectory clear. Three towering feet and ten thousand dollars of cake exploded into the atmosphere. Clouds of thick, buttery frosting rose and fell, and nothing was clear for a moment. There were assorted cries and gasps and one "Dear God."

The band fumbled and lost the song. Then there was silence, except for one long, unbroken screech from Boonz.

The only part of Spencer that was clearly visible at this point was the pin-striped legs. He didn't move for a solid ten or fifteen seconds, then stirred and pushed himself out of the remains. His entire torso was imprinted with a thick layer of icing and sponge cake, and his face was only partially visible under the mess. He swung his legs over and sat upright, wiping his eyes clean. Then he calmly adjusted his shirtsleeves, as if nothing was out of the ordinary, and stood, sliding a little on the masses of cream on the floor. He looked around in bafflement, as if looking for the imaginary passing cat that must have tripped him up.

"I seem to have slipped," he said politely.

They were outside now, Scarlett and Spencer, out in the little maze of shrubbery. The corner they had secured themselves in was a cozy green one with a bench and an unobstructed view of the skyscape. There was a heavy harvest moon above, and the city surrounded them in light. They looked down on the tops of tall buildings, down at cars and people, and they were at eye level with other skyscrapers. It was the kind of vantage point designed to make you feel like a minor deity, ruling over the city and all who inhabited it.

This corner of the terrace was probably designed as a lovers' nook, a place to propose, or a quiet site for high-powered business deals. Scarlett and Spencer were using it as a temporary hideout, concealing themselves behind a wall of potted trees. There was an awful lot of quiet behind them — just the muffled sounds of the swing band trying to grind back to life and the clatter of moving tables and hasty cleaning efforts. Spencer was scraping huge handfuls of cream from his body and wiping it into the topiary. After a few minutes of effort, he was starting to become recognizable.

"Do you need any help," Scarlett finally thought to ask, "or are you just going to keep rubbing frosting into that plant?"

"I'm probably going to stick with the plant."

"Nature's toothbrush," Scarlett said. "Or something like that. Do you know that cake cost ten thousand dollars?"

"Ten thousand? For a cake? Shaped like a boat?"

He scraped a bit more frosting from his shoulder and put it into the trouser pocket.

"Better save that," he said, patting the pocket. "That's got to be fifty bucks right there."

There was a noise behind them, coming from the direction of the potted trees. Max emerged from between two of them, seemingly from nowhere.

"You should leave," he said to Spencer. "I found you a door."

Scarlett went over and looked past him. Sure enough, behind the wall of topiary, there was an industrial door, a staff entrance and exit.

"You take this down two floors," Max said, "and then there's a service elevator that goes right down to the garage. There's a street exit down there. Everyone will think you vanished, like magic, or that you jumped off the building."

"This is a good plan," Spencer said.

"Yeah, you can't go back in there. Some people are really freaking out."

"You coming?" Spencer asked Scarlett.

"I think maybe I should stay," she said.

"Okay. Meet you at home."

"How are you going to get home looking like that?" she asked.

"Haven't figured that out yet."

Spencer nodded his thanks to Max, and vanished through the magic door.

"Well," Max said, "your family is fun."

Scarlett had nothing to say except, "I want to hide."

"So hide. There's space back here."

Scarlett poked her head through the trees. There was just enough space between them and the wall to stand up. Sure, it was a little weird to go to your sister's wedding party and hide behind a plant, but this night wasn't exactly on course. She forced herself through. Max pushed in as well, and they stood there, in their little wedge of space, saying nothing.

"Why did you let me off the hook?" she finally asked. "In Bio."

"What was I supposed to do if they kicked you out? You're my only friend, remember? Unless you're going to say you're *not* my friend. Then I'll be all alone in the world. Then I'll have to go to therapy."

"So you're not going to tell me," Scarlett said.

Max slid down the wall a bit.

"I thought you were like the others," he said. "One of those people who let your parents or whoever push you around and make you entertain. Your brother's in that show. You work for an agent. I thought you were one of them. I hate those people. But you're not. You're different. You're like me. You're difficult. And your family is a total bunch of freaks."

Scarlett was about to say something back to that last remark, but then realized it was best just to let it go.

"You think we're alike?" Scarlett asked.

"Yeah. That must make you sick."

"It's okay."

She felt all right here with Max. Perhaps for the first time in a week, or really, a long time, things were okay here in behind-the-trees land. He was right. They were alike, and at times, he was the only voice of reason around. Abrasive, sure. But he told the truth.

Maybe it was the adrenaline, or the view, or the stars, or the thousand shiny lights, or maybe when you're hiding behind plants with someone at a formal event, this is just how things go. . . .

It started with Max putting an arm over her shoulder, and her not shoving it off. Then they inched closer and closer, Scarlett ignoring the sounds of people coming out on the patio and calling for her and Max, obviously puzzled by their disappearance. The pressures of those outside voices pushed them together, until she was right up against his chest. It took minutes and minutes of slow forward movement, growing more and more comfortable with each other's closeness.

"Max?" she said.

"Yeah?" he asked calmly, as if nothing at all strange was happening.

She put her hands on either side of his face and guided his mouth to hers.

ACT V

*A **SPIES OF NEW YORK** EXCLUSIVE!*

WE LOVE A DEBUTARD WEDDING . . . as much as anyone else. Probably more than most. We love the spectacle of New York's richest and dumbest making the tie that binds. Like all the royal families of the world, our Society Friends always fail to notice that constant inbreeding makes Mother Nature cross, and this amuses us. Also, they have open bars full of top-shelf booze.

EVERY ONCE IN A WHILE . . . we get a truly exceptional account of one of these anti-Darwinian extravaganzas. Our in-boxes were exploding with reports of such an occasion. It seems that on Saturday night, Charles "Chip" Sutcliffe III, age 18, celebrated his marriage to a certain Lola Martin, age 18.

We would have enjoyed this story just as it was, honestly. Some early morning Procrastination Googling turned up the fact that "Chip" Sutcliffe is ranked number 98 on the "New York's Top 100 High School Scenesters" list on Gothamfrat.com. This list provided us with much joy! The little scamps had gone and ranked themselves! It's like those videos of cats eating with utensils — it's adorable when they try to act like people, even as they do it all wrong.

But that was hardly the end of this story . . . because the bride happens to be the younger sister of doughnut-magnet Spencer Martin, aka David Frieze, killer of our dearly departed Sonny Lavinski. Yes! He was there! And he didn't disappoint!

For reasons known only to himself, Martin took to the dance floor and performed an astonishing solo number, which concluded with his taking flight and doing a full body slam on his sister's massive wedding cake.

We would not have believed this story had it not been accompanied by many, many photos . . . photos we stared at for hours last night. Had the stress of murdering Saint Sonny finally broken him, we wondered? Had he grown tired of having other people throw food at him and simply decided to do it himself?

OUR SPECULATIONS WERE INTERRUPTED . . . by even more news of Martin. Our contact on the set of Crime and Punishment called to tell us that his name has mysteriously vanished from the call sheet and no one in charge is talking. What could possibly be going on?

We beg you to send in your tips. In the meantime, please enjoy our favorite photo of the wedding celebration. We have a selection of prizes for the best captions.

DAWN OF THE DESPERATE

Sunday was a murky day. A moody day. The sky was the color of the rinse water that Scarlett used to produce when playing with her watercolor paints when she was little, each dip of the brush leaving a milky touch of pigment until it was a thin, gray mess. Her dress from the night before lay deflated on Lola's bed. Her own bed was littered with all things Biology — a desperate scramble of notes on papers and cards, notes on her computer, her textbook, a mess of handouts. Much of this information was in her head, but in pieces — pieces that didn't connect together to make a picture.

And it was almost evening.

She could call Dakota. Dakota was at home studying as well, and Dakota knew what she was doing and had two Biology professors in her house. As Scarlett reached for the phone, she realized that if Dakota picked up, she was going to have to talk about last night. She would have to explain what she had done.

Aside from the possibility of her friends calling, which would obviously result in an immediate confession . . . there were other horrors. Mrs. Amberson would probably try to call her today about something. That was extremely likely. Or what if Chelsea chose today to call and tell her all about her wonderful new relationship with her good friend Eric? Or Eric. What if he tried to call again and get it all off his chest?

Or Max. What if Max called? That seemed least likely, but held the most terror. What if he wanted to discuss what went on out there on the terrace?

What *did* happen out there on the terrace?

Well, what happened was that she made out with Max behind a wall of topiary for about a half hour, that's what happened. And the only reason they stopped is that they were interrupted by a girl with a tray, who was startled by them and screamed.

The more she thought about it, the more she realized that the phone was her enemy.

There was only one thing she could think to do. She picked up her phone and walked it down the hall to her parents' room. On the wall just inside the door, there was a little chute that dropped five floors down to an opening in the basement ceiling. This is where they tossed sheets and towels; they fell into a wheeled bin that was usually positioned just under the chute. She opened the chute and tossed the phone inside, for a six-floor free fall. If someone had actually decided to wheel the bin over to the washing machine and do the wash, the phone was history. She stuck her head into the dank and stale void, but there was no sound, nothing to indicate that her phone had fragmented into a hundred pieces. It was probably alive down there somewhere. She hadn't quite figured out what she would have done if it had broken.

Probably ask Lola to buy her a new one. Maybe that's how things were done now.

As she walked back to her room, Spencer stepped out of the elevator. He also looked a bit lost.

"You didn't take any deliveries, did you?" he asked.

"Deliveries?"

"My script. It's not here yet. I called, and they keep saying it's on its way. They won't tell me what my call times are for this week."

"No," Scarlett said. "Sorry."

He nodded absently.

"I just took my suit over to get it cleaned. Mrs. Foo got really excited when she saw it. She loves a challenge. What are you doing? You look spooked."

"Studying," she said. "I have a Biology exam tomorrow."

He rubbed his unshaven chin, which was just starting to develop a shadow, and then poked a finger into his ear.

"Frosting got in there," he said. "I can't hear right."

On that, he drifted off to his room, and she went to hers and sat on the bed again. She closed her eyes, just to see what appeared in her mind — where her brain wanted to go.

It wanted to go to Max. It wanted to replay the whole experience over and over again.

She opened her eyes with a jolt and grabbed her textbook as protection. She had to learn. There was no more time, no more room in her mind for anyone.

Dakota was waiting for her on the front steps of the school the next morning.

"Can you just do one thing for me?" she asked. "Can you just explain . . . this?"

She held up her phone, revealing a large photo of a cake-covered Spencer.

"Oh yeah. Spencer, um . . ." Scarlett rubbed her eyes hard. ". . . he, um, the cake. At Lola's party. Sorry, I didn't . . ."

"Did you sleep?"

"Not really."

"I figured this might happen. Look what I have for you."

Dakota produced a large cup of coffee and pressed it into Scarlett's hand. This was the kind of friend Dakota was. Always one step ahead. Always with the provisions.

Scarlett took the coffee and sipped it, letting it burn her mouth. The morning was overly bright. She had a floaty feeling for a moment, and as she drifted back into her body, something seemed off.

"Oh my God," she said. "I'm not sure if I'm wearing underwear. I think I am. But I have no memory of putting it on. Dakota . . . *what if I forgot to put on underwear?*"

"Can't you feel it?"

Scarlett couldn't. She tried to get some sensation, but all was numbness. She shook her head.

"Reach around in the back and see if it's there," Dakota said.

Scarlett carefully reached around and felt just underneath the waist of her skirt, until her fingers hit a ridge of elastic.

"Why can't I feel my waist?" she asked.

"Everything will be fine." Dakota put her arm over Scarlett's shoulders. "Drink your coffee. I'll quiz you. We'll get through it."

"I made out with Max," Scarlett admitted.

Dakota slipped her hair out of the crooked ponytail it was in and played with the band, stretching it between her fingers for a few moments.

"In detention?" she finally asked.

"At Lola's party."

"At the party?"

"He just kind of showed up," Scarlett explained.

"And you made out."

"That about sums it up," Scarlett said.

Dakota finger-flexed a bit more.

"Have I always been like this?" Scarlett asked.

"You've always been entertaining, if that's what you mean."

"Of course," Scarlett said, picking up her notes and staring at the words swimming on the page. "That's exactly what I meant. And maybe . . . maybe he just won't show."

Max showed.

He had on a black sweater and jeans — slightly more neat and tidy than usual. He didn't say a word. In fact, he didn't even *look* at her. He just paged through his notes, and then when they got the word to clear their spaces for the test, he just put them away and looked at the model embryo in the corner.

She found herself burning with the need to speak to him, but just then, eight pages of exam were dropped in front of her, along with a look of "I don't know what the hell is wrong with you, but get it together" from Ms. Fitzweld.

Scarlett pulled the exam closer and opened it to find a lot of familiar-looking gibberish. In the first rush of panic, everything appeared broken. After flipping uselessly through the pages, she finally found something on page three that she felt like she could answer. The fetal pig diagram on page four *should* have been easy, but all the different pieces kept getting mixed up in her mind. Kidneys? Pancreas? Aorta?

She had to look through it three times to figure out where to begin, her brain working in starts and fits. She had just decided to answer the short fill-in-the-blanks on page five when she became aware of the fact that Max was moving, getting steadily closer, in millimeters. Her first instinct was to throw her arm around her test protectively, even though there was nothing written there.

Then she realized, he wasn't trying to copy. Max was offering her his test to cheat from. He was filling everything in with certainty.

Her head felt light and funny, and there was a pulse beating over her left eye.

Scarlett kept her eyes averted for the rest of period. As the time went on, more things came back into her head. At the thirty-five-minute mark, information came flooding back, and she tried to go back and fill in as much as she could. But it was too late. The bell rang.

"Bring them up," Ms. Fitzweld said.

Max said nothing as he slipped off his stool, and he didn't turn around when he walked out of the room. Apparently, whatever had happened was something he was prepared to sweep aside as brusquely as he did everything else — and maybe in the bargain, he would leave her alone.

"What the hell?" Dakota said, sliding up to her station. "What the hell was that? On page six?"

"I have no idea," Scarlett said. The test had been over for thirty seconds, and already the experience was fading.

"Did he bother you?" Dakota asked, indicating Max's empty seat.

"Nope. He acted like it didn't even happen."

"Thank God."

This bothered her, this indifference of his. How could he just walk away from her, ignore her, and act like they hadn't kissed? And, though she could never, ever admit this to Dakota, those kisses had been very good. So at the very least he owed her some sarcasm and contempt. Was that too much to ask? Would it kill him to display a *little* snide and inappropriate behavior?

"Yeah," Scarlett said, forcing a smile. "Imagine if I started dating someone you hated more than Eric."

"Don't make jokes like that," Dakota said. "The way things have been with you? Anything could happen. And I would hate to kill you. You're so pretty."

When Scarlett stumbled home, she found Lola in the Orchid Suite, going through her dresser. There was a pile of objects on Scarlett's bed — two sweaters, some pajamas, a scarf, a winter hat, a number of things from the Drawer of Mysteries that Lola had acquired during her stints working at the spa and the makeup counter.

There was no point in asking what this stuff was. She already knew. Lola was casting off her old things. Her clothes. Everything that was broken, shantylike, about the hotel. There would be no more hoarding of free samples of moisturizer or half-empty testers of fancy lotions.

"Hey!" Lola said brightly. "I'm just doing a little sorting out. How was your day?"

Scarlett decided not to answer that question. She sat down and looked at the neat little piles of Lola stuff.

"Are you . . ." Scarlett had no idea how to phrase this question. "Coming back? To sleep, or . . . Where do you *live* now?"

"Well," Lola said, refolding a sweater. "Chip went back to Boston today. I'll spend maybe four days a week up in the apartment in Boston, and the other three I'll be down here. Chip is going to transfer schools next semester. So I have until December to find an apartment for us. The Sutcliffes are . . . getting us one. Not a big one."

Even a small apartment in Manhattan ran to a million or two — at least any apartment that the Sutcliffes would consider buying. There were many things Scarlett could say about this, but she decided not to.

"I want you to know," Lola said. "I respect that this is *your* room now. I can't just barge in whenever I want. I'll always let you know, or stay in another room."

"No," Scarlett said quickly. "This is your room, too. I mean, when you're just staying here. I'm not going to move your stuff."

Lola looked over at her shyly and bit her lower lip. She shook out the sweater she had just refolded and did it yet again.

"I have to go over to the Sutcliffes'. We have some presents to open. Sounds like a lot of presents, actually."

"So what does that look like, when the Sutcliffes' friends give you presents?" Scarlett asked. "Is it kind of like what they find when they open up a pyramid? Do you go blind from all the gold?"

"It's a little like that. But I'm staying here for dinner. I think we're having pizza. Want to go down and ask Spencer what he wants on his? I think I just heard him come in."

Scarlett dutifully stood and went down to Spencer's room. He was standing by his bureau in a very strange position, leaning down on it, grasping his head in both hands as he intently read a script.

"So they finally sent it?" Scarlett asked.

Spencer said nothing.

"I'm supposed to ask you what you want on your pizza."

Spencer said nothing.

"Is there still frosting in your ear?"

He finally looked over at her, but again, did not speak. Instead, he held out the script, open to the last page. Scarlett took it. There was only one bit of dialogue on it. It read:

```
BENZO
That was Frieze's lawyer on the phone.
They just found him on the floor, beaten.
He's dead. The son of a bitch is dead. The
son of a bitch is dead.
```

MORE SURPRISES

Maybe it was the utter fear of what was awaiting her in Biology, but Scarlett once again found herself being more smart than normal in her other classes the next day. She was amazed to find that her interpretation of "Ode on a Grecian Urn" was not only in line with reality but actually insightful, especially considering that she had read it while walking to school. But eighth period loomed — the great end of the long day. Once again, there would be Max to face, and a test to get. The test came first. From the look on Ms. Fitzweld's face, Scarlett knew things were not good.

"This isn't really you," she said. "If you improve on the next one, I'll look into weighting it a little more heavily. I don't know what's been going on here with you and Biggs, but if you feel it's affecting your work . . ."

"It's okay," Scarlett said.

She opened her exam automatically. Seventy-eight percent. She'd never gotten a grade like that in her life. It was like free fall, a terrifying liberation. She shut the exam and the grade went away for a while. Max hadn't gotten to class yet, but his exam was sitting there. Scarlett pulled it closer with her pen and just lifted back the corner. He had a 94 percent. She flicked it away as he came in.

Once again, Max gave her the silent treatment. He picked up his exam as he sat down and shoved it in his bag without looking at the grade. For forty-five minutes, they sat beside each other, Max still for once, not rocking on his seat or playing with the electrical outlet. And when the bell rang, he slipped off again. This time, Scarlett took off after him. He headed for the practice room. She let herself in after him. It only occurred to her once she was in there that she had no idea what she was going to say to him, but he spoke first, eliminating the problem.

"I figured you wouldn't want your evil friend to see you with me," he said, putting down his things and settling himself at the piano. "I'm kind of an embarrassment."

"Could you maybe not call her my evil friend?" Scarlett asked. "Her name is Dakota."

"Whatever. Want to know something?"

"I . . ." Did she? Did she really? What if that something was a very awkward something? She should never have followed him.

"I have perfect pitch," he said.

That wasn't what she had been expecting.

"What?"

"Perfect pitch," he repeated. "Chelsea doesn't. Drives her nuts. My music teacher at school figured this out when I was little. She told my mom. My mom was thrilled that she had a prodigy on her hands, so she stuck me in music school. By the time I was eight, I took ten extra hours of music class a week, plus practice, on top of school. And then it just got worse. I used to like playing music before that . . . I used to love it. That school made me hate it. I had to go there every single day. People were always watching me play and telling me what to do and making me practice. I don't like people teaching me how to play. I know how to play."

"So did you tell her you didn't want to go anymore?" she asked.

"You've met my mom," he said. "You think that would matter? She knew I hated it, but she *told* everyone it was what I wanted. She told people I begged to go. She did to me what she did to Chelsea. It just didn't work with me. I didn't want to go to class anymore, so when my mom dropped me off at the school, I never went to my lesson. I sat in the bathroom and played video games. So then she took away my handheld. Then I just went and sat in the bathroom and did nothing. *Then* she started walking me to the class door and sitting outside. So then I'd go to the lesson and just sit there and refuse to play. This went on for maybe two or three weeks, and they said I had to stop coming. I won. But I don't play in front of her anymore, ever. That's my big secret. Now you know everything."

"I'm sorry," Scarlett said.

"Whatever. I don't care."

And he truly didn't appear to care. He knocked his hair out of his eyes and played a few lightning-quick scales.

"What about Chelsea?" Scarlett asked. "How did she get into this if you were the one who was good at music?"

"My mom must have figured that if she had one prodigy in the family, she might have another. She didn't. She stuck her in every single class she could think of to see what worked — singing, dancing, acting. You can learn to do anything if someone rides your ass enough."

"That actually makes me feel kind of bad," Scarlett said.

"Don't. I got out of it. Chelsea could have, too. But that would require a spine, and she doesn't have one."

"What about your dad?"

Max shrugged and tapped the keys noiselessly.

"He's kind of oblivious. My mom pushed her along, dragged her to the city all the time to go to auditions, and then she got her first commercial. After that, my mom quit her job and started running Chelsea's career full-time. It took her a few years, but she finally got her on Broadway. And that's . . ." He played a quick little trill. ". . . how we got here."

"But now that Chelsea doesn't have a show, are you going back?"

Max smirked at this.

"My mom's not going to give up," he said. "She'll ride that pony until it dies. She's going to make your boss nuts and demand that Chelsea go on auditions every fifteen minutes. You aren't getting rid of me."

This was the first hint Scarlett got that they might actually be talking about what happened the other night . . . with the kissing. *She* wasn't going to ask about it first. But Max just started to play, and she let herself out quietly.

When Scarlett got home, she remembered that she'd never rescued her phone from the basement. She hadn't missed it. Still, since she was passing the basement, it seemed wise to go and see if it was in one piece. What she found instead was Spencer at the foot of the steps, sprawled out in a way that suggested a broken neck. Many people would have screamed or fainted or called 911, but Scarlett merely steadied herself against the door.

"Please tell me you're faking," she said.

Spencer got to his feet and dusted himself off. He sat glumly on the washing machine and beat his heels lightly into the metal door.

"Just trying to work out a fall I used to do down here," he said. "Remember the summer, I think it was the year before Marlene got sick? And I had that old mattress down here? And I would just throw myself at it all day long. That's when I figured out how to fall down a whole flight of steps."

Scarlett remembered it well. That was the last time there were no problems, at least not that she knew about. She and Spencer spent hours down here. He had just gotten into Performing Arts and wanted to have a bag of tricks to show when he started, and she was ten and had nothing on her agenda except reading Harry Potter and eating Popsicles. She liked helping him out and suggesting things. It was fun telling someone to run into the wall a certain way and have them do it for you.

"Is that what you just did?" Scarlett asked, wincing. "With no mattress?"

"Yeah," he said, laughing strangely. "It was. I was an idiot to try it. I'm lucky I didn't kill myself."

"Are you okay?" Scarlett asked. "You know you'll get another job."

"I'm waiting for your boss to 'investigate the situation.' I'm not having my panic attack until she tells me I'm definitely fired."

Scarlett went over to the laundry bin. It was there, under the chute. She had to dig around for a moment to find her phone, but it was there, under a small pile of sheets. It had run out of charge, but it was intact.

"There's something going on upstairs," he said. "Everyone seems really excited about something."

He stared up at the ceiling, as if it could tell him what madness was going on in the floor above.

"Excited about what?"

"Something about Marlene. I got the idea they were waiting for you to get home."

"Oh good," Scarlett said. "That sounds promising."

"We might as well find out what it was."

There was indeed some kind of commotion. Scarlett's mom was on her phone in the bedroom. Her dad and Marlene were sealed away in the Jazz Suite. Lola was buzzing around the Orchard Suite.

"What's going on?" Scarlett asked.

"We have to wait," Lola said, but her voice crackled with excitement.

"Do not do this to us," Spencer said, leaning in the doorway. "We hate surprises now."

Lola gestured to him to come inside, then made sure the door was shut solidly.

"Marlene has been made Powerkid of the Year!" she said.

"The what?" Spencer asked.

"It means that she's going to be the official spokes . . . kid all next year, starting in January! She'll be in all the ads, she'll be meeting donors. . . ."

"You mean like the poster child?" Spencer asked.

"Exactly! That's exactly what it is!"

Spencer looked over at Scarlett warily. Scarlett closed her eyes.

"You two don't look excited," Lola said disapprovingly. "She had to do a lot to earn this. Hundreds of kids applied for this."

"I *knew* it," Scarlett said. "Marlene's been *doing* something. The politeness. The Princess Di books. She's been *practicing* being nice. For this."

"Wait a minute," Spencer said. "This big contest . . . Marlene just happens to win it a few days after your wedding? Are we really just that lucky? Pinch me!"

Lola started playing with the few remaining items on her dresser.

"The people at the party," Scarlett said. "A lot of them are big into charities. They run stuff. Did you do this?"

"I didn't do it," Lola said, her voice just a whisper. "It just happened. Do *not* say anything, okay?"

"How did it just happen?" Spencer asked.

"Chip's parents know the Powerkid people. It doesn't really matter. It's pretty much random anyway."

"That's not what you just said," Scarlett pointed out.

"This is a huge deal for Marlene! Do you want to spoil it for her?"

"Are you asking me that seriously?" Scarlett replied.

But Spencer was sighing and rubbing his forehead.

"Fine," he said. "We don't tell her that you got Chip to magically make her queen of the Powerkids."

Marlene herself came in a few minutes later. She wasn't precisely gloating . . . but the calm smile on her face didn't make Scarlett feel any more reassured about this news.

"I told them," Lola said guiltily. "I couldn't help it."

"It's okay," Marlene replied, her voice unnaturally formal and precise. "I don't start for a while. But I really want to get involved with reading programs. You know, encourage people to read. There's a lot I'll be doing. . . ."

She went on for a few minutes about her new post and duties. Sure enough, it all had the stamp of Lady Di on it. Visiting hospitals.

Having her face on the Powerkids holiday sticker and collection jars. Meeting celebrities. Being the adorable face of cancer.

"I have to go call all my friends," Marlene said, holding up her phone and parading out of the room.

"Remember," Spencer said to Lola, "a few months from now, remember that you did this, okay?"

"Oh, Spencer . . ."

"You won't have to live here," Scarlett said. She hadn't meant it to come out that coldly, but it was a fact. As usual, Lola tried to laugh it off, but it didn't come out quite right.

THE OFFENSIVE

It was five A.M., and Scarlett's phone was ringing. She sat bolt upright, her hand slapping around her pillows, her nightstand, her blankets, searching desperately for the phone before it woke up Lola. . . .

But Lola wasn't there, of course. It was just Scarlett, alone in the pearly half dark, an empty bed next to her. She found the phone on the floor next to her bed and slapped it up to her ear with too much force, causing further chaos in the head/skull region.

"O'Hara," Mrs. Amberson said. "Thank goodness. I need a little favor."

It took Scarlett a moment to process that statement.

"Are you there?" Mrs. Amberson asked.

"You . . . what? What time . . ."

"I need you to go over to my apartment . . ."

"No," Scarlett moaned.

"I need you to go to those Foo dog bookends I have on the bookcase near the window. They're the Chinese ones that look like dogs with lion heads, and they're propping up my section on Futurist and Expressionist theater. Go to the Foo dog closest to the window and . . ."

"No."

". . . pull its head off," Mrs. Amberson went on, not missing a beat. "It comes off, don't worry. I'm not asking you to break marble with your brute strength. But you have to pull hard. Inside, you'll find a roll of cash. Take it, get in a cab, and go to the courthouse downtown. It's the one from *Crime and Punishment*, the one where your brother shot Sonny."

As soon as she heard the word *courthouse*, Scarlett felt herself waking up. She sat up halfway, balancing her elbow on her pillow.

"Go in and speak to the *lovely* desk clerk. Just tell her you're there for me. She will be able to provide instructions. Oh, and Murray will need a walk and some food. I know it's a school day, but hopefully this won't take more than an hour or so. Have to go! I know I can count on you, O'Hara. Have to dash! I've made a wonderful new friend who needs to talk to me!"

Click.

Scarlett blinked and grabbed a handful of purple curtain, pulling it aside to look at the anemic overcast sky that had spilled over the still-sleepy city.

She got out of bed, even though this seemed like a bad move.

The midnight-to-morning doorman at Mrs. Amberson's building was more apathetic than Murray. He waved Scarlett right up without even looking away from his newspaper. He was the guy who greeted cleaners and workmen and staff in general . . . people who had to wake early and get things done. He could probably sense that Scarlett was an employee.

Murray the dog was curled up on the big white sofa when she entered the apartment, enjoying the quiet and the privacy. Her intrusion caused him such a shock that he rose vertically into the air. He didn't look reassured when Scarlett took the heavy Foo dog bookend from the shelf, squeezed it between her legs to get a grip on it, and pulled its head off. He tried to run away, but slipped into the space between two of the fat cushions, and the more he struggled, the more he sank.

Scarlett pried out the tight roll of cash wedged inside the bookend. Once she got the bills free, she gave them a quick count, just so she would know what she was carrying. It was seven thousand, one hundred dollars in all, mostly in hundreds. This was Mrs. Amberson's little emergency fund.

A half hour later, Scarlett's cab pulled up to the long set of steps that Spencer had thrown himself down, where he had pulled the gun. She walked over the spot where Sonny had fallen and up the steps, to where Mrs. Amberson was sitting. Her spiky hair was slightly flattened, and her black evening dress was a sharp contrast against the white of the steps and the building. She was a blot on the face of justice. She had obtained a cigarette from somewhere and was puffing away on it like she was afraid someone would snatch it from her grasp.

"I know, I know," she said as Scarlett approached. "I quit. I just needed the one."

She took one final drag of the cigarette, looked at it in disgust, and tossed it away.

"What happened?" Scarlett asked.

"Oh, the judge was quite reasonable. They released me on my own recognizance. Sorry to make you come down here for nothing."

"No . . . what *happened*? Why were you in jail?"

"There was a bit of a public altercation," she said.

"Altercation?"

"I suppose you heard what happened to your brother's character?"

"Oh," Scarlett said. "Oh . . . Oh no."

"I requested a little sit-down to discuss what was going on. So one of the producers and I had cocktails last night. Apparently, they liked him quite a bit, as an actor and as a character. But *apparently* the audience wants justice. Plus, there were issues with the writers, with scripts that were already completed . . . the usual back office nonsense . . . and the only solution they could come up with to move the entire story forward was to beat him to death."

"So," Scarlett said, desperately trying to piece this all together in the thin early morning air, "you met with the producer and . . .'"

"Well, I threw a drink at him, which was not considered appropriate behavior in the establishment we were in. And I may have slapped him just a tiny bit. Hence, the law. It's all part of the strategy, O'Hara. I wanted them to know that you do not play with the AAA. What a good slogan that is! Oh, I'm exhausted. But the night wasn't so bad. It's not the first night I've ever spent in a holding cell. Granted, the last time was after a night out sometime in the late seventies and I was arrested with seven other people who were dressed primarily in gold body paint. Half of them just thought we were in a different club called Jail. They kept dancing against the bars and trying to buy drinks from the cops. Anyway . . . you need to get to school."

Mrs. Amberson got up with the first trace of stiffness Scarlett had ever seen her exhibit. When she got into the cab, she luxuriated against the padded vinyl seat for a moment, closing her eyes in bliss and weariness.

"The battle is not over," Mrs. Amberson said, stifling a yawn. "It's not going to be easy, but it's not over."

"But Spencer is famous now," Scarlett said. "Can't he be on something else?"

"His flash of fame is a bit of a problem, O'Hara. It's going to be a bit hard to get him employed after this, at least for the short term. Everybody saw David Frieze. That's who Spencer is now. The most hated man in New York. Even the cake incident . . . that was covered all over the place. I'm not exactly going to be able to get him cast on *Sesame Street*."

"I thought there was no such thing as bad publicity," Scarlett said.

Mrs. Amberson turned and managed a smile.

"True," she said. "There is always a way. I try to embrace philosophy."

"Which philosophy?"

"As many as possible."

She fell into a light sleep, which was easily broken when the cab pulled up to Frances Perkins.

"My goodness, O'Hara," she said, rubbing her eyes. "This is your school? It looks like the setting of an Italian romance." She opened the window and leaned out to get a look at the cone-shaped tops of the two rounded towers that framed Frances Perkins.

"I am left breathless by the symbolism in this construction," she added.

Scarlett was at lunch before she noticed the seven thousand, one hundred dollar–size lump in her pocket. She accidentally pulled it out while she was in line for her taco. (Taco Fridays had gone down so well that Taco Tuesdays had also been instituted. Everyone loves a taco.) A freshman caught sight of it as she struggled to stuff it back in. She remained paranoid about it all day — too scared to keep it on her person, too scared to put it in her locker. In her mind, an unnamed god smote her boss with thunderbolts. Meanwhile, her phone buzzed all day with messages from said boss to come right over after school.

At least one part of this day was a little better than the one before — since they had spoken, Max was acting more like his normal self, doing his best to annoy Scarlett all period long in Biology. Moreover, he made a huge effort to make sure Dakota saw him do this. Once again, he positioned himself in the music room near her locker. Scarlett deliberated going in, and then impulsively opened the door.

"I have to go see my boss," she said. "She's been calling me all day. I just wanted to say bye."

"You say that like I care where you go," he replied.

"Later, freak."

"Whatever."

As Scarlett turned to go, she caught his reflection in the glass of the door, and he was smiling. So was she.

Spencer skidded alongside Scarlett on his bike as she approached Mrs. Amberson's building. The bike was slightly less wobbly than before, but not much.

"She call you, too?" he asked.

"Yeah," Scarlett said. "She must have news. Your bike seems a little better."

"Yeah, it is a little. I sat working on it all day. I had nothing else to do."

He got off and pulled out the lock to attach the bike to some ornamental gating outside the building. It still wasn't quite stable enough to even lean correctly, and immediately started to fall. Spencer caught it before it slipped.

"I would have missed this bike if it had gone," he said. "I have to admit it. It stands for something. I'm not sure what. I'm not even sure if it's good. But that doesn't matter. I *believe* in this bike."

"Hey!"

This was from Murray, who had stepped outside to survey his doorway domain.

"Yeah?" Spencer said.

"You can't lock that bike there!"

"Why not?" he asked.

"You can't lock that bike to my building!"

"I'm visiting someone in the building."

"You can't lock that bike there!"

"Just don't," Scarlett said quietly. "He won't stop."

Spencer sighed and hoisted the bike up, carrying it at shoulder height. It looked particularly pathetic being carried like that, its wheel hanging crookedly. Murray tried to block their way inside.

"You can't bring that bike into my building!"

"It belongs to 19D," Scarlett lied. "The *bike* is coming *in*. It's between nine and six, remember?"

Murray was furious to have his own rules used against him, but moved aside. He made them use the service elevator to go up.

"You're forceful," Spencer said. "I'm going to have you do all my talking for me from now on."

"I had a long day," Scarlett said.

Mrs. Amberson met them at the door. Dog Murray almost had a heart attack on seeing the strange man with the terrible machine on his shoulder.

"Come in," she said. "Sit down. I need to speak to you both."

This sober greeting alarmed Scarlett. She didn't think she was going to like the news she was about to hear. Scarlett settled on the sofa, but Spencer chose to keep standing and pace the room.

"I had a conversation with the producer of *Crime and Punishment* this afternoon," she said.

"The guy you got arrested for throwing a drink at is talking to you?" Scarlett asked, when she was done.

"Threw . . . what?" Spencer asked.

"I told you, O'Hara. Always do a little research. I spent a little time with some of the junior staff members of *Crime and Punishment*. As it turns out, the producer is well-known to have an affection for, shall we say, *commanding* women? Judging from what I heard, talking to him would produce no effect, but a direct strike would make a favorable impression. He thinks it's a sign of character."

"He *liked* that you threw a drink at him? You did that on purpose?"

"People are quirky, O'Hara. People in the entertainment business especially so."

Mrs. Amberson strolled over to the massive picture window and looked out on the view of the city. Scarlett was slouched low on the white sofa. She watched a large plane glide by in the distance through the flawless blue sky. From her perspective, it looked like it flew right through Mrs. Amberson's head, entering near the jaw on the left side, and flying out of her right ear.

"Is someone going to explain what's going on?" Spencer asked.

"As it turns out, they're casting the role of Sonny Lavinski's daughter, Daisy. She's fifteen years old and hasn't been seen on camera since she was a baby. She'll be a substantial part of the new story line. They think Chelsea is perfect."

"I'm out and Chelsea's in?"

"That's the current situation. I wanted you to hear it from me before it was announced."

They gave Spencer a moment to take in this news. He circled the room a few times and stared at Murray twitching on the floor.

"You know what really kills me?" he finally said. "No pun intended? It's that I could have done that scene. I'm really *good* at getting beaten to death. It's what people really want to see. It would make people like me."

And that's when it hit her — a flicker of remembrance first. Spencer working on the airline safety audition. A dozen ways to die.

"You can still die," she said.

Both Mrs. Amberson and Spencer turned to look at her.

"What are you talking about?" he asked.

"Do it *yourself*."

"What?" Spencer said.

"I'm saying . . ." As the idea took shape, Scarlett became more animated. "I'm saying you don't need the show to stage his death. You just do it, in public, like you did before . . . but bigger. You got yourself attacked in public. You jumped into a cake. What's a death? A million ways to die, remember? Like the tie? Get yourself beat to death in public. I mean . . . stage it. People already know the character is going to die. So just *do* it."

At this point, Scarlett was losing her grip on her thought. Mrs. Amberson leaned forward out of her seat.

"Go on, O'Hara," she said. "Keep talking. Don't stop."

"Getting people there, to wherever we do it, is no problem," Scarlett said, hurrying over to the computer and opening the *Spies of New York* page and pointing at the corner. "They have a box for tips. They would *not* ignore this. It would end up everywhere. Kill him big, in public, where everyone can see."

Spencer was looking away from them, but his eyes were flicking from side to side, like he was watching something in his mind.

"I'd have to die painfully," he said.

"Very painfully," Scarlett said.

"Painful is easy. I'm good at painful."

"A location," Mrs. Amberson said, standing up. "We'll need the right staging area."

"I'd need a partner, too," Spencer said. "Someone good."

Scarlett paused for a moment, then the answer became instantly clear. It caused her only the slightest pang to say it.

"Eric," she said.

Spencer looked up and nodded immediately.

"I need Eric," he said. "He could do it."

Once again, Scarlett was mildly aware of setting something in motion that she probably didn't mean to — but maybe, she wondered, that's what life really was. Making stupid plans and having to carry them out.

THE DEATH OF
SPENCER MARTIN

They posted it exactly as Scarlett wrote it:

*A **SPIES OF NEW YORK** EXCLUSIVE:*
This morning, something very interesting appeared in our in-box,
startling us out of a prenoon coma. We don't exactly know what it
means or who it came from, but we are sufficiently intrigued to
post it here. The message, in its entirety, reads as follows: Directly
following the broadcast of this week's *Crime and Punishment*,
the public will be given satisfaction on the very spot where
Sonny fell.

What does it mean? Will Saint Sonny rise from the dead? And
where is Spencer Martin, as he does not appear to be on the set?
The mind reels. As we get so little satisfaction and have such sad
offline existences, we are considering showing up. Would you like
to join us?

It had taken her a while to get that wording exactly right, and she
was proud of the result. *Spies of New York* got a lot of e-mails, so
she had to make sure to get their attention and make it seem

legitimate. They had posted it at eight o'clock, just an hour before the episode aired.

Scarlett and Mrs. Amberson stood at the base of the steps of the courthouse, waiting. Forty or so other people were milling around, and more people were dribbling in in groups of two or three. The courthouse wasn't a big attraction, so Scarlett assumed that they were there for the event. She hoped that none of these people were crazy, but there was no way of telling.

"You don't think that anyone's going to . . . kill him, right?" Scarlett asked. "I know this was my idea but . . ."

"It will be fine, O'Hara," Mrs. Amberson said confidently. "The police are on top of the situation."

The three police officers nearby were leaning against a collection of the stray crowd-control barriers that litter the New York streets, and a cruiser was parked nearby with no one inside. They probably just happened to patrol this area. They had one half-interested eye on the group, but their main concern looked to be their conversation.

"Where did you tell your parents we were going?" Mrs. Amberson asked.

"To see *A Midsummer Night's Dream*. I told them I was reading it for school and it counted as doing homework."

"Ah. Well, I don't approve of lying to your parents, but this case might be an exception. They've had a very hard week, with too many surprises."

"If they knew about this," Scarlett said, nervously wrapping her arms around herself, "they'd start chaining us to the radiators."

Murray was along for the ride, watching the action from the safety of Mrs. Amberson's purse. Every once in a while, his little head would appear just under her arm and the terrified, marble-like eyes would take in the scene. Then he would sink back down into the depths of tea-tree sticks and notepaper, convinced once again of the horrors of the world.

"And Spencer didn't tell you exactly what was going on?" Mrs. Amberson asked.

"Just that they figured out a way in and out, that it will start at 10:02, and we should meet them afterward at the meeting place two blocks from here."

More people came from the direction of the subway. Among them was a familiar figure, half hidden by a hoodie. But by now, Scarlett knew every inch of Max's outline.

"It's Max," Mrs. Amberson said, as he came closer. "Really, O'Hara, you've gone above and beyond the call of duty with that one. I remember when you were reluctant to spy on him. . . ."

"I don't spy," Scarlett said.

"Yes, of course. You know what I mean."

They quieted as Max approached. Mrs. Amberson pulled out her phone and stepped off to the side to talk. Scarlett got the feeling she was just doing that to give them some room, which was disconcerting.

"You always post where you're going to be," he said. "Stop flirting with me."

Before the kiss, that would have had a totally different meaning. It would have just been snide. Now, it had some real weight. Max seemed to catch on to this a moment too late, and his voice trailed off. Scarlett tried to come up with some kind of witty rebuttal, but finding nothing in her mind, decided to act like it had never been said.

"We just have to wait a few minutes," she said. "Then it starts."

"What's *it?*" he asked.

Before Scarlett could explain, a black Mercedes pulled up to the curb next to them. It was a car Scarlett knew well.

"Oh crap," she said.

Marlene got out first, followed quickly by Lola and her parents. Marlene's finger was pointing at Scarlett even before she left the car. She walked right up to Scarlett and jabbed it in the direction of her face.

"Told you!" she said. "I told you!"

"Aren't you at a *show?*" Scarlett's mom asked.

"I . . ."

"You!" Marlene noticed Max standing there. "Are you guys, like, *dating* now?"

There was obvious disgust, and maybe a little bit of jealousy in her voice. Mrs. Amberson had turned around and seen what was going on. She quickly concluded her conversation and hurried over.

"You're here!" she exclaimed. "We *just this moment* walked out of the show, and someone sent me a message saying that we had to get down here right away."

Scarlett's parents didn't appear to think much of this story.

"So," her mom said, "what *is* going on here?"

"Beats me," Scarlett said. "We just saw the . . . you know . . . thing . . . and we . . ."

"Let's try that again," Scarlett's dad said. "What is going on? If it involves Spencer, you know. In fact, this sort of looks like your handiwork. You're the one who brought *Hamlet* home, right?"

"Me? I . . ."

"Scarlett can't be blamed," Mrs. Amberson lied. "She genuinely had no idea. Spencer told me privately, client to agent. It's just a lit-tle show for the fans."

"Ten-oh-two," Scarlett said.

There was a murmur, and Spencer appeared out of nowhere, breaking through the crowd and running up the steps. The faithful were ready with the doughnuts, and they came in a steady volley. But Spencer was moving fast and missed them all. They fell against the courthouse steps and exploded into chunks and blotches of jam. A few people looked like they were going to run after him, but no one moved.

"People of New York!" he called, once he made it halfway up the steps. "Did you all come out to see me tonight?"

A chorus of hisses and boos and weird cheers.

"I know what you people want," he went on. "I know you're all upset about that *cop*. So, tonight, I'm going to . . ."

Eric must have been hiding behind one of the large Grecian pillars at the top of the steps. He came barreling from behind Spencer and jumped on his back. The crowd roared in approval. The fight began in earnest. The beat-down was spectacularly choreographed — they used everything they had. Body slams, punches, flips. But unlike normal, Spencer just took most of the blows, getting up again and again to suffer.

Scarlett's mom was wincing and shielding her eyes partially with her hand.

"I know he knows what he's doing," she said to herself. "I know he does."

The police moved closer and talked among themselves and into walkie-talkies, but they were smiling and seemed willing to let this go on a little bit longer, as long as everyone stayed where they were.

One man started to step forward, wanting to join Eric, but he was cautioned back. Eric took Spencer by the collar, pinned him face-first up against one of the grand Grecian columns, and started repeatedly slamming his head. Spencer broke away, acting woozy. At the top of the steps, he wavered for a moment, looked out over the crowd . . . and tumbled, taking at least a half dozen of the big stone steps or more, in the exact move that Scarlett had seen him do in the basement. The one he said was so very idiotic and dangerous.

"Oh my God!" Lola yelped. "I *hate* it when he does that! He had better not be dead."

Eric threw up his arms in triumph. He did a victory lap up and down. Scarlett was surprised to see Laertes and Hamlet hurry out of the crowd. They must have been called in to help as well. They rushed to where Spencer was sprawled and threw a sheet over him and picked him up, his body drooping in their grasp. The crowd parted as they brought him down the stairs, a few people cheerfully pitching the last of the doughnuts at the sheet. One person right next to the Martins had his arm cocked back and was ready to let fly, when Scarlett's mom stepped in front of him.

"That's my son under there," she said calmly. "You weren't planning on throwing that at my son, right?"

Eric ran down the steps and started high-fiving the crowd. When he ran past the Martins, he slowed just a bit to acknowledge them, then quickly sprinted away. Lola and her dad were speculating on Spencer's possible injuries. From the way her dad was imitating some of the body blows, Scarlett got the feeling that he had thoroughly enjoyed what he'd just seen.

"You know you're grounded," Scarlett's mom said quietly. "Right? Because I know that you did this."

"Yeah," Scarlett said. "I know. How long?"

"Let me think about it," she said. "I'm not sure I'm going to let any of you out of the house ever again."

There was no particular anger in her voice. She almost sounded like she was congratulating Scarlett on a job well done.

"He's meeting us around the corner," Scarlett said. "Can I just have five minutes? That's, um, you know. Max. From school. He just came down to ask me something about Bio and . . ."

She looked toward Max, who was still being grilled by Marlene.

"I'm Powerkid of the Year," she heard Marlene say.

"I have no idea what that is," he replied.

"Five," her mother said. "Not six. Five. I'm timing you. I need that much time to kill your brother anyway."

Mrs. Amberson guided the Martins off, throwing Scarlett a knowing glance over her shoulder as she left. This act of being left behind so publicly made Scarlett instantly self-conscious. Max must have felt the same way. He started playing with the strings of his hood, tightening it around his face until he could hardly be seen, then grabbing it and loosening it again. She let him do this a few times before she spoke.

"Marlene likes you," Scarlett said.

"Yeah. I'm thinking about asking her out. You cool with that?"

"Be my guest," Scarlett said. "She'll eat you alive."

Another silence. Another minute ticked away. Scarlett struggled to find some other remark, and had just about gotten one together, when she heard a familiar voice calling her.

"Hey!"

Chelsea Biggs was jogging down the sidewalk toward them.

Scarlett had anticipated that some people would read *Spies of New York* — but not *everyone*. Another miscalculation.

"Just made it!" she said. "I heard about it during intermission and . . ."

Her eyes fell on the hooded figure that had turned away from them. There was a moment of confusion when she realized it was her brother, then she shrugged, as if Max's appearance could be just chalked up to his constant attempts to annoy her. It was amazing how good Scarlett had gotten at reading the Biggs family signals.

"Anyway," Chelsea said excitedly, "Eric messaged me and told me what was going on. I can't believe I missed it! Did you guys talk?"

Chelsea really had no idea how any kind of normal human friendship worked. No one had told her that you weren't supposed to run up to heartbroken ex-girlfriends and ask if they'd heard the glad tidings that you had taken over their role.

"No," Scarlett said coldly. "I don't want to talk to him."

"Why not?" Chelsea asked. "Let him explain."

"I'm fine with it, okay?" Scarlett said. This was supposed to be a lie, but she managed to say it with such surprising conviction that she wondered if she meant it. She even managed to add, "I hope you guys are happy," without making it sound like she was placing a pox on the House of Biggs. These words, far from soothing Chelsea, only seemed to confuse her. She immediately looked at Max.

"What did you say to her?" Chelsea snapped. "What did you do?"

"Nothing," he mumbled. "You said you went out. That's what I told her. Because it was true. I don't even know who this guy is . . ."

"Don't listen to him, Scarlett," Chelsea said. "We did go out, but not that way. Eric came to the show. I found out he was there, because they tell me who uses my comps. We talked after the show. He told me all about you two, and he was all upset because you didn't show up. He said he's been trying to talk to you for days, but you don't answer. You're my friend. You helped me when the show closed. I wanted to help you, too. I've been talking to him, trying to get you two back together. He really misses you. He was so excited to see you tonight. . . ."

Dusty and dormant gears in Scarlett's brain clicked into action, attempting to make sense of all of this. Eric and Chelsea were not dating. Eric missed her. And Max . . .

Max had stalked off in the direction of the subway without another word. Chelsea shook her head.

"He's such a jerk," she said. "I am so sorry he did this to you. He . . ."

Scarlett didn't hear the rest, because she hurried off after him. He was taking huge, quick strides, and had gotten about halfway down the block.

"Where are you going?" she asked.

"Where do you *think* I'm going?"

"You just walked away! We were still talking!"

"I wasn't talking. I'm done."

"Why are you so *angry*?" she said. "What did I even do?"

Max stopped and faced her. He was doing strange things with his mouth — sucking his lips in, shifting it to the left and right. There was something so intense coming off of him that it caused Scarlett's pulse to jump and quicken.

"Fine," she said, holding up her hands. "Don't tell me."

"You should go," he replied. "Sounds like your *actor boyfriend* is waiting for you. Go on. Run."

He made a brushing motion with his hand, as if scooting her along. It was so absurd and childish that Scarlett accidentally laughed. He turned and continued toward the subway.

"See you tomorrow," she said as he walked away. There was no acknowledgment that she had spoken. Max's back was a wall.

She walked back to Chelsea, who was standing there, waiting patiently.

"Don't worry about him," she said. "I'll make him miserable at home for you. I can't *believe* he did that. Well, actually, I can believe it."

Scarlett started walking numbly in the direction of the meet up. Chelsea was still talking, telling her all the things Eric had said about her. The account seemed a little embellished, but the underlying message was clear: Eric wanted to get together with her. For real. Dating with a capital D. That's all she had wanted for so long, and there it was. And yet, some part of her just wanted to run back and grab Max and shake him until all his teeth fell out. All her impulses toward Max were so — violent.

When she turned the corner, she saw them a block or so ahead. Her parents were talking to the actors, whom they hadn't seen in a few weeks. They had gotten to know everyone during the show, and wanted to know how they were doing. Mrs. Amberson was talking excitedly on the phone. Spencer was rubbing one of his arms, but he was laughing. Eric held up a shy hand of greeting.

"See!" Chelsea said. "Please. Just talk to him."

Even from across the street, Scarlett could hear every word Mrs. Amberson was saying on the phone: ". . . I think if you check the coverage tomorrow . . . Oh! Have we tinkled? Yes, it's a standpipe, darling, I know. They can be very scary. . . . No, not you, Carmine.

But I think we should talk again in the morning, because this is a window of opportunity. . . . Get away from that disgusting pizza! No, no. No dairy for you! . . . No, not you, Carmine. Let's just meet for coffee at ten and discuss the future. . . ."

The merry-go-round was still circling.

Scarlett looked behind her one last time, but Max was definitely gone. So Scarlett and Chelsea crossed the street to join the group.

ACKNOWLEDGMENTS

For someone who spends most of her work time alone at a desk mumbling to herself, I seem to have many, many people to thank now that this book is finished. Even in making this list, I worry that I am leaving off dozens of people who do me everyday kindnesses that allow me to go on living.

My first thanks must always go to my agent, Kate Schafer Testerman (often known to the world as Daphne Unfeasible of Unfeasible Enterprises). Also, to my editor, Abby McAden, and everyone at Scholastic. These are the people who made this book happen.

More thanks to:

Justine Larbalestier and Scott Westerfeld, who not only read the book and provided critical notes, they also provide total life-support services in general.[1]

John and Hank Green, for being awesome, and always being such big supporters of me and my books. Best wishes.

The daily writing gang: Libba Bray, Cassandra Clare, Robin Wasserman, Scott Westerfeld (again), and Lauren McLaughlin.

Everyone at Springfield Castle who put up with me while I was working on the revision and running from the peacocks: Sarah

Cross, Ally Carter, Carrie Ryan, Sarah Rees Brennan, Jennifer Lynn Barnes, Diana Peterfreund, Robin Wasserman, Cassandra Clare, and Holly Black. (And a special thanks to Holly for reading the book between midnight and three in the morning, and then talking with me until dawn about it.)

My consultant on getting hit and falling down: Steve Copeland, formerly of Ringling Brothers Circus. My Gang of Four: Rebecca Leach, Tobias Huisman, Jordan Cwierz, and Chelsea Hunt. Alan Lastufka, for all of his technical help and support of Scarlett. Jason Keeley and Paula Gross, for feeding me. And to Hamish Young, who is an English person.

To everyone who participated in the BEDA project. There are about 500 of you, and it took all of you to make it work. A special thanks to Alex Day and Charlie McDonnell. Once you guys started doing it, then I had no choice but to continue or else I would be shamed on the Internet.

And to Dick Wolf. He knows why. Call me, Dick.[2]

[1] When they are in NYC, that is. Sometimes they retreat to their sky-palace in Sydney, and then I survive entirely by eating clumps of dust and burning my prize collection of antique telephone books for warmth.

[2] I mean, "You, Dick, call me on the phone or some other telephonic device." Not, "Please now refer to me as Dick." There are a lot of reasons for this, not the least of which is that I am female. Also, that would make my name Dick Johnson. I would never stoop so low as to make a joke like that. I have standards, you know.